POCALYPSE

AND EYOND

JONATHAN LOVEJOY

Armageddon Publishing

Cover: *The Reaper*, 1872
William Adolphe Bouguereau (1825-1905)

ISBN-10: 069231654X
ISBN-13: 978-0692316542

For every Elizabeth

For the Lord himself shall descend from Heaven with a shout, with the voice of the archangel and with the trump of God: and the dead in Christ shall rise first:

I Thessalonians 4:16

JONATHAN LOVEJOY

PART ONE

1

My name is Carmen.

When I was nineteen, my mother raped me.

2

$\mathcal{M}$y mother's breasts were gigantic and beautiful. And as it goes with my raping, that is neither here nor there except to me, and the pages of this Rose Diary—this journal I am condemned to live and die in. Under the rains of a fervent North Carolina sky, my music is silent at last so I can breathe, so I can think, so I can carry another burden other than my piano, and the otherworldly scratchings of it on paper.

My husband is seven years in his grave, thank the Lord, and his spirit rests with thee, O Lord. Chris' bones are left here to rot—to return to the dust from whence they came, which is today transformed to loose rock and mud. The pain of who we were—the burning agony of what we endured is at last fading into the past—turning into the powder that we once threatened to become, to be washed away at last I think, in this cold November rain. And this memory I do not cherish, that place we both lived, that lonely portrait in gray, which has haunted so much of my memory. But even while what I know of him, the monster that he often was—even while my memory of that man is dying, the winds howl and blow from a past a generation ago, to remind me that the pain I know, the burning that I was, ignited that day I came screaming from my mother's body.

This that I do, this feeble scratching, is like everything else I do—it is because I am afraid. How much of me hath drifted apart in terror, to reform, to coalesce again behind the bars of music! Was Mozart truly burdened as I, was my dear Rossini the bundle of nerves I am? I had sworn not to visit this place again—but in this departure—this Indian Summer's coldest goodbye, I am cursed to wonder at the aching that is still in my breasts, which were once heavy with milk after my child was departed from me. I must revisit again—by sorrow, I suppose, for I am unashamed before God, my private sins being long forgiven. What I do with my new mother, out of sight and secret from her meddling friends, is a perversion that I embraced before I was born, as did the roses we grow did so by predestination, knowing as seeds what lovely color they would be. The color of my heart is gray, worn ashen by the burden of years, where there is no sacrifice for my sin, but only what judgment He has for me. When lust hath conceived, it bringeth forth sin—whereby we need the mercy of God through Christ—for all have sinned and come short of the glory of God. And though we claim it to be so, we go on sinning with intent and purpose, being unable to cease from it.

The fires of warmth are my cottage just this moment, so that the secret of who I am is revealed that I am without modesty in my open blouse, with my own gigantic breasts spilled out for every rain and wind spirit to see. This, I have even done at night—looking up from the bars of music in a trance, to see my reflection in the nighttime prairie window—to see my blood sister—a woman with striking features, bulbous, pendulous breasts, the longest and shiniest black hair I have known, and a look of distant longing. A profound, indefinable sadness. And within this sadness I see the fear that has plagued us since we were children, and the longing to return to the place of innocence we knew as little girls, before the burning of blue and black fire. This fire burns hot in the cold evening day, my shelter from the cooling rain.

These words I now live and breathe, in the seventh year of Maria's birth and burial. Disturbed by my Mother Vera, my loyal guardian and protector. My pencil I have to put away, unguilty by the disapproving look on the cultured woman's face as she approaches me from the front door, having removed her coat and scarf soaking wet from the rain. Neither of us can know what lies around the next curve of time. Neither of us can know, as she watches me stand up from my writing table, breasts flopping free, undressing down to pure nakedness. Neither of us can know, when I sit back down, these unseen consequences, the road so often traveled, to remind us that we are not above God's Will, and that we will not rest in complacency, thinking we are beyond reproach. We cannot know, we cannot see Mother Vera's friend and her daughter, driving back down the length of the long asphalt road on our property. Getting out of her car frustratedly in the rain, in the darkening late afternoon gray, having forgotten some important whatever. We cannot see Vera's so called best friend, walking the short distance from her luxury car to my gray cottage, where the rainy early evening light is on. We cannot see the nosiest busy body in Martin County, creeping blonde haired curiosity in covert and cunning, away from the cottage door to the nearest window of the brick cottage living room. No, we cannot, we cannot see the dreadful, otherworldly shock on the face of cultured civility, as she watches Vera May Evans in tight, gray business skirt and charcoal blouse, bent over the shoulder of a seated, naked brunette, holding up the biggest breast she has ever seen, and sucking at the nipple like a starving child.

3

*B*renda Harrison stands at the window. Peeping. Peering in the rain, her business with Vera long forgotten. Brenda can see, with her eyes only, but cannot imagine what blood courses through my veins, nor what foreign land it hearkens from. She cannot tell of what emotion burns her lungs, be it the poison of revulsion, the heat of repulsion, or the cold icy mist of Envy's compulsion. If she is jealous, she cannot know it; for the full five minutes she stands there, she cannot know it. Nor can she know of the burning fire inside—of the itching that has appeared deep in my groin that I cannot scratch, nor can she hear the deep breathing from her best friend's nostrils. Does Brenda see the determined look on both our faces, while Vera strains lost against the back of the chair? While I writhe with my legs closed, one hand up on my stomach squeezing, rubbing and mashing it, the other hand at my other nipple? What builds up inside her, in the cold evening rain that has soaked her to the skin? Why does she not even feel the dreadful cold pounding into her, enough to make her breath appear in the dimmest fog? What is the source of terror in her veins, coursing past every firing nerve that heats her body up in the evening day? Can she see me grab the chair with both hands and put my head back to wait for my destruction? Does she see the expression on my face that warns of an approaching trauma inside my body? Does she hear my real mother's voice as I do saying *"wash me—wash me—in Jesus' name please!"* Each suck of my nipple pressing down further on the built up energy in my whole body? What does it do to her, when she sees me jerk in the chair, and hears me howl like a she-wolf in labor, watching her best friend pull and shake her head in loud grunting against my nipple in her mouth?

Brenda, are you still there? Can you see Vera kissing me now from behind, while I sit in the chair, holding both of her hands and trembling as you do now in the cold? Trembling as though I might never stop?

Brenda, are you there?

4

$\mathscr{T}$he flames that consume me burn so much hotter than most, to make me a prisoner within myself—these are the fires of Fear and Creativity,

my fear still being caused by the sound of strange voices, or the fervent memory of voices I have known. How many outside of the war line, apart from the River of Battle can know this—the post trauma that haunts every other ticking of the hours, throughout the day and into a sleepless night? What fear I have for the Lord is but a comfort—because I know he strengthens me—he holds me, he keeps me from hurt, harm and danger. And as for my continued apprehension, my constant nervousness at the collected humanity—I know that supposedly, he has not given us the Spirit of Fear, but of power, and of Love, and of a sound mind. Then why is it that my power is powerlessness and being alone—my love being only for God and Momma Vera?

And what soundness of mind can there be for one, whose house is Melody, where I am content to be alone? I can only be thankful when the white hot flames tinted blue and black are not ablaze inside—for I am able to better feel my earthly walk, and better able to breathe a little fresh air— to gaze up at the mighty stars in Heaven, and appreciate their beauty alone, without being tormented by some silly or sublime melody for my beloved piano. I have rarely ever transcribed these insanities from one instrument to the other, a whining violin is simply that, and not the plinking harp or tinkling and blinking piano key. Of this Divine gift I remain as ignorant as a child, though within this flame I am as wise as a serpent. And these two parts of the truth—the truth of the burnings I feel are who I am, of who I will be, and of who I have always been. Yes, the truth of who I am is *fire*— and for these 40 years, I have denied the third part of who I am, refused to accept the Third Part of the Truth.

The third part of all negative truth is cataclysm. And devastation to the soul. It is the flame passed from Evelyn Louise Daniels down to Barbara Jean Daniels. The woman who screamed when I split her in two as an accursed new born thing.

Extreme erotic sensitivity permeates my breasts. And this is profound, so much so that any prolonged squeezing, jiggling, wiggling or the like, and prolonged touching or stimulation by myself or another will cause me to shake like electric shock. How many other women share this gift of ecstasy, I wonder—to enjoy even the putting on or the taking off of a bra, the feel of their tremendous bouncing from a run or a jump, or even the vibration of a rough patch of road in the car. It is a gift passed down from my mother, I know, for I am aware of what deep and prolonged pleasures from this she hath obtained. From her own mother Evelyn first, in the mountain farmlands of Virginia. Then from herself, when she discovered one day in her bathroom during defecation, that when she pulled her nipple into her mouth, the lightning would strike inside her 15 year old body, to make it impossible for her to release her nipple from the sucking. This three pronged attack on my mother's body was gripping, as she bade farewell to what some would consider normal, and welcomed the deviant spirits to an indwelling, as she felt them upon her bowels, within her womb, and at the nipple pulled so deeply into her mouth. For my 15 year old mother, I see, a pleasure so profoundly irresistible as to be involuntary, to where she cannot imagine being elsewhere in space and time. Alone in her bathroom, away from her mother's punishment stick, the young girl lifts heavy, prodigiously overdeveloped breasts into her mouth, to ignite the fires that will burn our motherline for an eternity. This strange and wonderful gift, erotic breast sensitivity, I can only imagine is known to but few among us, perhaps even unique to my tragic cause, passed down from my grandmother Evelyn, to my mother Barbara Jean, to my own accursed self, and to my new mother Vera Evans; not by blood, but by these selfsame erotic spirits that torment my body and soul.

6

*I*n the Heart of Memory, Maria's grave is the point of origin. The beginning of this new inevitability, the place where I took Sorrow's Curse by the hand, and allowed it to escort me from here to the Gates of Heaven. Just as the rain fell when I buried my husband, today the rain falls as I see them put dirt over my daughter's body in the coffin.

The mourners are but two at this burial from seven years ago, so unlike what had aspired to be a prestige funeral when my husband died. There can be no sorrow shared when a mother buries her baby in the rain. Ironically dead, I think, the month that I was born. Carmen Maria Alicia Peele, carved on the gravestone too elaborate for a baby Carmen, who I send away with tears of understanding and sorrow, that to be absent from the body is to be present with the Lord. This baby Carmen, whose first name I bestow from myself as a permanent link to her, my own special curse bestowed, all of myself passed down from my own life, that her body be burdened forever with my feeble memory. Oh, how I had laboured within myself, not to have given her my name, because I loved her so, and if I loved her, how could I burden her memory with mine! I, a woman of chaff, yes I—a woman of straw, no better than one born in the dirt—oh, how I struggled to keep my name off Maria's grave! Had she lived, there is no way I could have done this to her, no, she would not have walked the Earth as Carmen Peele, but as Maria Alicia *Elizabeth* Peele. Yes, the accursed name my mother gave to me, that woman's name above every other name, whereby I suffered from days of my youth on the farm, through my time with my husband, and to now at my dead daughter's lonely grave. Little Maria Elizabeth Peele. Saved from this fate by Death, to leave this world instead as Baby Carmen, little Carmen Maria Alicia Peele.

As Mother Vera and I turn to leave this mud soaked mess of ground, where my daughter lies sleeping beneath the clay, the name Maria rises above all others in my mind, and begins to burn forever in my heart. And there is the most solemn and profoundly beautiful melody for a solo piano I hear, which I know to be her voice calling from the grave, as part of the overture that will burn in blue and black fire, at the head of the Opera that will bear her name.

These are the days of Brenda Harrison. Long before judgmentalism and hypocrisy took over, and infected her like a disease. Long before the rainy evening day at the cottage window, when she saw Vera taking her part of such unknown pleasures from me. In the hard and cold November rain, she is a bastion of strength for Mother Vera and me, her and her daughter together in the front seat of this rolling black luxury (do I care that it is called a Mercedes? I do not.) Her and her daughter in the front, smelling of some high priced perfume that tickles my nose. But so solemn and sophisticated, so worldly and world traveled, though not world weary at all. Unable to tear themselves away from our sides since old John Evans himself died, and I became a millionairess seven times over. What hope have they now, since my husband passed, passing the blessing of God from the spirit world to the natural one, with the banks holding another 15 million dollars in my name! What hope have they, but to bury their frowns and snickers so deep inside, to try and hide their natural contempt for Mother Vera and me. Oh, how the tables turn, when the lapdog becomes the mistress, and the mistress is not the whimpering dog at her feet! And though they are as relaxed and friendly around us as ever, with so much genuine helpfulness and goodwill, the two of them are often Death and Hell on my nerves, and make me as nervous as two sidewinders would, coming at me across a sandy desert terrain.

But Mother Vera is not unaware. She understands what evils there be, of what lurks in the hearts of women and men, and as always, she watches her back when Brenda and Catherine Grace Harrison are around, which they seem to be almost all the time. Ours is a place of constant coming and going, the brick farmhouse we still have not torn down and rebuilt or abandoned, while the grain silos are dismantled and hauled away, and all of the old farm equipment is being sold. How is it that we are able, I ask myself, to stay in the house where John Evans was murdered, and where Vera was beaten, raped and left for dead? I think it was part of our healing process, the catharsis and therapy for us, to establish joy and life where there was only death and sorrow before, which had been easy enough to do when this was still a working farm, as if we were continuing John Evans' great work, to carry out this farming legacy in his name. Evans Peele Grain and Storage, I remember, my husband had begun to imagine before he died, an idea left to him by old John himself. But men's plans are as feeble as the weather, which passes as the chiming of the noonday, or the tolling of the sunset, which echoes across the twilight, and the evening day of the approaching night.

In the Heart of Memory, our arrival at the farmhouse is a rainy one, one of us dressed in a coat as long and black as the shadows that haunt my night dreams. That have haunted me since I was a little girl at my mother's bosom. Yes, the darkest, the longest shadow that chases me is still that of Barbara Jean Coletti, whom the thought of can still bring a phantom twitch to my fragile nerves, and a tingling at my own breast and groin. And what Vera doesn't know, which I am afraid to tell her, is that the spirit of Barbara Jean comes to me under cloak of night, and even in the waking hours, especially from the burial of Carmen Maria, through this trip home, and now through our rain soaked walk to the kitchen where John Evans was killed.

As Vera fumbles with the lock while I stand stupidly nearby, feeling the eyes of everyone burning a gaze into me, I wish to open my dumb lips and tell Vera how terrified I am of going inside. Not because there is too much death here; that the sprits masquerading as our dead husbands (and now my daughter) live in the ceiling, the floors and the walls, no, not because of them, whom I have grown accustomed to. It is because I know that *her* spirit, that of the mountain woman, is waiting for me somewhere inside. Have I jumped from the sound of footsteps in the hall at night when Vera is away? Have I screamed a silly scream of pure fright from a phantom touch when at the sink, from a whisper and a brush across the back of my neck, even when I know there is no one in the house but me? I am glad to stand here under this umbrella, waving. Stalling. Grieving at the Charity Ladies' departure, because ghosts have less power in the company of fools. But are we any less foolish than they, that we choose to live in a house so conspicuously cursed, where Death comes to claim the fools who reside therein?

I watch the fine black Mercedes (a gift from Mother Vera to Brenda) turn and disappear beside the house, catching myself waving for at least a second after they're out of sight, wondering if Vera knows that I must again burden her with the truth of who I am, which is a woman tormented by the spirit of fear. When she opens the door to our space, the familiar daytime darkness, I know that I cannot say what is on my mind, nor can I speak of the shadow I just saw pass over the kitchen wall. As we walk inside, I know that she cannot feel the shadows as I do, nor can she fathom the heavy cold of their impending touch, or the terror they can cause at the edge of sleep.

"Are you okay?"

Some questions are overwrought with simplicity. As there is not quite time to address their gargantuan importance.

"I just have to go to the bathroom." My voice is low. Almost whispery. I see the girl, the woman I once was, the timid, frightened woman of straw, who had believed she was hardened with time, that her emotions had begun to grow a bark of protection, to survive among other trees in the nighttime forest wood. But I am learning that there is no greater amusement to the spirits that watch us, than our belief that we have left Buzzard Valley behind, just because we have seen the fluttering of a butterfly or two. Yes. This hallway, this house, *is* the Valley of the Shadow of Death, and here, as I always have, I *will* fear evil.

*T*he bathroom is a dream in soft blue marble, where I can let the hours drift me to another place in time while I bathe, sometimes resting in the tranquility of foam and suds in the large white Jacuzzi tub, watching the music pour from the sides of the tub in various shades of blue. Being in here always reminds me of the woman who raised me on the farm, how much she would have loved to float her breasts in the soapy water, while admiring the four white columns that rise to the ceiling around her. Oh, how she would have loved the luxurious blue marble walls and white porcelain while gazing at herself unclothed in the mirror, as I am apt to do—often finishing whatever piece that haunts me while bathing—shaping and coloring whatever it is with hardly much effort. Twisting, turning and dividing the beautiful melodies as I see fit. Admiring myself nude, repressing my urges, ignoring the epic sensitivity in my breasts, which I can feel at the taking on or off of my bra, which I have felt for as long as I can remember. As I stand here in the Heart of Memory, not as apprehensive as before, I am burdened by the dream memory of my mother upon the throne of our tiny bathroom grunting in travail, with one of her breasts held up with both hands, with the nipple sucked so deeply into her mouth. This, I watched many times over the years, often as the foreplay of what it was we had to do, with often myself sitting on the seat in front of her, nursing myself into bathroom relaxation.

Perversion is the behind closed doors stage I was trained on. Where I learned to perform forbidden acts with fire and passion, so that even today, upon my stillborn's final departure, I remove the wet bra from my impossibly large breasts, grown beyond the known keyboard, where it is pitched up to something in an unknown J chord, to where normal sized breasts are bloated to beyond recognition, to a size of tragicomic proportions, hung heavy in macromastic dimensions. Even before I was pregnant, they were too big. But now they have swollen to ridiculousness, with the culprit dripping sweet from one of my nipples as I watch, my black dress down to my waist so I can see. Are there others such as I who can feel the desire coursing to their groin through the mere touch and squeeze of their bosom, so that they must stand at the mirror as I do, and resist the urge to perform upon them? But today, they seem not as something for me to fear or hide, but something to adore and admire, to appreciate to the point of awe—something to worship as a gift from the Almighty God.

Standing at my bathroom mirror, in the aftermath of my daughter's grave, I lift one of the great breasts as a tribute and a comfort. Feeling, hearing the milk go down my throat in great gulps, to begin to quench a thirst I have felt for some time, thanking God for this private and wonderful gift of mine, feeling the spirit of my youth passed down from Barbara Jean Coletti, through myself, and to the memory of a daughter I never knew. Of this drink I must take, of the epic calling to my groin it doth make, I hear a woman's voice that cries from the four winds, and from the tombstones east of Appalachia: *this, do in remembrance of me.*

But I know not to nurse myself to completion, satisfying neither appetite: the thirst for milk, nor the thirst for my body's trembling. One last, hungry gulp I take. Releasing the nipple in a long, kissing pull. Eyes closed. A deep breath. One last swallow of the taste in my mouth.

I am taken back to days on the farm, to a time when most girls are in college or married or working some job or another. I was receiving an education in deviance, having developed a taste and craving for my own mother's milk, one to grow and match her own. Where this was concerned, the craving in our bodies burned hot enough to consume all pretense, until we both knew and understood without shame, that yes, my mother had to be milked every day; something which had caused a spark of flame in my body and spirit, so that for a brief time when I was twenty years old, the dripping of her milk was a glimpse of Heaven for my eyes, and a taste of Paradise for my tongue.

The taste of my own milk, the feel of my own nipple having been in my mouth, the sight of the steady drip, drip, dripping from the swollen breast in the mirror, all have conspired upon these cravings, to reawaken them, and to reaffirm their irrevocable dominance and severity. If I touch my breast again, if I pull at the nipple with either my hand or mouth, I will twitch and then double over from the explosion at the center of my body, which has haunted me since before my mother slapped me in the field and ended our perversion, in the days before she abandoned me. But this craving has returned again, like a ghostly soul resurrected, as the body of Eve digesting the forbidden fruit, and I know that I have been infused with power, that which is conceived and done in secret, which mankind is not capable of easily accepting, nor can even readily process or believe.

But the eyes of the Lord are in every place, beholding the evil and the good. And though I am aware of this, I stand again before him as a fallen woman, unashamed in my time, accepting of what triumph or transgression this may be, thanking him for what I am, for what I must do, and the blessing of mother daughter perversion I must endure.

9

A knock at the bathroom door. There is always so much to fear, from a fateful knocking at the door. She asks me if I need anything. Am I sure I'm alright, she says. *Come in,* I say. *I need to show you something.* The great mirrored door opens, and in steps a tallish, elegant blonde woman, her charcoal gray skirt stretched so smoothly across the widest hips, in perfect union with the lighter gray cashmere sweater, and the black boots below. The pinned up blonde hair enhances the eyes of winter gray.

Oh, I'm sorry, Vera says. *I didn't know you were undressing.* She tries to leave. To run from the spirits of shame and humiliation, seeing me only

24

from behind, the white skin of my scarred back exposed, my long black hair taken up in my hands, pinning it so skillfully and tightly away. *I need you to stay,* I say. Watching her cover her eyes, because remarkably, in the year and a half since my arrival, she has never yet seen me naked. And it was not something I had even considered, until after my husband died, but for the past five months since I buried him, this desire has been growing inside me as steady as a crop field, with no growth that can be easily detected along the way, but where the end of that growth is as epic as the changing of the seasons.

I have to show you something. In the mirror.

I lock eyes with the elegant blonde woman, seven years my senior, fabulous in forties femininity. Without a word, she closes the mirrored door, and she walks slowly across the tiles, her face somber, grieving against the oddness, the inappropriateness, and the tragic inevitability of this moment in time. I watch the elegant figure in gray, drifting up behind the woman in the mirror, the woman whose breasts are exposed for the all the spirits to see.

Vera steps up beside me, gazing at my breasts in the mirror, mouth partially open in shock, held immobile now, by a sight she has never seen or let herself imagine. Two of the largest breasts she has ever seen, but naked, with large dark brown areolas contrasting the white skin, with milk dripping rapidly from one nipple unflattened, and slowly from the other. She suddenly puts her hand over her mouth, and her face twists into a cry, which she immediately tries to straighten as a show of false strength, betrayed by the tear which pours freely from one eye. But the spirit of weeping grips her again, and her face twists, she covers her mouth, and her body begins to shake from the sobs I hear. *I'm so sorry,* she says. *I'm so sorry that you lost your baby.* And upon the last syllable, she goes into deeper sobbing, for a moment sniffing, giving in to her own pent up Sorrow of the Ages resurrected, called forth by this last link in the chain, the string of bad luck and tragedy which is her life and mine.

She stands close beside me, leaning over and kissing me hard on the cheek, which makes me have to close my eyes and take a deep breath. And when I open my eyes again, I see that both areolas have shrunken, pushing the nipples out to the fullness of themselves, with a slower, but still steady dripping from each one. Vera gets behind me, and wraps her arm around my waist, just below the low ride, heavy hangers of mine, holding on to me tight, and then tighter, which makes me lean back against her as if in rapture, my eyes closed again, breathing two deep and dramatic breaths of pure surrender. *I'm sorry you lost your baby*, she repeats. *Our little Maria.*

From behind me, Vera kisses my cheek again, this time with more power and commitment, breathing in deeply though her nose. Even the feel of the air rushing across my check is enough to make me have to resist a shudder, from the tingle passing from my cheek to my exposed bosom.

Vera! Mother Vera! What doth Barbara Jean have to do with thee! What bygone spirits do you awaken inside of me! These are the strains of Sappho, these are the flames in which I burn—take heed lest you be consumed by me! Motherline spirits of old passing through—from the Blue Ridge Mountains of Virginia, to the farms and fields of North Carolina, through our brick farming house, back into my body, waiting for the kiss, waiting for this moment in brief history. Forever waiting. Reaching out from me as I breathe, as the tears run down my face in quiet—reaching out from me, to keep you from moving your mouth away from my face—to keep me from holding my head forward and still—to move my lips toward you against my will, to press hard against your soft lips as though it could not be prevented, as if a force has taken over, to lock our mouths together like two magnets. And while this kiss relaxes me to ecstasy, I feel it twitch and tense your body to straining, like a predator whose jaws are clamped by pure instinct, and is unable to fathom but the taste of nourishment for her body. I am a prisoner too, Mother Vera, of this same instinct now, this instinct to submit and die to thee, and my tongue slides deep to yours on its own, feeling your lips clamp firmly around my tongue, sucking upon it, pulling it deep into your mouth and holding it there, feeding upon it, unable to breathe through the trauma of lightning to your groin. And what is the rough, animal grunting I hear, Mother Vera? What is it that I feel, as you begin to bellow loudly upon my tongue, our mouths locked together so that the muffled sound goes into my body as that from a vibrator, to activate every part of what is erogenous to my spirit; so that I balance as if at the edge of a cliff above crashing waves, resisting the force of a stiff and fervent breeze. But then, your rough voice stops and goes to silence, but you take tighter hold of me, still locked upon my tongue, readjusting your stance, in a move I have not felt since the days of Barbara Jean, and I feel the tremble begin in your voice on my tongue, and I feel it continue from the center of your body, until your whole body is vibrating enough to jiggle me from the inside out.

You stand here, doing the best you can to endure what is happening to your body, as the wave passes from a tremble to a violent convulsion at your groin, forcing you to release your tongue kiss so you can breathe, to slam yourself up against me from behind, and scream to God and Christ for the whole world to hear.

10

I open my eyes in time to see the strong anguish on your face at its peak, a face made more beautiful by the endurance of sensual agony in your body. You open your eyes, and I see you look away to the God you just prayed to, in disbelief of the power you just felt, and of what magnitude there is to the vow you have just broken.

God forgive me, she says, seeing my breasts in the mirror, enduring another wave through her groin, which squeezes her hips into me again, twitching her whole body, causing her to grunt once loudly in my ear.

Oh, Mother Vera! What have I done to thee! What spirit have I corrupted your body with! What is the aftermath you recover in, dear Vera, what is this new place where you attempt to breathe! Look heartily, Mother Vera, at the two big breasts you swore you would never allow yourself to see! I feel the small twitch again, this time hidden as you hold me, but the power of which is in your breathing, and the rhythm of your heartbeat I feel through the back of me. *The milk,* I say. *It tastes sweet.* In the mirror, I see your spent expression, from which you stare at me with deep knowledge and understanding. Without pretense, you step from behind me to take my heavy breasts into your beautiful hands, and the twitch which twitches every stitch is real, told in the loud gasp from me, and the single shock that unhitches a switch. Look at my face, Mother Vera, and you will see the addict reacquainted with her drug, that which once had control of her body in secret, and has come back to claim her both body and soul.

I move your hands away by necessity, staring you in the eyes like I never have, rolling your tight sweater up past the knife scars I see at the waist of your skirt, up over the two globes of yours pitched to G minor themselves, both higher and rounder than my own, hung heavy in the over-the-shoulder boulder holder in white lace. I roll the gray sweater up, leaving it on, then I slowly lift the bra fabric up, watching it climb higher, pulling your breasts up higher, higher and higher still, and then the round, firm G cup softees flop down to your chest, making you close your eyes and raise your head back.

And we stand here. Two Goddesses of the Bosom, breast obsessed breast queens, standing in the bathroom fully clothed, with only their breasts uncovered. *Put your nipple to mine,* I say. In the mirror, I watch two watermelon breasted women come together in cataclysm, the taller blonde unable to do naught but stare down at what is happening, hardly able to endure the reality of a libido risen again, to where it was but a few moments ago. She looks down at her breasts, at the large, meaty nipples which are her own, both tickling against the damp nipples of mine, shaking her head in denial that such profound pleasures are possible from such benign and feathered touching. Then suddenly, as if directed by an inner voice, she lowers her head to my breast, and I see the blonde woman in the mirror take the brunette woman's breast into her mouth, and I see my blood sister's face (my reflection) begin to anguish from the force of undiluted pleasure itself. I look down, watching Vera clumsily nurse the milk from my breasts, getting used to the taste, then taking it more fully in, and drinking deeper.

What I feel in my body is as one continuous plateau, which has the moment of its collapse preordained by Fate itself, as I can only stand and prepare for its arrival—knowing that this is the Nun's Intercourse, of those fortunate enough, those who have been blessed enough to partake of the fullness therein. And I watch this lust take over the blonde woman, who stops her nursing just long enough to take control of both breasts, then pull one into her mouth once again. When she does, I watch her brow wrinkle, to a mighty loss of breath and stability…

And I hear her begin to grunt slightly as before, her own breasts hanging naked below her rolled up sweater, making me reach over and tweak one nipple of hers. As she nurses the milk, as the lightning passes through her own nipple from my touch, she lurches forward a bit on my breast, unable to hold onto it, raising up and grabbing hold of me with a mighty yelping shriek, slamming herself repeatedly into the front of me as before, as if to stop her unendurable suffering. I hold onto her with all the strength I have, suffering the blast of another animal yelling in my ear, and the rough violence of her strong legs slamming her groin into mine.

I hold her there, feeling her breath, listening to the voice of defeat come out one last and lesser time, as her body finally relaxes itself to where she can think straight again, to where she can remember how to spell my name. Then suddenly, responding to her inner voice again, this accursed woman lowers herself to my breasts again, but this time with authority, holding my waist instinctively with one hand, and one of my breasts with the other. She melts me briefly with one deep, soft kiss. To my lips, then focuses on what must be done, this time nursing not for milk, but through the slow and steady bobbing of her head, to finally cause the collapse of the wide and eternal plateau therein.

And the sound of Mother Vera's voice moaning, the feel of the vibration in my breasts causes this rumbling quake to begin, and the Earth cracks from my feet to the horizon, and I see the wilderness around me begin to crumble, and I suddenly fall through this opening in space, unable to hear my voice begin the low, wailing sobs that must be, as if I am being tortured softly, as if I am being tormented from the inside out.

With strength and power, she holds onto me. Unamazed at the sound of a Weeping Orgasm, at the feel of the epic vibrating in my body, and the trembling it causes in my voice as it happens. But with mercy she continues, driven to nurse the life out of me, to drink every drop of suppression and sorrow from the reservoir of repression, as my wails, sobs and weeping have given way to outright screams, as I struggle to endure the waves of passion flowing continuously through my body.

11

The taste of Mother Vera's lips is sweet, which delights my mornings anew. It is safe to assume, I suppose, that our honeymoon has begun. After our marriage in blue marble, when the spirits gave her to me as mother and wife in the bonds of Holy Matrimony, seven years ago in the Heart of Memory. In my heart, she is my spiritual mother, as well as my wife, whom I am fully submitted to. And I am given to her as a bride before Heaven, in our secret marriage by the sea. My mind and my body both burn for her as they did for my mother on the farm, and I think that briefly, I am happy. It is a feeling that I am unfamiliar with—it goes beyond the silliness of laughter and fake joy. It is the feeling inside of Hope for the future, and the absence of pain and sorrow. It allows me to remember Maria's burial with longing unaccompanied by tears, and to remember my mother with a longing untouched by fear. But even as I sit astraddle of Vera in our Gray Palace (her master bedroom), both of us in the nude, our hands clasped tightly together, I know that this euphoria is fleeting, and that Fear and Sorrow are lurking in the shadows of our midst, waiting to lay claim to us again.

I have noticed when Vera is aroused, there is a rough edge in her response, causing her to become more serious, stronger and more aggressive toward me. Already, we are established as dominant and submissive, even in our first bedroom rendezvous, after our wedding by the sea. Our first encounter as woman and wife saw me on my back in missionary for the better part of a full hour, our gigantic breasts mashed together tightly and bulging in cleavage and to the sides of our bodies, with Vera on top in female superior, ending (as I recall) with her pinning my arms to my sides reluctantly as if it were something she had tried to resist, but finally giving in out of pure frustration, beginning a renewed slamming into me that rekindled her fire, and made her eyes roll back for the third and final time. It even brought my voice to the fore, which I try to avoid unless I cannot, crying out over and over again, as her strength multiplied upon itself in domination, my legs back and open wide, while she pounded herself into me without mercy.

Even as I sit astraddle her now, my mind is vivid with that first night underneath her, and the way violence had taken over her pounding. The sound of her orgasm had been unique, coming out in her voice in an angry yell, like a female soldier in battle, or a wayward teenage girl being paddled, whereas she is too angry to submit to tears, but cries out instead in rage and pain. This power, I know she felt, because she had taken full control of me both mind and body, which had caused her body to react accordingly. There is something about me, I know, that causes people to want to dominate me, even to bestow cruelty to me in some form or another. And though I know she would die before she would admit it, I know that inside her is a craving to dominate me with severity in our Gray Palace, betrayed every so often by the fevered violence of her sensual rage against me. But is it my own doing? Is it my own fault, having told her of the Evening Day, of the day I learned that to be born is to be cursed, and to live is to suffer?

I see it in her eyes sometimes. An aggressive contemplation, a sort of angry wondering about my mother and me, of how it can truly be possible that a birth mother is psychologically capable of bitter, deliberate sadism upon her daughter, from early childhood, even to beyond the twentieth year. I felt this in our first kiss, in our Blue Marble Wedding by the Sea, when I could feel the spirit of Barbara Jean Coletti enter her, and from the kiss alone, several years of pent up energy exploded into her body. It was the fulfillment of a forbidden dream—the receiving of a hidden heart's desire for her, to be in my mother's place at that moment, dominating the brunette daughter with the hourglass figure; the tiny waist, the wide haunches and big overdeveloped breasts—to dominate this woman as her mother did—to feel the softness of her lips in perversion, to taste her tongue in deviance—to learn that for Barbara Jean Coletti and me, what we did to one another, what depravities we performed as Mother and Daughter, we did them as unto God, without shame or remorse, away from the prying eyes of judgment and ridicule, no longer able to distinguish between what is hidden and what is forbidden, until we were made prisoner to the Spirit of Lust, which tormented Barbara Jean two fold, as the receiver of pleasure, and the giver of pain.

As I remember my mother's kiss from the Evening Day, as I remember Mother Vera's kiss in our Wedding by the Sea, I am suddenly pulled back into my body astraddle of Vera, both of us naked in the morn, and my body jerks one hard time suddenly, followed by a seizure of long and quiet vibration and trembling from head to toe.

12

*T*he winds howl through the November mist of rain, taking firm hold of my hopes drifted out in the weather, smashing them to bits up against every gray brick and stone. These gray skies weep again for me, as they do every year this Thanksgiving month, this month of birth and death for me. It is the month that the mountain woman was cursed by me almost 40 years ago, when she brought me home from the hospital and wept. And it is the month that I gave birth to Death, and buried her in a child's grave, and gave her name to the ages in stone. When I buried her seven years ago, I know, the music that burned an overture and opera suite, I know it was the grandest finale for my Operatic Stage, and not since have I been able to lift toward an overture a single quill or pen. Over one hundred of them, I believe, a century of joy and sorrow, laughter and pain condensed and heaped upon me for twenty years, burning out in supernova the opera without words *Maria,* the beauty and power of which conjures white fire tinted blue, and the coming of the end of the age I'm in. It is the spirit of The Italian Mozart (Rossini) in the modern day, with the heaviest moaning basses I have ever heard, that groan and sing among the golden colors from the brass, so smoothly dominated and controlled by the chorus of wind and string. The goddess *Semiramide* hath beseeched the god *William Tell,* to form the Goddess of Melody for the end of this age, greater and grander than both mother and father, to achieve a melodic inspiration unique in all of Creation, and a power and force unparalleled under Heaven. Although the world may never hear and will most surely never care, *Maria* is the greatest overture of all time, to precede the explosion of God's end time wrath and fire within. And thus spake Zarathustra, eschatology in the bars of music, in league with Tchaikovsky's tragic desperation of the Swan's Finale, to announce the birth of one greater than themselves, and the epic command by the Lord of Hosts that she be locked away from the world indefinitely, that it may not yet know the terror of the Second Coming of our Lord and Savior. Under this impossible burden I have written, knowing that there is no outlet, no relief from this suffering, yet I write under his Divine Anointing, waiting for the fulfillment of an unfathomable promise to come in. Somehow, I know that the existence of my pathetic self, the existence of my feeble life and poetry, and the existence of my agony in the bars of music, all of it has a significance that only God can foresee, and the death of Carmen Maria hath preceded the end of the world.

But the winds of the rainy November hath called to me again, drowning what few melodies there are left for me to write. Inevitably, the tombstones of this month loom tall again in my memory, so clearly seen in the mist of rain, calling me to gather my coat and step out of the lonely gray cottage, and take a stroll in the November downpour, with only a waterproof scarf of midnight over my head, to match the long black coat and low heeled black boots underneath.

Every now and then, in one of these cold, hard rains, Mother Vera has passed me on this long road, driving the silver gray Mercedes through the gate perpetually closed, to keep out the lost souls and demons who would do us harm. The reality of the world we live in is wickedness, and the evil that men do is on the rise like never before, and as the Evening Day approaches, evil men and seducers will wax worse and worse. It is the evil that bore me, that which tormented my mother and my late husband, that drives Vera to and fro, establishing Peele Houses here and there, where the battered women and children can go to rest. Not to be judged or patronized or condescended to—not to be shamed, nor to have their intelligence insulted, not to be passive aggressively threatened or bullied into leaving their husbands, but their time at one of the houses is a time of refuge and recovery, where the women are free to choose their own course of action—some secretly, ashamedly are in deep love with their husbands, and they so desperately want help for the cause of family, to have the demons of chaos and family discord sent away. And others have crossed a bridge that is washed out behind them, and may not bear ill will, but have inner knowledge and premonition that their marriage is over, and are dreadfully afraid. They have no money, they have no family, they have no place to go. And Vera is so adamant about the welfare of these women, that they be established with a house and a car if they so choose, wishing that she could make them all rich like herself, but being unable to do so. The poor will always be among you, thus saith the Lord, as is the curse of Adam and Eve, according to the will of God. As to his will for us, from life insurance policies alone, we were two widows with twenty million dollars to protect us from the grief of [our husband's] burials. Seven years after my husband was interred, a string of preordained investments have poured from Vera's uneducated mind, to confound the intellectuals holding our money in trust, to see our little farm girl fortune tripled—and only the Lord himself knows its ultimate end, whether it will be good, or whether it will be evil. So many have sacrificed their sweat, their sleep, their souls in hard labour and high education for even the smallest part of what Vera has earned by birth alone, to drive home the most spiritual truth there can be, that there is only Fate, Destiny and the will of God.

But this rainy walk calls me away from the fine cottage retreat, and the mansion of *Amherst Lake* newly built, the palace of *St. Carmen in the Fields.* My mind is turned to the blonde beauty who rescued me from the torment of Death, who is again touched by the depressive spirits that have haunted us over the years. She is such a tower of strength and elegance, a real world woman of beauty outside and in. And I wonder how many of the people who know her outside these walls, how many of them are aware of what churns beneath cultured civility? Of those things which are such a powerful part of who we are—those things that would burden all who know us with such profound shock and fervent disbelief? It is the resurrection of this spirit that has called me away from the bars of music, to walk this rain soaked road to the past, to the days of Vera's and my honeymoon in the farmhouse, after our trembling marriage by the sea. The rain spirits show to me again vividly, what things that there must be, to remind me that mankind cannot cease from sin, and that the only hope is Christ the Lord.

13

I can remember the woman coming home from one of her many charity visits, often in the evening day. The sound of her car (a silver Oldsmobile back then), makes me close my eyes in relief at the sink that she is finally home, to rescue me from the spirits that still lurk inside the house, though John Evans has been dead for three years at least, and the devil who murdered him is gone forever. I have been awakened from a deep sleep by her screams more than once, with her telling me it was Joe Little back from prison, crawling in through the bedroom window, or standing at the sliding glass back door in a storm. Of these dreams, I know so well, though they have nothing to do with the malevolence of a man.

Vera comes into the house from her rolling, silver gray refuge, somber expression lightened up just a bit at the sight of me at the sink, at the smell of southern fried delicacies cooked and ready to eat. *I went shopping today,* she says, placing the brown shopping bag with the lettering 'The Browne Bag Shoppe' to the floor out of my sight. She walks over to me and kisses me full on the lips, then hugs me from behind at the sink.

I had a dream last night, she says. *Its why I had to go shopping.*

Her hands undo the top of my flower made dress, an old souvenir I have bled in, a relic that I cannot throw away, with its tiny rose flower pattern over beige white cloth. She undoes the top buttons and spreads the fabric open, to reveal the gigantic cleavage underneath. I reach my hand back, my damp hand, undried, touching her head, while she leans it forward. As always, the taste of Mother Vera's lips is sweet, to nourish every part of my body.

The woman in the tight navy skirt and matching navy blouse pulls me from the cooking dishes at the sink, her big tittied farm girl, escorting me over to the kitchen table. *Wait right here*, she says, sitting me down as if I were helpless (is it that far from the truth?). She then gathers the three brown shopping bags, picking them up by the thin rope handles and clip clopping out of the kitchen. Smiling, saying *Stay there till I get back.* As I listen to the sound of the midnight blue, echoing away down the hall, I am hardly interested in whatever dress or skirt or new pair of shoes came from 'The Brown Bag Shoppe.' I'd rather be at my kitchen sink of relaxation, my hands in the soap suds too long, defying the logic of modern dishwashing technology. I'd rather spend an hour scrubbing all the pots and pans I ruined cooking breakfast, lunch or dinner, than spend five minutes fumbling with that dishwasher, which for some reason I despise. I think Vera is going to make me start using it soon, even though I'd much rather not.

Momma! I call. *I have to finish these pans in here!* But true to my nature, I cannot mention it again, knowing I have to sit bored at this table until she comes back. I guess I am a little curious as to what shape or style, kind or color the shoes will be this time, to add to the over 100 pairs of them she has already forgotten, from bright red to deep purple, more shoes in one closet than I imagine anybody around here has ever seen or has ever wanted to see.

And just when the living room piano begins to call to me, to tell me a *Fantasy for a Lost Shoe in A minor,* I hear the bedroom door open, and heels of a strange and wonderful new sort, I suppose, begin to come down the hall towards the kitchen, stopping just sort of my line of sight, *clip...clop...clip...clop...* stepping much slower and heavier, more deliberate than before, the sound of a woman who is beyond sure of herself, that her presence in the world at the given moment is perfection, as an artist who presents his finished work, whether it be praised or persecuted.

You can stand up now, I hear her say, which I half-heartedly do, engrossed more now by the piano's shoe than the ones on her feet. But when I step into her view, seeing her walk towards me from down the long hall, the shoes I see are only the midnight blue high heeled pumps I have seen before, inside of which are her bare legs, carrying the feminine mystique unclothed, the body of a tallish blonde beauty bald naked as she can be, hips and waist as strong and hourglass shaped as mine, with two very big, round breasts hanging firm and exposed, pale brown nipples pointing the way towards me in what is left of the daytime dark, and the dim light shining from the kitchen stove. But what has me standing frozen, with my hand over my mouth, my eyes burning the most bewildered and awestruck gaze of my life—is not only the pure, undiluted beauty, the secret, behind closed doors power of what I see. It is the picture of depravities coalesced, the rivers of possibility which have all met here, down from our family trees of origin, to form before me a naked, extremely shapely and fair skinned blonde woman, with a *phallus* hanging down from herself, an inch times ten at least, colored so nearby her own silken white skin, shaped and formed as clear as the chiming of the bells, according to this member of that which pertaineth to a man.

Dismembered, I am. Standing in the glow of unnatural luster, hands still nearby my mouth, but lowered just enough. In awe of the supremely beautiful smile of delighted wickedness on her face. Shaking my head 'no' once, unable to unwrinkle my brow, unable to fathom in these thirty three years of perversion and blood, that the real life sight of such a thing were possible.

Told you I went shopping, she says, still smiling, hung down below like hardly any men that have ever walked the earth could have dreamed, but in divine contrast to the strong and shapely hips upon which its straps are so tightly anchored, and the bulbous, bulging breasts above.

My mother would have wept.

You gon' put that big thing in me? I say, in full Carolina country. She is clever enough to respond only with a smile, escorting me to the table, facing me, then grabbing me by the buttocks and lifting me up, plopping me strongly onto the edge of the table.

I had a dream last night, she says. *I guess you could call it a vision, it was so clear. The bathroom door was open, and I saw a woman as beautiful as you, shaped just like you but taller. Her breasts were even*

43

bigger than yours, if that's possible. Her beauty was magic, Elizabeth. Her breasts and hips were...

Vera pauses, shaking her head in memory. In memory of what I know. What I myself have seen.

She was standing in front of the mirror totally nude, and she was strapping on something like what I'm wearing. I think it hung at least a foot long, I'm not sure. The picture of her turned slightly to the side, looking down, both hands pulling at the straps, with that big cock *hanging down. Elizabeth, I know it probably shouldn't have been, but I think it was the most beautiful thing I ever saw. She was like a goddess. And then she started putting up her long black hair, still looking in the mirror, and she said... "you're going to have to fuck her." Then she started to suck one of those giant breasts of hers. Then I felt an orgasm coming into me that would have made me scream for sure, if I hadn't woke up in time.*

I nod my head. Resigned. Resignated. Unresisting. Unprivy to what Vera had just done in the bathroom out of my sight, stripping to the nude quickly, then choosing the medium sized member she brought, grabbing it with both hands while naked and closing her eyes in a rapturous sigh, looking beyond the ceiling towards Heaven in epic gratitude. Stepping into the harness, strapping on the big ten inches as quickly and completely as she could. Marveling for a moment the powerful sensation coursing through her body; waves of pre-pleasure sent by the merest touching of it, feeling the base of it pressed perfectly enough against her groin to be a new extension of herself, as if the nerves inside her were responding to it as if by magic. Standing there for but a second more, shaking it back and forth with her body only, finding that even this benign motion sparks a craving deep inside. From this, Vera had walked into the bedroom again, returning to her heels of midnight blue, than walking down the hall, feeling a spark of sensation at her groin with every step.

But Momma it might hurt.

We can go slow, baby, she says, voice trembling unbeknownst, a desperation in her eyes I know she is not aware of. *I can just push the tip in for now. Okay?*

Okay.

At the table, standing nude in front of me, she undoes the rest of the top buttons on my dress, sliding my white bra straps and the dress down from my shoulders, taking both of my big bazooms out, then lowering her head like a thirsty animal at a watering hole, taking one into her mouth with a violent and complete sucking, pulling it hard into her mouth with full strength, with activates my own breathing to irregular ins and outs, so that the kitchen is loud with the voice of my pre-raping. The taste of the nipple, even without the flow of milk at this moment, is too good to her body and spirit, causing her to take hold of me with both hands and moan in pure frustration which I can readily perceive, releasing the nipple once in a hard, loud suction, then again this same suction and popping sound many times more. Then she moves my underwear cloth down below, and I stare into her eyes for support as she looks down at the death of New Chastity, pushing the oversized thing into me until it is halfway in, the elephantine thing, this horse dong of a member, drawing power from the grimace on my face, my endurance of the pain from being split nearly open in this raping.

You okay, Baby? she breathes, with no intention of stopping on this side of the grave. *Yes,* I say rather loudly—a whimpering, pathetic 'yes' born from shock and fear more than pain. I grab onto her, then press my face hard against her cheek to prepare myself for the rest of the sliding, which is but a moment from completion, holding on for dear life and breath while she takes a final thrust, pushing the tenth of a century up inside me. The completion of this journey brings a loud cry from me, to cushion the slight agony of violence, which causes her to bellow a loud and rough *oh, yeah* exclaim of pure victory, staring me in the face with *Momma's in now baby,* repeating it ad nauseam. She hugs me without consolation, pushing, grinding her hips, bellowing constantly from the energy of Pandora's Box opened, and I can see from the look of violent anguish on her face that she is every bit as surprised as I, but the surprise of agonizing pleasures that shoot through the body and spirit, when deep and unknown depravities are discovered.

She can only grab tighter the fabric of my dress, and start to lose herself in a pumping that had already begun in her spirit, even before her body's motion was activated. The rough, uncomfortable force fills me up to my womb, and I cry out as she shakes me backward and forward from her hips slamming into me on the table, stopping once to kiss my lips and every inch of my face, her entire body tense now from muscles pulled tight in waiting, a strength greater perhaps, than what she is normally capable of, a strength built up to a spiritual plateau, the unique powering of her body by her brain at this moment, to feed her the energy of Amazonia, the agony of a warrior woman's desire.

At the edge of this tragic outcome for her body and spirit, I hang on helpless and dumb, not quite touched by the hand of Testros as she at this moment, holding on in loud, high pitched yelps, as her impossibly violent pumping reaches a full head of steam, followed by a yell from her not heard since before Salem lost its sanity, and then this witch's cry continues like the sound of the word 'back' yelled to infinity, up the loudness scale and down until it dies, replaced by a most powerful and low pitched bellowing, a blustering cry I can feel running through both our bodies, while she licks, breathes and kisses my shock and tears away.

14

A flash in the Heart of Memory. But a brief moment in the flow of time, when I am at the kitchen table of loving violence, frightened into a last gasp of fear by a phantom dressed in black opening our kitchen door, this, the ghost of my future self come to judge me. And in this pouring rain, I am that ghost seven years hence, pulling open the door to the old farmhouse, catching a glimpse at Carmen seven years before at the table, making eye contact with the ghost of my past self; enduring the profound spark of fear I have felt since before the mansion was built. Those days were a sensual beginning for us that was so auspicious, so filled with bright as lightning potential, that it has arched across time and our brief history. Pure energy, enough to supplement and satisfy the love we already had, which is enough to carry us from here to our lonely graves.

From the mansion and my gray brick hideaway, down the long asphalt road, to the kitchen of the old farmhouse I could not let Vera tear down brick by brick as she desired. In this mausoleum of old melodies and memories I am drawn to every day now rain or shine—to walk the proverbial lane of memories, that lie in wait for me in the farmhouse of death.

Forward and backward over the timeline, this place pulls me along without effort, like the familiar ghost train of legends past, present and future. Before this rainy November, where looms my fortieth year, I had not been back down this road for three long years, hardly even leaving the bedroom of my big mansion home. Avoiding even my House of Melody, which is the gray cottage I just walked from. The place where just two nights ago, these rains fell hard over the evening day, when Brenda Harrison saw perversion through the gray cottage window. Engrossed in a melancholy symphony called *Rossini in Vienna* (my 105th numbered so-called symphony) heavy on inspired melody and misery, of the Crown Prince's failure in his own mind to achieve Mozart, but not realizing how far beyond him his own voice flashed and thundered to exceed that same Mozartian brilliance; the pain of living, breathing, dying in the shadow of the King of Melody—this 105th (and likely the last) symphony of mine was formed fully, and ready to flow from my mind to the paper, where I can still write with the lowly pencil and my notebooks.

And why did I know my blouse must be open, my breasts exposed in my little world while this symphony came to life? Even as a young married woman, I often undid the top of my dress and pulled my breasts out to write in the heat of summer, in my old comfort cushioned chair—this most likely when my mother was heaviest on my mind. But this habit usually came when quartets were written, where the cello's lonely voice would solo her spirit words of fear and sorrow. And perhaps it is that this symphony would be so heavily accompanied by my mother's voice, to the breaking of every rule, this Symphony for Cello and Orchestra in F Major—perhaps it is this which pulled these mammalian memories from their holding place that twilight, when Vera found me there. Not for quite some time was she inclined to what she did, the reaching over my shoulder to grab the heavy breast, pulling it up gently over the shoulder to begin the heavy sucking, this without the milk of our years in this House of Death.

By what strange coincidence, what terrible twist of Fate itself descended such howling bad luck to us that night, when the nosiest, most gossiping busybody in [Martin County] just happened to be at the cottage that evening, having shined car lights that we hadn't even seen through the rainy daytime twilight? By the Spirit alone, I can see, hear and feel all that there is—whether in the heart of my memory or any other, or by that of the Holy Spirit upon my imagination. But in my own feeble brain and recollection, I only recall the return of Depravity's touch in the center of my body, as Vera stood over me whilst I sat at my music desk, taking the greater part of pleasure by the sucking alone, pulling the sensation up from my groin through the nipple into her mouth, until I could sit still and quiet no longer, closing my eyes, closing my legs tighter and pressing my hand against my womb alone, then suddenly convulsing, twitching hard one single time, then a series of quiet, single twitches with eyes unopened, feeling the great and magnificent pull of energy from within.

As Vera had moved from my breast to my lips, to taste from my tongue the brief reawakening of ourselves, as her hand gripped a handful into the big, soft flesh at my nipple, resting still and quiet as we breathed together, I know the sound of these chords of hypocrisy, the green tint of these bells that chime, which had gripped Brenda's spirit like a vice, until the threat of light-headedness caused her to have to look away from the kiss inside, and stumble through the rain back to the black Mercedes, where her daughter Catherine Grace sits in waiting.

15

That sneaky, watermelon breasted bitch, I hear her say, hearing her true self echo in the wind, from their origin in the confines of the luxury car.

What?

Unable to gather the strength for a response, she only takes a deep breath, her heart and mind burdened by the truth of what churns beneath cultured civility.

Mom—

Just drive, Brenda says.

There can be no end to the blast wave, the explosion of envy and feelings of betrayal. If the Brenda spirit did not have enough reason to hate me before, she has been granted this unbelievable gift, that she can see me as an immoral, sweating slut caught behind closed doors, having cast some kind of white witch spell on her rich best friend, keeping her trapped in depravity forever.

"Daughter my *ass,*" Brenda says, in the aftermath of a jealously that runs too deep, to cause the proverbial frost of green ice inside.

Ignoring Catherine Grace's own bewilderment, Brenda's mind begins to glow, the cold Theatre of her mind, aglow with the image of my naked breast sucked into Vera's mouth, a sight that she tries to convince herself is repulsive, but finds that she is unable. Then she is suddenly confronted by the Italian Girl in Carolina, the old-time Woman of Straw, that *"big-tittied country girl,"* she had called me, remembering the day she first met me in the Baptist church, back when my husband was still alive, having literally melted right in front of me with *"Vera said your husband was good-looking but good LORD,"* she had said, making all of us laugh inside the church that day, having only said that I was 'sweet' when she hugged me, her body stiff with underlying resentment for me, that Vera was no longer her lapdog, but a wealthy woman of means by John Evans' timely death, and was now someone to be admired and respected.

I can remember when Vera had begun to talk about inviting them to this old farmhouse for barbecue on the same summer day, a year before my husband died. I remember how I was unable to stop staring at Brenda Harrison because she made me nervous, feeling the heat from her poisoned stare, a long glance directly at my bosoms, then my face, then my hair. But then another look at my husband washed the poison away, unable to be in his presence without becoming a puddle of strawberry ice cream.

I think that my husband was one of the most handsome men of all time. A true Adonis, but having been born under a cloud of grief, and raised in a downpour of domestic abuse and neglect. What was left of him, when Vera rescued us from the grave, was a beautiful shell, a man with no self worth, no confidence, and no hope for the future. He just stood and smiled whenever we were confronted, hardly speaking at all, so that he was impossible to know beyond a soul of great kindness, and a heart of epic love and compassion.

Brenda's mind flashes briefly to the soul of goodness I knew and loved, standing beside the *"fat-breasted gypsy"* he was married to. This day forms a point of origin in the Brenda Harrison mind, allowing the spark of energy to arc across time to this rainy evening of her drive, to strike her heart with the profoundest hatred for me imaginable. Seven years late and a dollar short, she is, to ride this train from ignorance to the Truth. And she must endure the agonizing trauma of revelation, like a woman fallen into dangerous surf over a pier, then to have that pier be smashed into splinters by a passing, malevolent boat at the edge of her rescue. She must stay in these precarious waters, these waters of endtime revelation, and suffer the choking they must provide. Her survival depends on the mercy of God, as Fate splashes and rolls her ashore, where the coughing truth burns her lungs in near drowning.

Brenda Harrison rides the rain soaked streets of this town, wondering how it is that her life has come to such a state of affairs. When Conrad Harrison went bankrupt, Vera was there for her like no other. When he suddenly began to disappear later and later into the evening after work, Vera was there like no other. And when he finally left her after twenty four years of marriage, when her daughter was in graduate school, yes, Vera

Evans had been there like no other. Brenda and Vera had both braved the years of pent up rage and fear, their tense, sado-masochistic bond kept alive by synergy, keeping them drawn together by forces they had no power to control, even though there was such underlying jealously, resentment and dislike between them. All of which had begun to fade overnight—when Brenda's husband spent the night away for the first time, then told her over the phone they were going to have to talk. So much of Brenda's superior attitude had faded into the sunset of her dead marriage, until finally one day she invited Vera into her daughter's shrine of a bedroom again, and while they hugged in the aftermath of trauma, Brenda had sobbed like a broken woman. Accepting Vera's hearty, sensual hugs with such profound gratitude, like shelter from the downpour of a cold, winter rain. *I'm here for you Baby*, Brenda's wealthy friend had said, feeling Vera press hard against her in Catherine Grace's old room, her body soothed to tingling by the sound of Vera's voice, by the scent of her hard candy breath, by the taste of it at her lips, by the feel of Vera's big, soft breasts pressed against her own. These sophisticated, middle aged charity queens, whom their friends believed had no problems that could break them, alone together behind closed doors pressed together in a hug meant for their eyes only, Vera's body on fire from the weeps and sobs she feels from her friend, who until this moment had shown no such vulnerability, no such submissiveness and humility. And the quiet, brief kiss they had shared, had gone straight to the center of Brenda's yellow blonded, high class self, lighting a fire of renewal, and a belief in her heart that what her and Vera now had was special, best friends uniquely committed under the sun.

From that fateful scene three years ago, when the Harris divorce was final, to Brenda's rainy arrival at her beautiful suburban brick home a few nights ago in Grand Harwich Estates (a home she would have lost if Vera had not intervened), Brenda sits still in the parked car with her bewildered daughter, unable to fight spirits of disillusionment and despair.

"Are you alright?" Catherine Grace says.

Brenda turns to look at her daughter's pretty face, drawing small comfort from its benign, ordinary attractiveness, enhanced by hair, makeup and an expensive looking white silk blouse and earrings. A tall, thin, blonde young woman of educated, complicated and suddenly antiquated appeal.

"Kiss me."

Catherine Grace leans over, in the quiet confines of their little space, and presses her lips lovingly to her mother's cheek. But Brenda can only turn and gaze a quiet, judgmental stare, having still found no comfort, not even in her daughter's kiss, nor suddenly in the car that Vera Evans paid for, nor from the glow of the soft light fixtures in back of the lovely house that Vera saved from foreclosure.

"Like you meant it," Brenda says. "Kiss me. Like you meant it."

"I *did.*"

"Okay, forget it then." Brenda opens the door in a huff, the car light flashing onto their lonely, isolated, focused event. Catherine Grace grabs her mother's arm, conceding to this latest insanity, telling her mother to close the door again. The lithe blonde daughter breathes a sigh, leaning in to her mother's cheek again, pressing harder this time. But not hard enough.

"There, you feel better?"

"No," she says, looking her daughter in the eye. "No I don't."

"What do you want, Mom? What's the matter?"

"I want you… to kiss me… like you *mean* it."

Oh, what secrets that bear revealing, what secrets are there, still waiting to be revealed! What sights and sounds might give birth to pain— oh, what secrets lie hidden in the rain! They hear the fervent increase in the November rainfall around them, both burdened by the Autumn cold, the sudden strangeness and tension born. From this twilight rainfall, there is another spirit come to life, dormant abilities sparked by sights of the forbidden, causing Brenda Harrison's body to give way to the heat of a new flame, as she breathes deeply the scent of her daughter's expensive perfume, holding her by the back of the head, pressing their lips together in desperation and grief.

"I need your tongue," she says.

"But Mom—"

"Please."

In the driving rainfall, at the fall of the Carolina night, Brenda Harrison takes her daughter's tongue into her mouth deeply, to fill the void left by Vera's betrayal, as she longs for the taste of her best friend's tongue in her mouth, and the touch of Vera's naked breasts on her skin.

16

The Lesbian, the Lesbian

The Lesbian snack

I kissed another woman's lips

And now I can't go back

The Lesbian, the Lesbian

The Lesbian snack

I touched another woman's hips

And now I can't go back

17

The rain falls in weeping over the Mother Daughter Dynamic. Over the mother weeping from the ghostly pain of a great depression—building these last three years since her husband left—having held on to her daughter like a static cling fabric, already making allusions to this night so many times over these last few months—the strongest being on their mother daughter trip to Myrtle Beach, and a long, tight hug in their bikinis in the hotel. But these were of a benign sort; the kind that all mothers and daughters can hide in pretense of moral and emotional support. Unwilling, or unable to cross the line into what the public would hath deemed as forbidden. To unlock the last taboo. The last great secret of mankind's enduring legacy of perversion. The last revelation before the end of the world.

Mother Daughter Perversion. It is a hidden river that flows beneath the surface of who we are in public—shades of which can be seen in some public mother daughter displays, and the sensual way they carry themselves. And this perversion may not be limited to the incestuous mind; there are some who channel this subconscious energy in mother daughter camping trips, mother daughter beauty pageants, mother daughter fun ship cruises and the like, ad infinitum, to satisfy the energy of this craving, of what some recognize as an unnatural closeness between them. It is a shameful secret that so many of us bear alone, having been put upon by our mothers, who often because of a deep and abiding depression must have an outlet for a corresponding libido, where a deep and abiding lust resides. In the house at Grand Harwich Estates, in the rainfall of yesterday's grieving, Brenda Harrison is in disbelief at the expanse of feeling inside, the great, rolling pleasure from her lips to her groin and back again—standing in the middle of the living room floor in a deep hug and kiss with her daughter. It is a new drug of choice, I think, rather than what medicines come from the prescription bottle—so tragically born not purely from herself, but from the sight of the great breasted secret she saw at my cottage window.

In the kitchen inside the old farmhouse, still lost in the daytime dark, my heart races from the sound of a woman's voice I hear, this, the weeping and sobbing of a suburban charity queen, holding her daughter tight after the deep kiss, her voice shaking under remorse and regret, saying *I'm sorry* over and over again, telling her blonde, pretty daughter how much she loves and needs her, and how much she can't live without her. I am one with the Catherine Grace mind, holding the woman in her mid-forties, enduring the moaning, mourning sobs, of the kind she has never seen or felt from her mother, feeling the strange sensations of her mother kissing her neck like a desperate lover, not knowing where all the tears and incessant loud sniffing could possibly be coming from all of a sudden—why suddenly after all these years the mother daughter line must be breached now.

I want you to suck my nipples.

Sometimes, the words that flow into the air are a jumble of sound, the jibberish of a language unlearned, so that the brain cannot process their meaning all at once, to spare the heart and soul the shock and trauma of it.

"What did you say?"

"I said I want you to suck my nipples."

"What... wh…"

"I don't understand what the problem is all of a sudden. You just had your tongue in my mouth a minute ago."

"I know that, Mom. God, when you say it out loud…"

"I don't see anything wrong with it—with a mother and daughter expressing themselves in private every once in a while. Its nobody else's business but ours."

"Mom… really?"

Brenda harnesses what dominant power she has left, burning the mother's gaze of judgment into her tall blonde daughter.

"Mom we're just deep kissing. And it was kinda nice, I guess. As strange and twisted as it was. I guess I kind of liked it. I'd die before I told anybody about it though."

"So I'm gross and disgusting now, huh?"

"Of course not. But Mom, what you're talking about doing—its…"

"I *know* what it is. And I still say that between a mother and daughter who love each other… maybe there's nothing wrong with it at all."

"This is… this is coming from somewhere," Catherine says. "Either something you've seen or read, or something somebody told you…"

"I *told* you Catherine. Its because I love you. I've been thinking about it for a long time."

"Since Dad left?"

"Your father being gone has got nothing to do with it."

"Then what *does* it have to do with? You didn't start acting like this until after you got back in the car from Vera's house. Are you mad because you couldn't find her? Her car was there, you could have just knocked on the door. You were at the window so long I thought…"

When Brenda tucks her thin, pretty lips in and looks away, what spirits of instinct and revelation there are take hold of the Catherine Grace mind.

"This didn't all start until after we left Elizabeth's house. What does that have to do with this? Why are you all of a sudden acting so strange?"

"Is it strange," Brenda says, "for a mother to demand and accept her daughter's kiss?"

"Uh…*yeah,*" comes the brutally honest Whip of Truth. Snapping the air lightning quick. "Weird doesn't even begin to describe this."

"Well… I think it's beautiful."

"Out with it."

"Nothing's wrong, I said."

"And I said *out with it*. Unless you want me to drive back home tonight."

Brenda concedes her daughter's impatience, and her earned right to know. She glances at Catherine's powdered and perfumed prettiness, and turns to the portrait over the fireplace; of a barefoot country girl holding a sickle of death, walking through a field at either sunrise or sunset, distracted by the song of a lark somewhere out of sight.

"Youknow how beautiful Elizabeth is, right?"

"She's the best looking woman I've ever seen."

"Well, she's even more beautiful with her clothes off. Her breasts… are as big as a mountain."

"Excuse me?"

"You heard me. When I looked in the front window of her guest house, I saw her at her livingroom desk. She was topless. No… completely naked. I didn't know breasts that big were possible. You just don't see that on a normal sized woman. Her shape is a gift from God. I've known her for years, always knew she was top-heavy. But I never dreamed…"

"Is that why you're suddenly so miserable? Because you saw Elizabeth naked at her desk? Are you really that jealous of her?"

Arms crossed, Brenda lowers her head and nearly cracks a smile, amused at her daughter's epic lack of understanding.

"What I saw tonight," she says, "Is the end of the world."

Fully perplexed, Catherine Grace follows her own bewildered gaze over to her mother.

"I'll admit, that's pretty amazing. And to tell you the truth, I'm sorry you didn't have a camera. But its not really that big a deal. She'll never know you saw her."

"Yes, but *I'll* know. Its too bad we can't just plug printers into our brains. Then *you'd* know."

"Know what? That Elizabeth Peele's got a pair of the world's largest breasts, I *know* that. Big deal. Everything about her is weird anyway."

"I saw something else too. Something I never imagined. Something I'll never forget for the rest of my life."

By the barefoot girl in the field, nearby the phantom song of a lark, Brenda Harrison steps down from a life of practiced hypocrisy and pretense, to ring the Bell of Truth, to tell the Third Part of the Truth to her daughter, which is cataclysm. This is the whirlwind of destruction, gathered in the images of Vera and me in my gray cottage—a whirlwind of impossibilities and what is unimaginable, blowing through the lives of the mother and the daughter, after having shared their own kiss already, their House of Denial damaged even before this revelation—about what churns beneath cultured civility. Brenda feels the tingling energy in her body as she talks, and is hardly aware of the change in her daughter's expression, from self-assured bewilderment to shock and disbelief, then finally to somber awe and devastation.

"I think I understand," she says. "Are you going to tell Vera?"

"I... I can't."

"Then what are you going to do?"

"I'll tell you what I want to do. I want to *fuck* her."

"Who, Vera? Or—"

"Elizabeth."

The two of them are suddenly lost in the Heart of Memory, to where my helplessness takes form in long, dark hair.

"I don't know where the Hell she came from. But I wish to God I could run a pole up her white ass and send her back."

"Why? Just because of what you saw?"

"How would you feel if you caught Yvonne Brown with another woman's tits in her mouth?"

The mere mention of her best friend's name causes Catherine to stiffen at the possibility. The idea that even in this rainfall, Yvonne could be taking shelter under a stranger's roof. Whether it be man or woman.

"Yvonne likes men."

"Honey, they all like men, until the right woman comes along. Don't you know that? Or has Yvonne's big, floppy tits never caught your interest?"

A stern, cold look from the daughter. No answer.

"That's what I thought."

"Are you accusing me of being a *Lesbian?*"

"I'm accusing you of being…a woman. I'm accusing you of being my daughter."

"You always think something's going on between me and Yvonne. What about you and Vera?"

"What about me and Vera?"

"You tell me. You're the one who's so mad with her because of what you saw, that you had to kiss all over me to get over it. If she was just your best friend, if there was nothing else there, you wouldn't have cared less if her and Elizabeth had something going on."

"But I *do* care. The same way you'd care if Yvonne stuck her light-skinned tits in another woman's mouth."

"Stop *saying* that. I *wouldn't*."

"Why can't you hear me say it? You don't have to lie anymore. You don't have to try to cover up, Baby."

"Mom, I'm not a *dyke!*"

The last word comes out in a choked scream. Burdened by tears, and a heavy weight of frustration and sorrow.

"Then why are you crying?"

"I'm not—"

This last word is choked away. As a stick of dynamite at a dam, whose lit fuse has been cut and thrown away at the last second.

"Like mother. Like daughter. Your best friend has a busty, hourglass figure. My best friend has a busty hourglass figure."

"So what is that supposed to mean? Its just a coincidence."

"I felt you holding back when you kissed me. I felt it but I could also feel that explosion underneath. Something you've had dormant inside you since you were a little girl. Something you've been fighting your entire adult life. Running from one man to another, getting humped and dumped by one pathetic, empty promising loser after another, wishing to God that you didn't have to play their stupid games anymore, wishing you could just settle down and be who you really are inside."

"Oh, my God," says Catherine, nearly laughing. "My Mom's coming *out.*"

"You call it what you want. You make fun of it all you want. All I know is that all of a sudden, this very minute, I don't know who the Hell I am anymore."

"You're Vera Evans' *bitch.*"

As if pushed down upon, and powered by a spring, Brenda's arm moves quickly on its own, to slap her daughter's face to oblivion.

"What gives you the right to talk to me like that? I was the one who laid in the hospital screaming until they had to split me open with a fucking razor blade to pull your big, bowling ball head out of me until I thought I was going to die. I was the one who shitted your big headed white ass into this world and then fed you and raised you and spent tens of thousands of dollars on you while you whored your way through your so-called childhood while your father didn't give a damn if you lived or *died!* And who the Hell are you to judge me, the biggest fucking closet dyke on this side of the Appalachian mountains! Oh, you think I haven't seen it? Everybody's fucking seen it! Everybody was too polite to say anything about your spoiled, pissy little Tomboy ass! I was the one who taught you how to dress, I was the one who taught you how to stop dressing like a fucking *boy!*"

Catherine Grace Harrison braves the storm. As a tree in the throes of a violent wind, whose branches twist and sway to the outer limits, to the far edges of their calling.

"I was married for almost 25 years, and I raised a daughter who grew up and got her PhD, while most of the little bitches you went to high school with are worried about 30 hours a week at JC Penney. So just because I have rocked myself to sleep for *years* with the thought of Vera Evans sitting on top of me bald ass naked and shaking like goddamn shock patient, I have earned the right to keep my *fucking* sexuality to myself! I want to fuck Vera Evans? Huh? Then you want to fuck Yvonne Brown! And no, I am not gay, and if I were it would be my right, and my fucking business!"

In the brief and sudden calm, the angry mother strolls heavily to the sofa and sits down, resting her head in her hand, leaning on the soft cushioned chair arm away from her daughter. In devastation and ruin, the daughter walks defeatedly towards the stairs.

"Where are you going?"

"I'm just gonna go pack. I think I should get—"

"You will *not* abandon me! Did you hear me!"

Brenda stands up quickly and hurries over to her daughter, grabbing her arm.

"I had to put myself back together after your father left—and I will *not* go through that again. Now you get your ass over to that sofa."

"You can't talk to me like this. I'm a grown woman, I have a life."

"You will get over to this couch," she says, pulling her hard by the arm, pushing her hard down to the sofa. "You will sit here and you will shut the *fuck* up, and you will fucking respect me as your mother!"

In the aftermath of violence, in the uneasy calm of rage subsided— Brenda Harrison walks to the other end of the plush sofa of charcoal gray, and sits quietly in the evening day, in the dark'ned twilight rain.

Vera's life is guided so intimately by dreams. It is the beginning of who we are, and who we always have been. Even before I ever knew she existed, she had dreamt of me; face, hair and sorrow alike. And this dream energy had leapt, then drifted across the miles to where I lay in misery. And there were times when the echo of this fine woman would whisper my name, and add to the mysterious nature of my life—not knowing whether to be frightened, or whether to be comforted by her. She once called herself a 'dream queen,' which might mean different things to different people, I suppose. But to what I know of Mother Vera, it means that the spirits of what is meant to be flow in and out of her dreams like petals in the wind. And this oddity, this abnormality, this gift of unfairness to billions of others, this Divine advantage of hers in life—she has accepted. Whether it is the grandness of world stage finances, a sixth sense on what stocks to buy and when to sell, or whether it is the intimate, private world of our domestic—of what dinners are prepared, or room is redecorated, or what new pleasures will take place in our bedroom.

Standing in the old Gray Palace (bedroom) inside the brick farmhouse at the end of the road, the spirit of Barbara Jean Coletti touches my heart again, to display the wild origins of my new mother and me, the untapped violence released from both of us during that time. We were four years together as mother and daughter wife in this house, where we played out our end of the world drama unseen. Behind these closed doors, I can still detect the erotic pain we suffered to coalesce, when the two of us came together as one. This, even while the milk of our perversion still ran, bloating my breasts up to gargantuan proportions, from which they have never subsided, even though the milk itself has long gone. In those days, I was as my mother had been—a cow to be sucked and milked, to be pounded and pulled upon, to be wrestled to naked submission, to be pulled over the knee and spanked to tears fully clothed, or even paddled by my own request, so that I could feel the burning fires of my youth on the farm spread to my groin and barren womb while my tormentor took her portion of a spiritual daughter's milk, her violent and satisfied portion of me. And I can remember in those days, how the lust and craving I had was woven into pain, so that I needed for Vera to treat me roughly, especially at times my breasts, grown to Barbaranian proportions, flopping and hanging down in forbidden girth, many times too large for my frame, seen unclothed by

Vera's eyes only. I had trouble making her understand so often, that the controlled, firm spanking of my nipples is a pain that rises to pleasure in my body. How the perfect twisting and pulling of them is a suffering that phases to sweetness inside. That the loud and boisterous yelling is the agony that must come out of my voice, while the pleasure grows and takes Agony's place inside.

Sitting here on the king sized bed in Vera's old bedroom, gazing at the figure dressed in black I see in the mirror, I am unafraid now of the daytime dark, by what is left from my mother's visitation; a shuffling in the kitchen, a doorknob rattled, even a footstep or two. What of these ghosts that have haunted me all of my life—what serious harm can they do? For I have known the depths of fear, even unto torture and death, and I know that my days of Hell on this earth are over, and my mansion home is the arrival of Days of Heaven. Here, in the ghostly daytime dark, the theatre of my mind thrusts me into the Heart of Memory again, where Vera and I stand intimate in the front of the mirror, with nary a stitch of cloth to cover our bodies. Before Heaven and Earth, when we are concealed from the outside world, we are not ashamed before the Almighty, who will judge the right and wrong of what we must do.

For I am not a child, as I was on the Coletti farm, abused as a toddler and an infant, breasts suckled as a 12 year old, twisted and spanked raw as a teenager. I am come of age, having survived a 13 year marriage in Hell, and my sensibilities have been tried by fire. What I do, I do willingly before my Redeemer, who hath forgiven all of what sins and wickedness I have done.

Even at this moment back in time, the strong woman stands behind me at the mirror, sucking the deep bruise onto my neck as her hand rests still at my groin. I must call upon his Name in my mind, to pray for the strength to endure what I know is going to happen to my body. The sucking at my neck, each pulling of her lips away is very loud, as much a part of what arouses me as a touch, a pinch, or a squeeze. I take my own breasts into my hands, allowing Barbara Jean to flow inside, taking one of the great globes up to my mouth for a single long and mighty suck, enough to cause the sweet fountain to flow. But what nourishment I need will not come from the milk today, but from what pain I can receive from Mother Vera, which she does not know she is called by God to give me. What callings in life we have, we all perform unawares, whether on the world stage, or whether it be done in secret.

I whirl the most gigantic self squeezing that I can upon my own breasts once, twice, then a whirling again once more, until I grow impatient enough to take Vera by both wrists, and guide her hands to my bosom. *I want you to hurt 'em,* I say. Instinctively she squeezes, but nowhere near to my satisfaction. *I want you to squeeze harder,* I say. *Like this.* I put my hands over top of hers, and bury her hands into the flesh, telling her to grab the nipple and pull. *Harder. Harder,* I say. *Pull my nipple until it hurts.* Of this, she reluctantly complies, watching carefully the reaction on my face, to see my brow wrinkle slightly from the pain. And I know that it activates the dominant craving she has, which has flashed many times before, as she pulls on them again, this time harder I feel, which relaxes me to a higher state of being. *Squeeze 'em,* I say, *I need you to squeeze 'em hard.* In her compliance, I still sense a fearful reticence, the intrepid holding back, as if she is cautious, afraid to cause me harm, although I know how badly she has been wanting to. It is time for us to descend. To go deeper into the depraved truth that I am, the truth that was created by my birth mother, truth that is too deep to be spoken. *Twist them. Harder. Harder. Twist the nipples like you're angry with me. Punish me for being a gypsy slut...*

Vera allows the understanding to kick in, and she gives both nipples a mighty twist, sending a pain through me where I have to take a breath from the shock, and push back against her and groan a deep, gruff voice. *Oh my God,* I hear her say, leaning back to kiss her roughly on the mouth, to feel what energy is born from her by Fate, when she causes me great pain for the first time. *Do it again,* I say, *like you want me to cry from the pain.*

Baby, are you sure, she says, to which I say *yes, please,* feeling the lightning bolt stab through me again harder than I can easily handle, and I must scream a short, quick burst of pure shriek, which is pain, and the sound of agony leaping from my body into the room. But she continues, to hear me break down in something close to regret, though the pleasure from it is almost equally unbearable. Somewhere in the noise of my own shock and weeping, I hear her exclaim roughly to God again, and I feel her body spasm against mine, and shake violently enough to remind me of Barbara Jean in an earthquake.

19

*I*n the rain of the present day, many years from that awakening inside her, I wonder how much of what happens to us is pure chance, and how much of it is meant to be. Where does the will of man end, and the Will of God begin? What diversions, what deviance lives inside the hearts of women and men, so solemnly suppressed and sworn against, waiting to erupt like a fountain of volcanic mist, like the breath of a white dragon up from slumber, burning blue and black fire from within? Of these fires, the flames in which I was formed, the fire in which I was born and raised, by what Divine plan were they carried across the timeline like a burning comet, to crash into the life of this beautiful woman whose house I'm in?

How is it that I languish in the Heart of Memory, whereas she stands behind me as never before, in the aftermath of her strongest orgasm to date, vision hazed, swallowing once from spit gathered in her mouth, both her hands still clamped so hard to both of my gigantic tits?

I'm sorry I hurt you, she says, but breathing it so insincerely, still in disbelief that such an orgasm is truly possible, grown and flashed into her body from my screams alone. It is the Coletti touch, the ghost of Barbara Jean fully arrived, and I nearly smile as I lean back against her to relax, unafraid from this manifestation, of the spirit of Sadomasochism in our midst. *I need you to spank 'em,* I say, to which she clumsily obliges, hitting them awkwardly from the sides, making them jump and swing, which is good enough for now. *Now squeeze 'em,* I say. *Squeeze 'em really hard...* and she buries her lovely hands into the soft flesh like balls of bread dough, giving them both a good firm squeezing wet with the milk, but only to the point of firmness, rather than the hardness I require. *Go harder,* I say, pushing against her hands, teaching her to lift the big things high up into her hands in rough firmness, then a gigantic squeeze hard enough to make them sore. This, I need repeated over and over, which relaxes me back against her, grabbing her long blonde hair with my hand lifted behind me.

Spank 'em again, I say, waiting to see the inadequacy, the feeble and nonexistent effort. After she begins, I reach down to show her what I mean, and begin to spank the front of my own breasts with the same fever a mother spanks the behind of her naked daughter with. But the pain can only make me breathe just so much in the false response, to show her of what erotic nature this may be. *You have to punish me,* I say, somber and deliberate, while she takes a good hold of my body with one hand, and smacks good and hard the front of my breast with the other, again and again, until the sensation is on the edge of being right. *Harder and faster*, I say, snapping at her just a little, enough to make her get up and go, spanking my areolas with enough continued force to make me push and cringe back against her. She stops at the near edge of my endurance, to watch me writhe, to feel me writhing, feeling her own energy rising again.

And when she resumes the nipple spanking, it is with purpose and without mercy, forgetting herself in the negative emotion, this by revelation, by predestination, raising her hand high up with every swat to my nipples, bringing down hard and fast each punishing blow to my tits, spanking me as though I deserve it, hard enough to make me have to push back against her, hard enough to make me have to release the struggle, hearing my voice come out on its own, but shocked when she does not stop, crying out again in a flash of regret, then suddenly feeling a hard tug at my hair, and her lips clamped forcefully to mine. As I groan deeply, the sound muffled by this dominant kiss, I feel her spirit take over in malice, which is sadism unleashed, with both my breasts now being squeezed to their proper point of pain, to where I understand that I have caused it to happen, that I have triggered the crossing over into pain and punishment. I suddenly feel a double whack, both her strong hands slamming hard into both my breasts and squeezing, with a force that takes me back to the farm. A touch of fear flows through as she does it again, fear and pain merging in conduit from my breasts to my groin. She takes my ear to her teeth just enough, biting down a firm hold, then slamming both hands in pure violence, repeating it while holding me still with her teeth clamped at my ear.

I am transported backward though space, to when my mother would do this very same thing, sometimes when I was at the kitchen sink or at the cooking stove, or simply naked in her bedroom on Sunday morning. Of this violence, I am so familiar, having been trained to love it as a comfort, and as a source of Divinely wrought pleasure for my body. From this powerful whacking, we work ourselves into a steady rhythm, me with my arms back, grabbing Vera's hips for support, her bashing both hands to both my breasts in hard, slow and steady cadence, working me up to a threshold of pain I have not felt since before my mother left me, carrying unbelievable sensations to the center of my body, causing me to need the continued slapping violence at my breasts until my eyes roll back and my mouth hangs open in the awe of slow motion falling, and I feel an explosion of energy that makes me push backward against her and begin to scream a deep, woman's scream, very loud and forceful into the room, something far beyond the call of Agony, in the mixture of pleasure and pain.

Vera's strength gathers itself, through the rising of the sadistic mind, causing her to slam herself into the back of me at the hips once, and then once again, now holding on to my breasts like two great handles of support, to steady both her and me alike, for the pounding that now must be. The manner of this orgasm is incomplete inside me, holding me to a torturous plateau of whimpering and straining against the unending grip to my womb, a grip of pleasure caused by pain. I feel the dampness, the swollen nature of this woman's self behind me, pushed at my backside in a fervent straining of herself—grunting from the effort—that gives way to a faster pounding against me, rocking the foundation of my sanity, until I am crazy with shrieks and begging, while the slamming against my backside rolls this phantom energy inside to infinity.

20

These are the fires of goodwill that burn. Those in the Vera Evans mind, burning blue and black fire. In the daytime dark of the present day, standing at the bedroom mirror of dreams, I can see us as clearly as I could then, blonde woman in the pinned up hair, so comfortably in her own Amazonian skin, so comfortable running to and fro, spreading time and money all over Creation in the name of charity. Fueled now by what fires in her soul that ignite, energized by the darkest memories humanely possible. Of the shotgun blast that blew her husband out of this world, of the cold knife blade in this very room, that nearly sliced her out of this world as well. A survivor of a brutal rape and attempted murder, she is, these are the goodwill fires that burn. In love with one who was a prisoner of that evil spirit, that venerable domestic evil that is surely from the devil—in love with me to the core of her heart and soul, in love with a woman of straw, poverty, ashes and soot. This misery torments the Vera Evans mind, motivated by epic Fear and Depression: volunteerism unfettered, unleashed, with no G.E.D, no Associates Degree, no Bachelors's Degree, no Master's Degree, and no trek in a desert to a Ph.D. Hers is the freedom of passion without pay, to help those who are less fortunate than she, time and money spread throughout Creation, done in the name of Charity.

And does it matter of the burning in her soul, the agony of what was revealed to her in gunpowder and cold steel, what was revealed to her in blood? Does it matter of the way the blood ran from the cut flesh of her back, when the killer's belt sliced it open in sensual rage? Does it matter of the way her backside suffered a splitting of its own from the raping, from the Sodomy of the Farmer's Wife, which made her understand the echo of Hell on Earth, and the power of the Curse of God over mankind? Does it matter that Charity and Goodwill are but a grand medication, an inner need satisfied to her own soul's content, as well as the contentment for others? What energy fuels the Fires of Goodwill—the fires in which we burn? What are our motivations for what feeble charities we give?

At the mirror of our time, I see what flowering of seeds planted have grown, as I see myself in the nude in sorrow, as a prisoner again of violence, but this time of my own making, when I gave her permission to exact a punishment on me she had felt in her dreams the night before. As it was when she endured the whipping of death, I too stand in front of the mirror, dimly lit by the soft lamps inside our Gray Palace (bedroom). I brave the fear resurrected, the nerves I have suffered my entire life, watching the reflection of her face in the mirror, studying the shameful determination, the irresistible urge to see me broken under the lash, to try as she might to see me as my mother and my husband saw me for 30 years; as a beaten, bruised and battered woman.

Is it ironic that such a compassionate woman, such a beloved and kind woman in public—is it ironic that a charity queen buys a black leather belt in pretense, smiling when the sales woman says, *we've got to buy 'em something sometimes don't we*, walking out of the men's clothing store as if she had left the Brown Bag Shoppe, unable to make eye contact? Is it ironic that she stands with this belt in her hand, with me looking in the mirror, afraid, raising the belt so high in her hand, and bringing it down with all her strength on my naked backside? What is the irony, of this Woman of Charity and Goodwill, studying the quick rising of a red welt, feeling the lust in her body grow, then raising the folded belt, and whacking it across my buttocks again. The pain, I must admit, causes me to cringe a bit, shocked when she says sharply, *stand still.* The tone in her voice is one she has never used with me before. It is a soul of bitterness uncovered, where tolerance and civility go to die, and where fear and resentment are born. I feel the third flash of heat to my hips, causing me to immediately tear up from the extraordinary pain, which seems to go past where pleasure resides, to where there is only sorrow and fear.

But these tears can only serve her sadistic purpose, the punishment part of her awakened, the belt suddenly the phallic extension of herself, stroked by the striking of it against my hips and thighs, to raise her inner woman to plateau. After the fifth, sixth and seventh stroking of folded leather, she stands close behind me, looking at my tears without remorse, nor even the tiniest echo of compassion or pity. *I'm gonna have to whip you,* she says, to which I nod my head while the tears fall, feeling her squeeze once against my backside, to help relieve the pressure in her building.

In the mirror, I see the strong, naked blonde woman take hold of my naked blood sister, and I feel the Call of the Whipping Leather against my skin. She grabs tight hold of my upper arm, and begins to lay the belt across me in classic form, spanking a fear in me I have known all my life, as the types of fear are many, among these being the Fear of Pain. It causes me to whimper at every flash of leather against me, some at the small of my back, my sides, my legs, my thighs, and most decidedly at my hips and bottom. Her grip on my arm is tremendous, the force of the blows is traumatic heat to my white skin. *I... told... you,* she says, *I...told...you...I was...going...to...whip you...didn't I...*this, to my loud, pathetic response of *yes, Momma please*, a bit confused by the fervor, by the fevered pitch of it all. She spins me around and grabs my other arm, her face nearly unrecognizable to me, now facing the front of my welted body, where my breasts hang exposed, above my tiny curved waist, above the widened hips, and the shaven, shameful front side of me.

The first blow strikes my groin, causing me to scream loudly, and try to pull away from the whipping. What kind of person must I be, to inspire hatred in even the ones who love me?

Vera brings the belt across the front of my thighs too many times for me to count, even up to my waist, and across my swinging breasts at least one times ten. When this last blow to my breast is struck, the Spirit of Violence departs in satisfaction, and the angry woman stands boldly in front of me, judging me, still holding the belt, telling me sharply to *go over the mirror and look at yourself*, which I do obediently, hands up to my sniveling mouth, arms covering the front of my heavy hangers, well fed hips exposed to her while I stand at the mirror red-faced and weeping. It is the burning of black fire tinted blue, having leapt from the Vera Evans mind to my skin in agony, the blue and black fires of goodwill that burn.

21

I am a future ghost in the room. Gazing at two lost women, but perhaps not lost souls, on the road from here to Heaven. For whatever heavenly reward these two must partake someday, their time here is burdened by the Curse of Eve, and the sorrow her husband brought upon mankind. I see a woman of extraordinary manner and appearance at the mirror, heavy breasted, upside-down-heart-hipped and weeping. Standing alone, arms crossed over the heavy bosom. In the Heart of Memory, her future ghost is pulled inside, until I am a prisoner of my younger self, standing at the mirror in sorrow. I turn to look at Vera's confident, casual walk to the closet; big, strong hips switching the motion she is accustomed, hanging the belt somewhere inside her walk in closet outside my view.

Although I have received many times worse over the years, I have never liked the whippings, as they burn my skin with a fire too hot to endure. Even my breast is welted in several places. The raised, elongated impressions of the belt are everywhere, though none are given place to blood, as were those when I was wed to Barbara Jean in hatred, or to my husband in rage. They itch and tingle everywhere, across the cosmos of my body, reminding me of how the stars gradually appear and begin to twinkle on a hazy summer's night. As Vera returns from her closet, there is a flash of the same resistance I once had for my mother when the whippings would end, and she would return to me from the tiny closet space in her bedroom. Even then, my nineteen, twenty and twenty one year old self were so often at one of the mirrors unclothed, arms crossed in front, refusing to touch a single spot of itching or burning, staring at the crisscrossing of bloody welts from my shoulders to my thighs.

Vera steps up behind me, and I turn and hug her immediately, sobbing, telling her how badly the whipping hurts my skin. She holds both sides of my face while I hug her around the middle—kissing my forehead and eyes, kissing every inch of my cheeks, then resting her lips full to mine, breathing in through her nose, kissing my bottom lip, then the top, then both lips in sensual unison. *That was a good whuppin' wasn't it, Baby?* Reluctantly, I nod my head, though I really want to shake my head 'no.' *But you didn't like it much did you?* Again, I nod my head. Politely. *Don't worry,* she says, studying the welts on my backside in the mirror. *One day when you're in the mood, I'm gonna let you return the favor.*

I won't do it.

How come?

Because I know how bad it hurts.

But you've hurt me before. You've twisted my nipples hard enough to make me scream.

I know.

I'm going to have to be honest with you, Baby. That belt turns me on. I came twice while I was whipping you.

I didn't know that.

Now I know why your Momma whipped you so much. She had to.

And now you have to, I say. Not hiding the irritation. *And that belt hurts.*

Maybe I won't hit so hard next time.

Or maybe you won't hit me at all next time.

She smiles a little. Breathing a quiet giggle once through her nose. *Not much chance of that,* she says. *You jiggle and wiggle too good. And you don't know it but you're probably one of the world's most beautiful women.*

No I'm not.

Think what you want, she says. *Doesn't matter to me. I know the truth. You're lucky I don't try to put you on the world stage, Honey. Your face. Your body. Your music. You'd be world famous overnight.*

I don't think so.

I do, she says, pressing her lips to me again—eyes wide open. She steps back a little, turning me around. Staring at my bruised, welted bottom.

Put your hair down, she says. I do it, but in a bit of a stubborn huff, my whole body itching from the painful welts. When I am done, she studies my bottom again, below long hair as black and shiny as a raven, grown halfway down the length of my back. *Of all the beautiful women I've seen,* she says, shaking her head. I simply cannot agree, looking down and away to my mother when I was sixteen…

> *"I'll bet you think you're pretty when you*
> *look in the mirror, don't you? But you're*
> *one of the ugliest bitches I think I've ever*
> *seen…"*

I need you on the bed, Honey, Vera says. She escorts me to the bed, in the power of her easy command, with her one hand at my lower back, over where one of the painful itches resides. Lay on your back, she says, which I do gladly, breasts wobbling into place, with me holding them slightly with my upper arms, to keep them from flopping over to my sides, which they can do mightily. Vera stands still at the edge of the bed, all frivolity having drained from her face again, unafraid to stare me in the eye with a solemn, serious look. She rubs her own backside, unbruised, sliding both hands up to her waist and closing her eyes, cupping and squeezing her own F Major chords, firm and round, set higher than those of my mother and me, pulling on her nipples and pinching them while she stares at my breasts—this, in the like manner of what I saw on the farm so many a rainy day and night.

She climbs slowly to the bed, her lovely, fortyish face burdened with this craving from within, to at last be rid of this wrath of energy stored. *Spread your legs,* she says, rubbing her hands once across my forbidden self, making me twitch once, an involuntary spasm, as I have never manufactured a bedroom twitch in my life. She runs her hands up both my thighs, my legs spread wide, sliding herself forward onto me. Looking down in tense, intense concentration, spreading herself open with her hand, to where I can see the little lady member hanging down, having enlarged itself in our time, three quarters of the fourth inch which became my mother's. Vera touches it to mine, her body jerking a mighty twitch, with her having to breathe and say the name of God, asking me did I feel that. It is nothing I haven't felt a hundred times before, when the spit is from clit to clit, to elicit this twit from tit to tit.

Yes, Mother Vera. I feel the same lightning bolt as thee, seeing the same look of shock and anguish you have on your face as me. Vera pushes the rest of herself against me, the little phantom, fem phalluses rubbing together now, Vera grinding her hips slow and hard, saying the name of *God* once more with force, so that every spirit knows by which her gratitude and awe is born. The power is such that only a divine reverence for it is possible at this moment, an energy that even I can feel, this Waltz of the Tribades differing in power from any other we have known. She reaches down to one great breast of mine, down to one great tit, pulling the nipple into her mouth once and high up, releasing it back to wobbling in place, grunting once from the completion of feeling it provides. She lays down lightly on top of me, so careful not to break contact with our points of origin, her head to the side of mine in tense, intense concentration again, her hips grinding down and up, down and up, sliding and pounding against me as I have never quite felt from her wearing no phallus, with only that of her woman's self sliding against mine.

I hear the grunting, the fevered breaths of impending madness in my ear, as I relax with her on top of me, pumping herself into an altered state, her body pushing and slamming into me now with too much power to stop, flashing my mother's beauty to my mind (of when she had her own breasts pulled into her mouth), causing me to strain to maintain an inner shriek from the sudden burst of pleasure into my body, pounded to what I suddenly cannot easily endure silently. This sound carries into the Vera Evans mind, to reawaken what had only stirred a moment before, and she is soon a prisoner of her bodies' own involuntary reaction, though a deep and powerful bellowing from her voice, not a yell or scream, a sound which lasts throughout her bodies' spasms, and lurching thrusts slammed hard against me.

22

*W*hat is the nature of sadism! Why must cruelty enter the caregiver's mind! In the bedroom of the old farmhouse of death, I sit still enraptured, or rather imprisoned by the Heart of Memory, by the time nearby the death of my husband, and the cold shadow of my daughter's grave. It is when the depressive spirits had greater control over our minds and bodies, compelling us to do their will and bidding. Vera had sworn to herself, made a solemn vow that she would have no part in what depravities I was born and raised under. Telling me this on our private wedding night back then, when she learned the true nature of what is forbidden. *I swore to God I would never let it happen*, she had said, before bursting into tears beside me in the bed, repeating over and over how sorry she was, being totally conflicted, between the brick wall and the concrete barrier, with no escape from between the rock and the hard place. Does she abandon me emotionally and rebuild the boundaries between us? Does she continue to swim these Waters of Perversion with me, to pull me under as in the teeth of a Great White Shark, to bleed me, and drown me, and devour me in the Waters of Sin? Does she attempt to climb the rock face wall to the top of the cliff, or does she swim the treacherous ocean waters to freedom? Vera Evans learns quickly, in the bedroom, In The Mists of High Above, that there are no choices in life that are not predetermined, and one will do that which it is meant for them to do. And it seems that very thing one swears is an impossibility, that is exactly what becomes impossible to avoid.

On our wedding night, during those tragic days in this very house, I had to endure watching her get up from our marital bed, burdened under otherworldly sorrow and tears, going to the bathroom in great weeping, a mourning that would not be comforted. And I had lain there stupidly, drowning in guilt and discomfort, so sorry that once again, I had brought the curse of God on someone I loved. I can remember turning over in the bed, to give place to the drowning waters, the Spirit of Despair I have always known. Even now, so many years away from where the spirits began, I am again tormented, visiting my life's suffering upon another, and I resign myself to this pain, allowing the first tear to rush to the pillow.

We have come together in what I thought was love. Why then, O Lord, do I still suffer? Why is grief, this Divine wedding present to me? I am cut by every sob and cough and sniff I hear from her in the bathroom. And just when I commit my soul to a fervent repentance for whatever evils I have done, I feel the bed dip under the weight of one whom I love. I turn over and see Vera sitting there, her face in the glowing aftermath of tears and suffering. I raise up to hug her as quick as I can, pledging my sorrow, asking her to forgive me. And I can remember that she told me it was her who needed to apologize, not for falling into our behind closed doors calling, but for making me feel guilty because of it. *I love you,* she says. *And for the things we're going to have to do, I swear before God, I am not ashamed. And for these things we do, I can never be sorry.*

From across the gulf, from deep inside her suffering, Vera reaches out to me, and we embrace as mother and wife, pledging our love to one another for all time. Of this love, I see and remember, at the beginning of our wedded bliss, at the beginning of our marriage in pride and secret, coming together humbly before the Lord in our hearts, in the bonds of our Spiritual matrimony, giving our souls as a loving sacrifice again to him, as a marriage done by him for us in secret.

23

*T*he cold, dusty smell. The old, musty space within these middle class walls is a never ending curiosity to me, through I can feel the tiding of a ghostly end, with no more melodies left to brighten the pseudo-fanciness I see. Every book, every nook and cranny of John's office-den hybrid, the three guest bedrooms, the Gray Palace (bedroom) I must now leave behind—every little trinket and forgotten treasure of an old life it seems has been left behind. Vera asks aloud many times how her and I could have possibly stayed here for so long after John was killed. Maybe it was because it was all we had left when he died, despite the embarrassment of riches he left behind. Vera had wanted us to move out immediately, but

I told her that Chris had loved the house and property the way it was, but was afraid to tell her. Without ever knowing that I told his secret, Vera had suddenly 'changed her mind' about us moving, and the three of us had many days of joy, trying to turn this place into a home.

The piano that had brightened this place is in my gray cottage now, a brilliant little white Steinway, where so much of more than 1700 pieces of my insanity have been displayed for my eyes only. The living room here seems emptier to me now, though I'm sure I'm the only one who noticed when the piano was moved to my gray brick cottage down the asphalt road. A long, lonely road to another world. Many steps away from the road of dirt and gravel near this brick rancher I'm in at this moment, where my husband and me took so many long walks together in the evening day. For him and me, those were Days of Heaven, when the cure of chaos and family discord, where the demons of violence could no longer torment us. I often would like to speak or write his name, but I do not, so that not even his memory can be disturbed from his heavenly resting place for too long, so that he may truly rest in the peace of God, and even his memory may walk by the waters of the River Valley, along the shores of Cerulean Sand. That part of me which was him, that part is long gone, from a life I can never relive again. As though the bridge from my mother's farm to my husband's life is washed out, and I must always skip beyond that part of the timeline in darkness, to the light of my new life, which began here in this farmhouse seven years ago. My life with my husband is a picture in twilight and darkness. One which I cannot easily remember, as though it were the product of a long and terrifying dream, extended from my life with Barbara Jean herself, which was a nightmare I still so vividly recall.

I stand at the window of this beautiful gray bedroom. Lost in a tempest. Tossed upon the winds of time and history, the history of my feeble life in the country, the painful scars that cannot heal, which are the souvenirs of my time. *This place is a dump,* Vera had said, the last time I brought her here, which had lashed me across the heart. *I want to watch 'em haul it away brick by brick.*

Please don't, I had said. *It's a beautiful history of us. Its who you were. Who I had always wanted to be.*

Too many ghosts in here for me, she had said. *I don't see how you can stand it. It gives me the creeps.*

Maybe that's why I like it. Because its creepy.

I'm not saying you're creepy, Elizabeth. I'm saying the memories that live in this house, on this property, are creepy as Hell. And frankly, if I never step foot in here again it'll be too soon...

As I survey every life of this misty November rain, I am comforted now by this mausoleum, this graveyard house of darkness, this palace of faded, bygone hopes and dreams dead and long since buried. And maybe it is creepy. Maybe I am strange for being drawn here—for even considering taking the old brick steps back into the kitchen I once thought of as palatial. But something will not allow me to give Vera permission to tear this place down, no more so than the gray stone markers of a cemetery, the gray concrete and marble monuments to man's time on this earth as grass and weeds, clipped and fallen to Earth as fertilizer for the soil, or dried up and blown away like dry summer dust at my feet. For now, this is still my conduit to days long gone, and places where I am still condemned to visit and hide. From these unholy spirits, there is no need for me to tremble any longer, no need for me to run, even from the monumental scraping of chair wood across the kitchen floor, or the epic stomping of bare feet down the uncarpeted hall towards me. Of this demon, I have known, which I will refuse to acknowledge with even the turning around from this window, for today, I know that God hath not given me the Spirit of Fear, but of Power, of Love, and of a sound mind.

PART TWO

24

*B*arbara Jean Coletti walks the miles. From where her Lovely Bones had lain undisturbed, deep inside the North Carolina woods. She takes every step in power. White skin glistening. Breasts hangling, dangling down heavy and hanging. Swinging from the effort of feet jangling dead, crackling twigs and wet leaves in the forest. Eyes angling upward. Mouth hanging open from the strain. This, the agony of reanimation. The enduring pain of rebirth. The madness of reunion. A spirit called forth from somewhere. Reunited with the physical world. Whether the soul is that of the woman whose body is reborn, only God is allowed to know. But of the madness, the fear in this beautiful creature's eyes, the terror in the immortal soul that lives, of this I see vividly and plain. Dropping to her knees in lighting strike to every muscle inside. A woman of Amazonian beauty. Strength in feminine form. Unable to endure the suffering of otherworldly stings to every muscle, in the drowning November rain.

Crawl over the forest floor, Dear Mother. Endure the burning in thy breast. Struggle to breathe air into the lungs afire, beautiful woman! Struggle to pull thyself up to thy feet. Crawl as a mountain haint, Dear Woman, shake and crawl in the manner of the great slavery story that was told. Whether or not that Beloved be real, I do not know, white woman. Crawl to me in the truth of what is real! Of this, what human being can ever know of thine life, Dear Woman, what feeble mind can grasp this otherworldly refrain! From the cold, wet forest floor, thou art born—now to this cold and wet forest floor thou shalt remain! Lie flat upon thy stomach, dear Woman of the Leaves. For thou art not yet fully aged—thy beauty is too profound for the human eye—take your part of corruption by the Curse of God, by the Curse of Sin, on the nighttime forest floor of rain, underneath the hiding Forest Moon.

Lie still, Dear Woman. Endure this part of unearthly suffering—that which none but thee have done, that none but thee have breathed, and lived to tell the tale. Sleep now, Barbara Jean. Take thine otherworldly slumber in the rain. Rest, in the final rejuvenation of thyself, deep inside the Carolina Forest Wood.

25

*A*t the window of my daytime mausoleum, I open my eyes again to the misty rain, having succumbed to the spirits that roam these unhallowed halls. Waking up from the most powerful waking vision I have ever had the misfortune of seeing, where I saw my mother reanimated like a sleeping beauty, un-zombie-like as in horror fantasy, but as a real live woman of the woods. I can still hear the loud, deeply laboured breathing from her open mouth, as she stumbles through the cold, daytime forest in the November mist, dropping to her knees and falling to the ground, laying still on the forest floor in the rain, still breathing loud and tortured breaths. And even though my faith is strong, though I look to the Cross for strength and protection, I know that the power of Fate is absolute, and I cannot resist the Spirit of Fear at this moment. Cold, prickly needled on my skin, a wave of frozen energy through the center of my body turns me against my will, and I finally begin to walk slowly out of the Gray Palace (bedroom) towards the Hall, braving the terror with each step, but refusing to run, knowing that panic brings a fate worse than death. I draw upon the training of my years, when I would listen to her walking from room to room while I was closed up in the bedroom, listening, praying she would forget that I existed, where I hid in the bars of melody and prose.

I step forward, unlively, endeavoring to persevere, to endure, to suffer the new jangling of my feeble nerves, as the cold grows around me in the hall, and a whispering voice begins to speak in an unknown tongue from the walls. *Oh, God* is the whisper from within me, as I have to take a livelier step down the hall toward the kitchen, at the edge of something close to a dead run. And this starting gate is opened by a strong tug upon my hair from behind, and I am suddenly a brunette-maned horse after a hot shriek, bursting into a full running through the old kitchen and around the counter, my outstretched hands reaching for a doorknob that is so close and yet so infinitely far away. By the mercy of God, I am transported, warped across this kitchen time, to finally be at the back door, hearing the fullness of demonic laughter in deep chords as I open the door quickly, closing it hard behind me in the pouring rain, walking quickly down the brick steps to the music of my mother's voice inside calling me a *fat breasted bitch*, holding on to the rail while I take each step quickly and carefully, then hurrying across the grass to the asphalt road nearby.

On the long road to the future, the asphalt road to our mansion home, I stand wet and dumb in the rain, having been shaken to the core of complacency, down to where I live, to where bravery and unbelief is not possible. I do not believe in ghosts, as they have been created by mankind's fears and fervent unbelief. But what ghosts there are roaming this earthly plane, I surely believe, are the Spirits of God or the Spirits of the Devil, both who masquerade in earthly form as the dead; as dearly departed souls of the living. But these powers to persuade the human mind, the power to persuade my mind—this is so profound as to be absolute, so that one cannot distinguish this loved one as an angel or a demon, but as the ghost of their lost loved one resurrected.

Every day of my life in that old shack my husband and I called a house, that ply-board and kindling wood I lived and died in—every day I lived in that house, I was made aware of what possibilities lie just beyond our reach—that lie just beyond our realm of sight. Oh yes, those were ghosts, by definition—the ghosts of past pain and suffering in that house and on that property, built in 1910, under the passing of a comet bright enough to be seen in the daytime, and another one seen only at night, this one not seen again for a lifetime, that will shine again when my bones are interred, perhaps bright enough this time to portend the coming end of the world.

And perhaps there are tiny echoes of this approaching comet in our own lives, seen by an accursed few, who have seen the bright and sparkling flash of a meteor in the sky, streaking through the heavens on a fervent summer's night. On the 1st day of the November I'm in, I saw such an omen, so brilliant that I checked myself to see if I was awake or dreaming, seeing that I was fully awake and observing a fireball in the sky. Standing on the balcony of my great southern mansion home, overlooking the prairie field beyond, I saw a so-called shooting star appear from Heaven—half as bright as the hiding full moon—streak across the sky from high above, a star of blue-greenish tint, burning across the prairie in the dead of a cold

November night, until it broke up into a shower of sparks and smaller pieces, vanishing over the far and distant woods beyond. And when this happened, my soul was suddenly gripped by an uneasiness I had not felt in many a year, since the days we lived in the Brick Farmhouse of Death. I regretted with all my heart that there was no camera of any kind, maybe even to have caught the moving picture of it and sent that to a news station to play for a jaded and disinterested latter day people. But such a thing would be too mysterious, I think, too strange and fearful, and meant for my eyes only, which have grown accustomed to the otherworldly sights from God.

Something bad's gonna happen, Vera had said when I told it to her, breathing a deep sigh. *Are we going to die?* I had said, asking the question honestly, but knowing that the two of us are not meant to die just yet. *Ask God to protect us from whatever it is,* she had said. *Because I've been having weird premonitions for a month now. I haven't felt anything like it since before John died. That thing you saw is like confirmation of it. All I can say is... just pray until it passes. And hope that its not one of us. Do you think its you or me?* I had lowered my eyes, to wait for the Spirit to say 'yes,' and prepare one of us to have to bury the other soon. But there was no wave of premonition through me concerning Vera or myself, as the path to our tombstones stretches far beyond the horizon, to where the ashes of my southern Earth comet lay.

Knowing it was somehow married to the end of the world happening I just ran from in that house. Knowing that they portend a time of great fear and sorrow for Vera and me, and that we are likely to witness an event that the world beyond us could neither believe nor understand, as I am certain that the likes of it will be such as what has not been since the beginning of time.

26

To massage my gigantic breasts from behind is her ultimate diversion. To feel the heavy weight of them rise and fall in her hands. Lifting them up, dropping them, listening to them flop down against my skin. Even when all other kindnesses and cruelties have come and gone—the softness of kissing, the roughness of an over the knee spanking (which I am overdue), or those things that descend us further from what is normal—even after all other things have passed, it seems that our return is her behind me standing, massaging my breasts to comfort oblivion. This, the destruction of one, or both of our bodies' tranquility, often bringing one or both of us to a shaking, to a rolling back of the eyes, and an inner or outer cry to the heavens for mercy. It is our special place we can go, I think, to escape the cares of this world, and the incessant emotional demands of this life. This too, was where my mother and I lived for two years before she abandoned me. Every squeeze, every gentle tug at the nipple takes me deeper into the knowledge and memory of her—the way I used to stand behind her this same way, and exact comfort cushioned punishment on hers unclothed. Every part of her body was sensitive, I remember, and most significantly her bosom. Every squeeze and tug on mine seems to be a squeeze and tug on hers in my memory, when we stood anywhere in the house, but most often at the mirror, of course, so that she could watch my hands working magic on them.

Sometimes it would start over her clothes in whatever country blouse she was wearing, graduating to it being pulled up or unbuttoned, then off. Continuing with my hands over the impossibly big bra, squeezing over top of it, pushing the white flesh inside in astro-cleavage, cleavage pushed up to the heavens, a mountainous bounty of breast flesh spilled over. *Undo my bra,* she would say, when she could take no more foreplay, and I would oblige this, unlatching the industrial strength thing with care and skill. Sliding it away from her milky white shoulders, down her smooth upper arms, then down and away. Revealing to both of us the center of our mother-daughter energy. Two impossibly large, even humongous breasts, excessive by most standards, grown to watermelon sized proportions, but shaped and formed as perfect examples of Olympian breast beauty, the highest form of macromastia that can be imagined—breasts huge enough to draw ridicule, but when seen nude, hung so perfectly enough as to cause awe and disbelief. All negativity towards breasts such as these would be lies born of jealousy, envy or spiritual hypocrisy, all of which she has dealt with all her life, forcing her into seclusion with me, going into town only to shop for food, and the occasional necessity we need. This remarkable anomaly of hers, that puffs her blouses and the tops of her dresses out, the source of her greatest public shame and humiliation, is the source of her greatest behind closed doors pride and pleasure.

In the Heart of Memory, as I feel my own breasts being worked by Mother Vera, slipping me into further relaxation, I can feel the weight of my mother's breasts in my hands, the feel of which I have come to need for my own comfort and peace of mind. Whether or not she knows this, I may never know. I only know that it is my solemn duty, my most fervent obligation and calling, to work her sensitive breasts into an orgasmic fever, to where she is able to speak her vulgarity with such freedom when it happens. *I wanna taste 'em,* she says, and I know to raise one breast up to her mouth where she can reach, and pull the nipple into her mouth for one quick and mighty sucking.

I wanna taste 'em, I say to Vera, obliging myself alike in kind when she pushes mine up to my mouth, pulling the nipple in for a long drink of the phantom milk, my real milk having long since gone away. Releasing the nipple in the hard kissing, pulling sound, hearing my mother tell me to pinch her nipples, which I do, telling Vera to do the same to me, hearing my mother begin to moan pitifully in the Theatre of my Mind, hearing her say *Oh, God, I'm going to cum in my tits,* hearing this give way to a sound from her as if she has been twisted to agony, a pitiful, weeping, sobbing noise, which reaches into the core of myself from Vera's touching, and causes me to have to do the same.

In the Heart of Memory, I see my mother's eyes rolled up to Heaven in blindness, as Vera gazes at me in the mirror while she squeezes, wondering what manner of magic she has performed, to make me fall back against her so violently, and look toward Heaven with such shock and ecstasy in my expression.

27

On the asphalt road of Amherst Lake. In the aftermath of trauma, I am still at the mirror of our mansion home in my mind, in my bedroom refuge of golden oakwood and crystal. At the towering oval mirror, my arms go up to my hair, watching Vera devour one of my breasts at the nipple, standing behind me and to the side, bent down, holding one of my breasts up, sucking on it hungrily, with loud suction noises filling the room without shame—her face grimaced from the effort, I see, savoring the taste of it, amidst the feel of it in her mouth, and the pressing of her body's lower self against mine. Oh, how many such scenes as this, did I stand in front of mirrors to see! How many times did Barbara Jean stand to the side and back of me! Her head lowered to my breast, her lower body pressed so diligently! I can feel the strain in her body as she presses against me, unable to stop drinking the phantom milk, the sensation causing me to have to breathe in voice, in the throes of this post orgasm wave. But Vera's pre-orgasm is apparent, in the heightened breathing through her nose, the tense muscles, the tighter holding on to me, the almost painful hardness of the nipple sucking, her mind on fire with thoughts of everything from Brenda Harrison hairbrush paddling a spoiled, uppity daughter—to thoughts of my own mother in this same position, isolated on the farm, sucking my soul dry from the same nipple. It is not many ticks of the clock, it is not many seconds hence before I feel her naked self pressed bone hard against me, followed by the earthquake trembling, and the deep and fervent grunts muffled at my breast, still suctioned hard into her mouth.

Nursing my breasts has always been a devastation to her, every now and then even giving her a Witch's Crown, which can have her twitching fully clothed, being touched nowhere else on her body but at the mouth by the front of my breasts inside. So much of Vera's behavior has phased into my mother's when we are alone, but not in hatred or hypocrisy such as she. As Vera releases the nipple one last time, gazing at it in post trauma, I hug her, knowing that even the violent spirits that threaten do so in the shadows of the spiritual monument we have built, which is our everlasting love for one another.

$\mathcal{B}$enda Lynette Harrison rides the wind. The cold, November wind of a woman scorned, and a daughter's epic betrayal. Burning in the memory of natural lines crossed, natural barriers breached, and what devastation it has caused. Suffering the third part of the truth as she drives west to Chapel Hill. The third part of the Truth, which is Cataclysm. The truth that the other side of Heaven on Earth is Hell on Earth, and a journey through fire and brimstone. These are the flames of earthly torment. Of earthly pain and suffering. The fires of a motherline corrupted by blue flame, the fires of blue tinted black. When the white flame of purity is colored as the blue of the ocean. The fire of forbidden lust that burns. These flames await on the other side of the barrier. Waiting to consume those who might cross over into them. Those born in the white flames of ignorance. Those who do not know. When the souls find a breach in the barrier—beware! Woe unto them who wish to cross over, where the wilderness burns with blue and black flame! For the other side of Paradise is Hell, and woe unto them which go in thereat! Whose bodies are not given to the heat of this flame, and are consumed forthrightly therin!

Brenda Harrison rides the wind. The November wind of a woman scorned. Of a daughter's epic betrayal. Imprisoned naked in the snow of an irrevocable memory. Driving the fine black Mercedes in the November rain. Eyes alive with a vision. Devastation lighting the theatre of her mind. Recalling the night when she learned the truth, that this is the End of the Age. When the Brunette Woman of Music was in her cottage, sheltered from the rain. When the Blonde Woman of Charity held the music woman's breasts to her mouth. Nursing the music woman into a trembling. Brenda Harrison relives this tragic scene, and the hammer it took to her fragile sensibility. Of what churns beneath cultured civility.

The cosmic jealousy. The end of the world envy. A blast into the Wall of Perdition. The barrier to the forbidden. Seeing her best friend suck the breasts of another woman. A woman who is her daughter in spirit. Seeing the modern mother daughter dynamic concentrated and displayed. Shining like a burst of sunlight. Blinding revelation. Then the instant cooling, soothing light of moonlight unleashed. A light too irresistible to look away from. And then the horror of this light glowing the color of rust. Deepening. Look away, Dear Woman. You cannot. The beauty of this light turning dreadful to look upon, as this moonlight has now turned to blood.

Brave the flood of fear, Dear Woman! Gaze the Heart of the Modern Mother Daughter Dynamic! Languish the Heart of Memory, Woman of Straw, on your fervent trip West in the rain!

Brenda Lynette rides the wind. The cold wind of a woman scorned. And a daughter's epic betrayal. Still lost in a humiliation beyond endurance. A humiliation that kills. The humiliation that blasts like a grenade in a suburban living room. Annihilation. Ruin. The scene of the clumsy, cold kiss she forced upon her own daughter that night. To cope with what she had seen. The kiss that stood in proxy of a hug, or a holding of hands. The kiss that stood a feeble ground, as a Mother and Daughter in the ruins of Joplin. After the Great Twister has come and gone. This that exploded a breach into the Walls of Perdition. To where they can now see the light from the blue and black fire.

Brenda Lynette remembers the underlying, unspoken disgust on her daughter's face. The insistence that she had to go back to Chapel Hill, early to complete the duties of her office, as professor at the Carolina blue university school. The pride of the Tarheel State. Brenda cruises the miles to this earthly promised land. Driven by that selfsame demon which is common to man—that can neither be resisted nor understood. A naked woman in the frozen snow. Grieving to be warm.

The rainfall of this November trip splashes mightily. Lulling her mind to road sleep. Watching each lonely pathetic set of lights drift by like wandering eyes of the dead. Ghost eyes. Eyes that go forth in the gloom, forever seeking. But finding none but places they have already been. These Mercedes eyes of gloom go crying through the rain. Driven forth by the vision. The vision of her attempt to complete a forbidden journey that night. Having surreptitiously spoken—*would you mind if I slept in your bed tonight,* convincing her daughter that it is so she could get a good night's sleep. Standing at the bathroom mirror before bed. Gazing at short-haired, blonde sensibility. A conscious seared with a hot iron. The hot iron of lust.

About what we did, she says, from the bathroom, *maybe we don't need to take it any further, but I don't think it's wrong for a mother and a daughter to share deep kisses in private.*

Don't start that again, the daughter answers. *I hope that's not why you're sleeping in here because if it is—*

If course it isn't, she says. *I'm just putting my mind at ease about what happened, that's all.*

Gaze at thyself in the mirror, Woman of Straw! Gauge the burning of blue and black fire!

Into the bedroom, she takes a darkened step. Moving casually to her daughter's bed. Standing there a moment, wielding the knife that cuts through a complacent heart. The knife that cuts through tension. Sliding in the bed—nerves a jangle of chimes undisturbed, ringing through her body without mercy. Her daughter beside her, laying on her back. Rambling about her time at the Chapel Hell university school, to politics of university teaching, the impossible road to job security, let alone tenure. At the end of the Classical Studies Adjunct road, she is. To soon turn onto the Associate's Highway to Heaven. In love with foreign languages and cultures—the leisure of travel, the tranquility of European country sides in the summer, secret admirer of Carmen Coletti, fearful of the power in her expression at the piano. Dreaming of watching her play for her in the nude, at a farmhouse in the Italian country.

Brenda lays beside this Woman of Knowledge, this accursed woman. The woman who is her daughter. Rolling over without shame, without mercy. Kissing her daughter goodnight on the mouth. Not releasing this kiss. Punctuating it with a touch to your daughter's thigh, Dear Woman. Rolling over on top of her as if pushed by a phantom. Pressing down upon every inch of her. Moaning hard at the wave of lightning energy passing through. Having to make water—feeling as though you may piss yourself— though you just completed this a moment ago in the bathroom. Beginning to writhe, which plunges the daughter into a fearful discomfort, which she escalates into resistance. Arms flailing now, her arms pushing against you, while your hands are clasped at your daughter's head. Locking your lips to hers. Savoring the violence of this kiss. Unable to unlock your grip. Unable to see the terror and rage in your daughter's eyes. Caring nothing for the weak punches to your back and sides. Nor the angry pushing at your face that has begun—the epic silence, broken only by the sound of heavy breathing, the grunting of female voices. Losing the kiss now as she turns her head, her anger kindled against you, her strength growing.

This, Dear Woman, is the spirit of combat. The fight born from your actions. Energy risen up against your spirit—the Spirit of Rape. Fight, dear Woman. Fight in this land where tears are inconsequential. Where fear is irrelevant. Press your aching groin to hers, Dear Woman, feel the bulging bone below. Push upon it, Dear Woman, use the force of a greater strength you have. Hold her down. Listen to her begin to cry. Hold her down Dear Woman. Feel the epic sensation rise within thee. Of a kind you never understood was possible. A kind which takes over the muscles and the nerves. To push and spread energy to your spine and your brain. Now brave your bad luck, dear Woman of Straw, as your daughter's fingers make a perfect pinpoint stabbing to your eye—to shock your body from a growing erogenous stupor, where a lifetime of repressed energy had lain in wait. Feel the light of this forbidden depravity fade. Fall away from the Catherine Grace victim. The skin white angel of your wildest and most dreadful want and need. This spoiled blonde creation of yours has poked the eye of your vulnerability. Roll away in a different kind of screaming, Woman. Lie on your back defeated like a she bear in the grass, after the divinely guided poking of the sharpened stick. Hold thine eye, Dear Woman—beseech Heaven as to your precious eyesight.

Now scream after her, Woman, as she runs from the bed to your room, closing the door and locking it behind her. At the door of the upper room, where you suffered the years of a dead marriage for so many suburban years. Bang on the door, accursed woman. Scream at the Catherine Grace child—make terror in her soul, with the desperate rage, the vitriolic pounding, the acidic slamming of both your hands at the door, your eye already swollen, already profuse with tears, a deep scratch underneath it, leading to the bluest eye. The bluest eye now red with suffering. Have you ever felt such pain, as when your daughter hath poked you in the eye? Now brave her screams. Her screaming at you that you are sick. That you are disgusting. That you're crazy. That you're *doing this because of Vera and Elizabeth and its fucking twisted*. Dear Woman, forgive her vulgarity, Accursed Woman. It was born from thee.

29

*B*renda Lynette Harrison rides the wind. The cold, November wind of a woman scorned. And a daughter's fiery betrayal. Cruising the shimmering lights of the new city, in the rainy late afternoon. Finding her destination—along the road to her future. Parking in the late afternoon lot, seeing a silver gray Sonata sitting there. Shiny and sensible—her daughter's rolling, trolling treasure. Catching her at the weekday afternoon office hour—always the last to leave. A necessary evil it is, if the brass is to be shown. If they are to be made known of her lust for this prestige. The rising tide of tenure.

The Woman breathes a sigh, glancing into the bluest eye again, this time in the rear view mirror. Touching the bloody scratch barely set to healing. Observing the red pool of blood in the white marble of her eye. *Who did it to you,* they'll surely wonder when you walk. *Who gives a damn,* you'll think. *Who gives a damn,* you think, as you open the door in your trench coat of midnight blue. Carrying the gift in the clear gallon apple juice container, the heavy and rightful teachers offering. *Why is this woman with the navy blue umbrella and a messed up eye walking around here with a jug of apple juice? Where is she going,* they'll ask. *Where is she going,* the older lady professor asks. Matronly, bespectacled. Unpretty. Undeterred by the blonde, middle aged pretty in her stylish coat and private party drink. Coming to roam the halls of her campus. Where no earthquake could crumble the solid rock of her tenure.

Is Professor Harrison in her office, you say.

I'm sure she'll be there 'til at least seven. She's the last one out everyday. Pardon me for asking, Maam, but are you related to her?

What questions beg a severe thrashing, Dear Woman! What questions ask for scorn and ridicule!

I'm her mother, you say. *Thought I could get her to take a late afternoon sip,* you say, holding your prize.

Looks delicious, the matronly scholar says. Whining a fungalooga smile. *What happened to your eye, Honey.*

'*I tried to fuck my daughter last night you nosy bitch*' is the key. A key hidden in the doors of secret. Unturned by those who might peer inside, to see what manner of latter day depravities are displayed as pictures on a wall, behind the closed doors of eschatology.

The story's too long for me to tell right now. But you seem like you're genuinely concerned about it. Thank you for that.

You're welcomed sweetie, take good care of yourself. And take a big sip for Miss Dot now, that's me.

Okay, you chuckle. A full, toothy grin. Dr. Dorothy's spirit reflected. Returned to her, unfruitful.

Your smile fades as the Queen of Academia walks away. An aging mother, she is. Unburdened by shyness. Lifted up by barriers fallen down. The barrier to public performance and self display. Watch the Woman of Learning walk away. Marvel her need to read. To gather information. To spread it into the air like pollen. Watching it fall where it may. Marvel after her a second more, Dear Woman. Of her calling to these hallowed halls of learning. As she hurries away, stupidly uncovered in the rain, with only a sweater and a quick pace for protection. You turn away from her failed condition. Her condition of over achievement. The tower of self importance, drowning in the Autumn rain.

Walk the halls of learning. The Halls of Academia, Dear Woman. Focused on your daughter, in her office of high aspiration. Clip clop the hallowed corridors of schemes. Where otherworldly ambition comes to live in a drunken stupor of knowledge. Where exalted dreams come to die an empty death. Every door of every empty office is a portal, is it not? Where tortured souls travel through to the Land of Self Delusion, ever learning. Never coming to the knowledge of the Truth.

30

*B*renda Lynette Harrison rides the wind. The cold wind of a woman scorned. And a daughter's fervent betrayal.

Take those last steps, woman. To where the portal of your daughter's disbelief lies in wait. Turn the corner of this chapter, Brenda Lynn. Let the walls echo the coming of the end of the world.

"Mom," she says bewildered, looking up from her book, gauging her mother's knowing smile, and understanding expression on the edge of a wink. Place the teacher's gift labeled as from the apple tree, the sip of reconciliation, the unfermented wine of surrender. A mother-daughter who have breached the wall and survived. Whose latter day closeness must be affirmed. Watch her tired cynicism and bitterness fade, as you plop the apple juice container onto the desk. *Apples for the teacher,* she says. Standing up, while you unbutton your coat to leisure.

Now, Mother. Watch her complacency melt away like snow splashed by hot water. Watch her complacency give way to horror, as she watches your full nakedness go on display, having worn no clothes but boots underneath your coat. Tossing your coat onto the chair by the closed door. Satisfied at the epic shock, the painful, fearful humiliation on her face as she watches her mother naked in her office, bent over, fiddling with the coat on the chair, slight bosoms dangling to their requisite points, nipples exposed and hardened, white buttocks visible in full.

The mother turns, gauging the daughter's terror and epic confusion, at why the mother has a sample perfume bottle to wield. Now gauge the look on your daughter's face, Woman, as the stream of liquid hits her squarely in the eyes, making her hesitate as to what manner of magic this is, that sends her face to blazing agony, and takes her breath in one big gulp of air. Now, Dear Woman. Watch her grab her face in realization. Now feel the vibration of the *omigod* grow in rapid succession. Feel this third *omigod* vibrate your groin, Dear Mother. Feel your daughter's loud scream in your body.

Watch her back away from the desk screaming. Slamming backward into the window sill. Screaming again as a fire victim, still holding her burning face, as even your own eyes begin to water from the blast of *pepper spray* in your daughter's face. Now what you must do, dear Mother, you must do it quickly. Now, you may open the professor's gift to quench your thirst. Turn the yellow cap until it opens, Dear Mother. Dear Woman, open the drink of thy latter day thirst. Watch the splashing of it pour violently from the jug into your screaming daughter's tight blue blouse. Breathe the rush of this wine into thy nostrils.

Watch her now. Soaking wet and gasping on the floor behind her desk. Cough, Dear Woman, while you step away. Pouring a trail of this wine slightly away from your daughter's feet. Watching her struggle to look at you through eyes that cannot see. At last, dear Mother. Have this drink with thy daughter. Click the lighter flame, to where it may burn without ceasing. Drop it to the floor. Jump back, accursed Woman of Fire! Run from the heat of this small explosion of orange fire and smoke, that quickly engulfs your daughter's legs, then instantly every inch of cloth on her body, veiling her from head to toe in a flame of fire.

This is not the juice of the apple, Dear Woman, that blazes hot as the fires of Hell! Grab thy coat, dear woman! Close the door quickly. Locking it, so there can be no quick release of this soul on fire. Hear her begging screams for you, dear Woman, see the echo of fire through the frosted glass door. Quickly mother, put on thy cloak of midnight! Cover thy nakedness in scorn! Slip the coat of dreams upon your cold white skin—in the halls of learning thou art hiding in!

A shock to your nerves! A shock to every nerve, Dear Woman, when the woman on fire slams so hard against the glass—unable to find the strength, the faculties to unlock the door and turn the knob to freedom. Watch, Dear Woman! Watch the fiery creature inside slam with all its burning might against the glass, unable to conjure enough strength to break it. Now watch, woman. Watch the charred arm slide down the glass and away. Listen! Hear the feeble scratching at the door unseen, underneath the orange fire that burns within.

Now turn and walk, Mother. Clip clop long, booted heels down these unhallowed halls again. Breathe. Breathe the taste of pepper spray from your mouth. The pain of gasoline fumes from your lungs. The smell of fire and smoke from your nostrils.

Hurry, Woman! Turn the corner of this final chapter, and stroll the last mile quickly. To the double doors that have presumed to stretch themselves so far away. But you know they are there for thee. Step lively, Dear Woman. Praise Heaven for the fresh air in your lungs. Stretch forth thine fearsome hand of judgment to touch these sacred doors. Now breathe in deeply, Dear Woman, as you emerge from the deep, opening the doors into the cold. Seeing the breath of deep Autumn, frosted from thy dragon's nostrils. From the lips where resides thy dragon's tongue.

Look down, poor woman. Look down to where her office window still glows the orange light of a dying flame. The fire of a dying life inside. Now open the wired midnight cloth, Dear Woman. Savor the pounding water above, sheltered from touching a single hair of thine head. Walk swiftly, but calmly, Dear Woman. See the Mercedes luxury call with such a sweet invitation to thee. See the Mercedes luxury call, invitingly, to thee. Touch the handle, the stylish modern woman, Woman of means. Woman of Education. Woman of Charity! Woman of Straw!

Slip inside Mercedes luxury, Dear Woman. Luxury colored so appropriately black. Slide into the cloth interior. Colored so mournfully charcoal gray. Lean thy head back to rest, Dear Woman. To remember the sight of your daughter's body engulfed in flames, the smell of her burning skin, and the vibrations from her screams in the pit of your stomach and womb.

Brenda Lynette Harrison rides the wind. The cold wind of a woman scorned, and a daughter's fiery betrayal. Cruising the miles in contented luxury. Three hours and 25 miles down east, to the suburban house in Grand Harwich Estates.

To her pills and a glass of wine.

31

A glass of wine relaxes her enough to slap me. A habit she returned to after we buried Maria, her pills and a glass of wine. A good hard slap to my face in the bedroom, enough to flash purple in my brain, knocking me to the bed. Then slamming down hard on top of me, her face merciless with irritation, smacking me with her open hand in my face very hard, several times more. Hard enough so that it scares me sometimes, and I try to block her hands, which only irritates her more. This I do now, with her grabbing both my arms and staring at me, her expression twisted to a frown, and a stern look about the eyes. I can smell what is left of the red wine on her breath, the secret little sips she takes every now and then, when she knows she is going to have to hurt me. The entire process, from the sipping glass to the burning in her body—relaxes her to the core of her spirit, the way that a nicotine addict is bathed in tranquility by the poison smoke in their lungs.

Vera breathes in the slapping of my face repeatedly, the pulling of my hair, the hard pinching of my sides or my outer thighs when she lays on top of me, to remind me of these sessions from Barbara Jean, who used closed fists on my face rather than open hands every now and then. I knew that I was in trouble tonight anyway, when I saw her in her big bathroom, pulling the medium strap on about her hips, the one that hangs a perfect inch times eight down in front of her. The one that I know I like the best. I had disturbed her time in front of the mirror, touching the member in fascination while she tightened the straps. Standing dim-wittedly beside her, watching her in the mirror unawares, until she said *"go wait for me,"* rather coldly. I know she watched me walk out in the mirror, seeing my blood sister's [my reflection's] wide and wiggly bottom leaving her line of sight. I had noticed the wine glass half empty, two-thirds empty on the bathroom counter, though I had pretended not to. Not that it bothers me when she takes a sip, I don't know why it would anyway. She has no desire to be drunk with wine, therein to excess, but only to assist her in her nightly relaxation, which so often involves hurting me in one form or another.

Tonight, she had stood behind me, hands clasped behind my neck in the classic wrestling hold, which humans seem born knowing how to do as well as a bird is born knowing how to fly. In our Carolina mansion, in the confines of our bedroom, Mother Vera flies on wings of eagles, having stood behind me when our session started tonight, bending me over in the wrestling hold, her member hanging down unpushed up inside me, with her drawing epic feeling from this wrestling hold alone, breathing hard to conceal her bodies' inner devastation, which I felt twitch her muscles twice while she held me bent down. The strength of the hold reminds me of Barbara Jean, though not the spirit, as the intent is clearly devoid of malevolence, as my mother performed her bodies' fervent need in bitterness. Vera's is the bitterness of competition rather than conflict. The venom of a lady wrestler upon another in aggressive contact. The wrestlers do not hate one another, necessarily, though their need for violence and victory is paramount, above all things, until this craving is achieved. So too, it is with Mother Vera and me, the violence of sporting combat, where the emotions of violence are channeled to achieve a competitive victory. For Vera, this victory is a physical and emotional dominance over me sensually, which her body is trained to leave her wanting badly almost every night—

And when several days passes without this dominance, my consequences become more severe. She has learned to control her bodies' reactions to her quick and powerful orgasms, which often seem to come from nowhere—especially when she stands behind me, with me bent over in the wrestling hold. And when she wears the member, it is because she has a big energy built up inside, feeling the need to channel through the phantom lady cock of my own Mother's wildest dreams.

As I lay underneath Vera now, writhing from the pain of my sides being pinched to death, and the fat of my thighs being pinched to bruises, I remember that the need my mother suffered from was penis envy, but of the kind concerned only with behind closed doors sensual expression. The enema nozzle. Her hairbrush handle. Even the epic and exalted banana fruit. How many times has she not been able to contain her inner woman, and held one of these between her legs tight, to watch me stroke it for her until her body spasmed and convulsed, or to push the enema nozzle into my rectum from behind, or to watch me choke on the yellow banana fruit pushed down my throat? Oh, what Heaven would she have been in, if she could have strapped her envy about her hips!

This same envy is one with Vera's body tonight, as she rests it deep up inside me, at the end of the better part of a half hour, my face sore from the many slaps, my hips sore from the punches, with her locking her lips firmly onto mine, so that she can pass the wave of energy from her body into mine. She pins my arms to my sides, hardly moving at all, and I notice that the trembling of her body is magnificent, as is the deep vibration of her muffled voice in my body.

32

Hello, Vera.

Precipice. It's a ridiculous word, isn't it? Hardly ~~conveys~~ tells the truth about how a person really feels, does it? It hides a person. It hides the feelings. Precipice. What the Hell does that really mean, anyway?

The reason I ask is because, well, it's the word that comes to mind. The only way I can effectively describe what I feel. But is that really the truth? Couldn't I just say the word "cliff?" How about "edge?" What about "dead end?" I hesitate to say, "poetic nonsense," when I say the word "precipice." Because a certain ambiguity in life is necessary to preserve order. To preserve the public decorum. We just can't go around saying the whole truth, can we? We just can't go around telling the whole truth about everything.

But what happens when you reach the end? What happens when you know you've taken the last few breaths of life you'll ever take? When we go over the precipice, are we ashamed to look at one another in the eye, and scream while we fall to our deaths? I can already see the edge that's come and gone. And I know I have to scream before I die.

I killed my daughter. I burned that bitch to within an inch of her miserable life, and I think she will die tonight. And I hope that we will see each other again in Heaven, her and me. I killed her because

the world cannot use another empty,
status seeking, social climbing bitch who
could care less about anyone but herself.
Been there and done that. So I knew what
it was I had to do. When I saw the evil in
her eyes. The hypocritical, self important
smell on her stinking diet breath. The
bony, underfed ass and nonexistent, tiny
tits were enough to make me sick. Women
are not supposed to starve their curves
away. But I taught her to do that, didn't I?
I taught her to despise hips and breasts
for herself, although I believe the desire
for them on other women ran deep. Yes,
Vera.

    I believe my daughter has been fucking
her best friend for years. She's a rather
~~exotic looking~~, no, she's hot as Hell, with
an ass like Jello and big, wobbly tits to
match, both coming off a tight, young
athletic body you just want to lay out on a
dining room and serve dinner on. Starting
with cool whip on her tit. Or maybe, her
clit? Will you think less of me Vera, if I
use such a dirty word? What about desire,
Vera? What about the curves on a
woman's body? Do they really matter
though, when Love is the main issue? The

main point of attraction? To say that I've been attracted to you for years is redundant. I don't think there has ever been a person you've met that has not been attracted to you in some way. I don't think attraction can ~~adequately~~ say it just right.

I love you. It is probably why I was such a bitch to you for so many years. Because you were prettier than me. Because you were nicer than me. Your husband was richer than mine. And then, to top it off, here comes that crow haired angel thing from Mt. Olympus you live with. A god and goddess, her and her husband were. You remember her husband? Of course you do. Did you ever get a chance to fuck him? I hope not. But who did you fuck, Honey? Was he dead, the first time you sucked her breasts and made her cum? Which brings me to why I know now that I love you. I knew it the moment I looked in the window two weeks ago, and saw you nursing her giant titty like there was milk in it. (Have you tasted her milk? Is is sweet?) I kept myself from fainting in the rain that night. I stumbled to the car where the living corpse who was my daughter was waiting. I couldn't tell her what I saw yet, but when we got home, I kissed her deeply. Then I kissed her deeply again in the house. And that night, I tried to make love with her in my bed. But she stabbed me in the eye and ran from me. She locked herself in my old bedroom, and she told me I was doing it just because of what I saw you and your daughter doing.

I don't like your daughter. I don't understand her. Please forgive me for saying it. She's sweet and far too attractive for words but she's somber. Strange. Scary. Old school Goth, if that makes any sense. In the eight years I've known her, have I ever been alone with her? No. What can you say to Wonder Woman in real life, in polite conversation? I would tell her to keep her lilly white hands to herself, and get away from the woman that I loved first, before she ever knew your name.

Tell Elizabeth that I am afraid of her. She's just a little too good to be true. Tell Elizabeth that she is the truth. That she shines a light onto people's souls, forcing

*them to confront the darkness within. So
then, Vera Honey, how can I compete with
a goddess?*

*We are all at a precipice, then. Aren't
we? It's as good a word as any, I guess.
It's where I was at the beginning of this
letter. This letter to you. Whose eyes I
long to gaze into. Whose hair I have ached
to run my fingers through. Whose body I
have hugged tight in my dreams. Whose
breasts I have kissed in the moonlight.*

I love you, Vera.

Goodbye.

33

The types of Fear are many, and uniquely distinguished. Among these is the Fear of Lost Love. And the Fear of Abandonment. In the grand living room of our mansion home, where melodies resound the Great Music Hall, I sit with Vera on the plush gray sofa, in the wake of Brenda Harrison's letter read, her name echoing ungently in my spirit, even to the jangling of my feeble nerves in brief. I suppose Vera sees me gazing down at the hardwood floor, at the image of myself lying there on my back dead, having collapsed from the strain of another broken heart, after Vera has blamed me for her best friend's journey over the precipice, and her downfall into insanity and death.

The news of Brenda Harrison's departure, the news of her death had been bad enough, which Vera saw first on the local news here in our mansion, while I was cooking dinner. Telling me by the grand kitchen stove that Catherine Grace Harrison had been burned to death at her school, and her mother was found dead 100 miles away, an apparent victim of herself, and the pain of whispering voices within. These same voices that have haunted me since I was a little girl, telling me to drink bleach and window cleaner, (window *clear*, Mother called it), to put a sharp knife to my own throat, or to make me a rat poison cocktail and swallow it whole. *Don't eat,* the voices sometimes say. *Starve yourself to death. God wants you to die.* And so I understand from whence they cometh, these epic voices of melancholy, so capable of pushing a person over a precipice, indeed.

And even though I am wealthy by earthen standards, rich beyond the Dreams of Avarice, I sometimes lie in bed when Vera is away, wondering how I'll ever have the strength to wake up again. I think if Vera had not given herself to workaholism and volunteerism, she would have surely been a partner in the depression that haunts me like shadows in a cemetery on an Autumn moonlit night. Among these tombstones I drift, the ghost of a woman dead to this life, seeking the comfort of another soul in misery.

Upon the reading of this letter, this cry from the grave, I rise up from the stupor of the punch, this blow from having heard that Brenda Harrison was in love with my Mother Vera, adrift across the massive hardwood floor, to one of the Cathedral like windows many steps away. Refusing to look back at the woman I love. Drawing upon the strength forged within, from the part that is a tempered heart of steel. Behind me, I hear the folding of the handwritten letter—then the steps which seem to echo around me, reverberating softly, perfectly in my Great Music Hall, where these high ceilings and hardwood floors seem to capture and reflect every sound to a ghostly dimension.

Vera steps up beside me, gazing with me across the Great Lawn, past the marble statue of a woman who stands steadfastly playing a harp, nearby the long asphalt road that leads to the iron gate East of Eden, in the company of every rising sun. Although the trees afar off hide the sun's earliest and best morning horizon from me, the rear of our house is the Prairie Green, with a view that stretches forever, to where the sky touches the ground itself, so I can see the red death of every sun, and the blushing light of every red or violet cloud, or when their draperies are caressed in amber.

"I never loved her," Vera says. "I admired her. I needed her. Sometimes I even felt sorry for her. I always knew that the way she treated me was because she was miserable."

"She didn't look miserable."

"I know. Maybe that's part of why I loved her so much."

"You said you didn't love her.'

"As a friend, Honey. As my best friend, so I thought. She had a Master's Degree. I was just a farmer's wife who didn't even graduate from high school. I don't have a single degree to my name, you know that?"

"You have a nurse's certificate."

"To be a Certified Nurse's Assistant. Anybody could get one."

"I bet you I couldn't."

"Really? What can a PhD in musicology teach you about composition?"

I open my mouth, but I can't speak. All I can do is lower my head, then look back at the white marble muse on the front lawn.

"I'm sorry, Baby. I'm just… she's not even here anymore. And she still makes me feel like a loser."

You're not a loser begs the tip of my tongue. But to no avail.

"John and me," she says, "we loved each other. But sometimes I wanted to run as far away from that farm as I could get. And I almost did, too. And then I met you. You made me realize how empty, how superficial and shallow my friends were. How ridiculous my life had become. And I learned that I didn't know God, either. After I met you, I asked him to come into my life. Christ, specifically. I asked Christ himself to forgive me. And I believe he did. After that, I just accepted that Brenda was who she was, and nothing was ever going to change it. Funny, after I stopped trying so hard to please her, she started warming up to me. After her husband left her, I even think that maybe, she even started liking me a little. The divorce changed her. She even cried in my arms when Conrad left her. But that's as far as it ever got with us, Elizabeth. Just a hug and a cry."

Brenda! Woman of the World! Take thy ghostly caress from my lover's heart! Thou art passed away from this life, thou wast taken away in misery! Get thee hence, fly to thine eternal reward beyond! These are the generational curses, I feel, channeled from myself, from my accursed self, through to my real mother first, when her best friend Valerie Kirkland committed suicide herself. Was this woman Valerie secretly devastated by me, by my mother's relationship with me, when Valerie's ex-husband took her daughter away? And this curse has catapulted itself across the years, arching the shape of a rainbow over the timeline, to land in devastation into my new mother's life, landing split splat on the Community Woman's body and soul.

Does this woman lie dead because of me? Had she not looked in my window that night, had we seen the flash of their car lights (which surely came when Vera's eyes were as closed as mine), had we welcomed her into my gray cottage with but a smile and a friendly greeting, what course of events would have transpired therein? When a blessed life meets a cursed one, Miss Brenda, who shall be the better for it? What light or dark spirit shall be the victor?

\

34

*B*renda Harrison, I do not know thee! What I know of thee in the Heart of Memory, is the lust and contempt thou hast for thy daughter! This same lust and contempt thou hast for thy friend! Touch me not, Dear Woman of Straw! I will see you again soon enough, in the Cemetery Valley of Green.

"We were right at the edge," she says. "All of that old bitterness was fading. I remember that day when I came home late. I stopped at the cottage because I saw the light on. Didn't you notice my car lights when I drove up?"

"No."

"I guess we were both pretty occupied, weren't we? We didn't see or hear her drive up at all."

"We weren't supposed to see it."

"Hmmm?"

"The lights. Any other time we would have seen the car lights. Or heard the engine. But when my eyes were open, I was too busy staring at what you were doing. I don't think it was dark enough yet anyway. If her lights were on we wouldn't have noticed unless we were looking outside."

"I didn't hear anything, either. She couldn't have parked that far away."

"The heat was on that night. You know how noisy it is. And I was moaning a lot, remember? You hadn't done that to me in so long. If I had been still and quiet, maybe we would have seen her."

"I always wondered about there being no shades or curtains on these windows," she says.

"All my life, since I was 21, my windows have been bare. Do you think she told anybody?"

"I don't know. And I don't really care. This is our property. Our home. And by God we have the right to do whatever we want here. And right now, I want to feel your mouth on my breasts."

I look over at Vera immediately. A deliberate, questioning stare.

"You heard me, Baby," she says, prompting me to kiss her firmly on the cheek, taking hold of her arm with both hands. The look on her face is abject sorrow, mixed with a sudden stern refusal to give way to any sobbing or weeping.

"Aren't you going to cry, Momma?"

"It'll happen when it happens. We still have their funeral to go to. Right now, I think I just need to go upstairs. You want to go upstairs too, don't you?"

What she doesn't know, is that my mouth has already watered enough to make me swallow once, when she told me what she wanted to feel. In this, in what we have between us, my own need matches and exceeds her own, though I am practiced in the waiting, until she has her fiery axe to grind. But in the moments that lead up to our rendezvous, I am often overcome with shyness, which is my most natural form, when my entire body becomes excitable to her touch, and the easy power of her command. It is the same energy my mother and I displayed, both dominant and submissive, where I was trained that lack of response would not be tolerated.

Holding on to her, I turn further away from the window, my attention focused on her now. Touching my nose to her cheek. Kissing her earlobe, sucking it just so. When I grab firm hold of her bosom, over top of the snug, flower made dress that fits her silky smooth, from her breast to her bottom, when I give the fabulous F cups a squeeze through her dress, her voice deepens in a quiet release, as I go back and forth between them, defiantly squeezing them both over top of her favorite ivory dress with midnight blue flower pattern, squeezing for every disembodied soul, and every spirit that has found us favorable, or unfavorable to look upon. My other hand is cupped at her big backside, a strong, wide wallop of womanhood, it is, to reveal even what the Women of Color take for granted (a white woman shaped like a tall, big-hipped black woman), reminiscent of what my mother bathed and packed inside her underwear. It is her best feature, her F cups notwithstanding, as many over the years have come to know, whether she is in her farmer's wife jeans, or one of her big wig charity dresses, always stretched so smooth and tight across her bottom. She does not try to conceal the bigness, the fullness of her backside with false modesty, all of her skirts and dresses do justice to the word 'voluptuous,' as it applies to her shape and form.

She is bigger than me. Taller, stronger, more athletic waisted, her waist not given to the profound inner curve of mine, which exaggerates my lower half even more. Her breasts are high and round and full of support, her waist is firm and curved inward just enough to provide the angle of her hip spread, which is considerable. Vera the Body, she has been called by at least one of her friends, a woman who tries to compare her own big curves to Vera, though her heavy proportions are not as perfectly formed. "Dumpy" is that woman's fate, I'm afraid, with none of Vera's true hourglass dimensions to display.

At the top and the bottom of this hourglass, my hands bide their time. Working her breasts and her hips to only the beginning of relaxation, and the start of what stimulation they require.

35

Whack!

The blow sends an echo around the room, a shiver to her groin, and an undeniable quiver to mine. "Oh boy," she says, eyes wide open now, glancing towards me. "Better hold off on that," she says. "Wow."

I am obedient. Grabbing her big bottom for a mighty pinch and a wiggle. Understanding fully the unwelcome nature of a premature orgasm. I lean to her mouth, pushing full lips up against hers, breathing in, holding onto the North and South of her world. In the sphere of a woman's libido, there is the Northern Hemisphere, where I have lived my whole life in grieving. And there is the Southern Hemisphere, the Valley of Perdition, the life and death for most women ever born. But even among these, few reside so whole heartedly in the South Western part, where the hips and buttocks reign. Most are a prisoner in the East, the South Eastern corner of a woman, where the sensations are the sharpest, and the easiest to abide.

But there are a few who can feel power in the South West Corner, who understand how a good rub, a good wiggling, and a good smack and whacking of the buttocks is like ringing the doorbell to be let in. Those who don't know why (butt women, they are), who don't know why a hand across their backside just right can send waves of pleasure through their body. Though I am a breast woman by preference, my hips are sensitive enough to work me over as well, though I never really need for that to happen. And I have pulled Vera into this [Breast Woman's World], even from the very beginning when I showed her my lactating breasts in the old blue marble bathroom, which when she first placed them in her mouth, it crumbled her body to ruin, then reformed her, and made her slam herself wildly against me. This, with only our breasts exposed, I remember.

So, by choice and by calling, we are breast women. Slaves to the electric pleasures they provide. But I am sometimes convinced that Vera's attentions have roamed south many times, which she tends to ignore on account of me. But in the early years of this, hardly a greater pleasure I know she ever achieved, than when she could take the belt or paddle to my backside, in a tight skirt or with nary a stitch on, where she could watch my hips twitch and tremble under the strain. And she has always lived to take her dresses off with her hips towards me, always standing with her legs together, letting the dresses fall gingerly to the floor. Then her stockings, and her underwear besides. Then, hands smoothly and quickly across her naked backside, to relax herself into the spirit of her and me. I know that as it is with me, she is inherently a breast woman *and* a butt woman, and I think that sometimes she holds back a fervent obsession.

Still standing beside her at the big cathedral window, I rub and squeeze the ample bottom, wiggling it energetically, feeling in my heart that the two of us are in for hip pains and pleasures long overdue.

"Lets go upstairs," she says, to which I happily oblige. Following her lead, as she turns from the cathedral window and walks across the living room cave, where my Bosendorfer sits beautiful and silent. I watch the beautiful blonde woman with the pinned up hair and pent up sensual energy back there. I watch the tall, strong hipped woman take every Amazonian step in full confidence, as if I am not even following behind her. Climbing the staircase with purpose, hips rounding out the bottom of her dress. Smooth and wide, I am content to notice, wishing I could hear the sound they make from another good smack of the hand. Not many days hence, I think, I am going to lay the paddling wood across her backside, fully clothed and fully committed to causing injury unseen. But for now I lag behind, in the wake of my determination, still aware of my place as the slave to her as my mistress, wife, and mother.

36

*T*o the top of the stairs we flew—we flow—to the top of the staircase we have flown, past every innumerable portrait of Christ and womanhood. Past the giant picture by Ciseri, of Christ before Pilate, one of many such spiritual snapshots from the annals of time, drifted from the Earth's memory into mankind's stubborn reality. *Ecce homo*, Behold the Man, who was brought sinless before the scribes and the chief priests, and then the Roman Procurator, where he was condemned to die a slow and agonizing death, to be scourged for the shedding of his blood, and then to be made to carry his Cross, burdened under the bleeding wood, dragging it on the Road to Golgotha, then lifted up from the Earth at Calvary, nailed to the accursed tree. I take each labored step, in the burden of my life's calling to isolation and misery, past the portrait of myself Vera commissioned in my 40th year, wearing a sinful dress the color of blood, my hair as black as the feathers of a raven, my cleavage in bountiful form, my skin the color of ivory cream. I hardly recognize the features of extraordinary appeal, which seem to me a different woman from what I see in the mirror. But Vera insists that the goddess-like woman in the portrait is me, which I find amusing only because it's the most beautiful woman I have ever seen, but knowing that the fish eyed, blood-lipped, clown skinned woman in the mirror is who I have grown accustomed to. The woman who herself is deserving of beatings, and rapings, and many orgasms forced upon her against her will.

Following Vera down the upstairs hallway, gliding to the upper room, I am convinced now that perhaps I may be slapped around again, or held down and have my breasts bitten, or perhaps strapped with her leather belt until I am again bruised and bloody. In the fervent and fierce apprehension of this, at the bare edge of what could be called fear, we take the last steps down the upstairs hall, the strong, lovely charity woman, Our Lady of the Hips, followed by the fearful, somber woman of music, Our Lady of the Bosom, walking obediently behind her, past photographs of women in perpetuity, mothers and grandmothers and aunts beside the occasional husband, these pictures skillfully dispersed among the dominant theme of Christ the Redeemer, scattered conspicuously throughout.

We take our last step, past Sallman's Christ in the field of lambs, past *The Good Shepherd,* turning into the Queen's Chambers, Vera's gray and crystal palace, where tall dark wood posts mark the four corners of the king sized canopy bed, under the glowing crystal chandelier. Across the softly lighted room, I see the Charity Woman's reflection stop and turn, watching me close the door behind us, facing needlessly away from her, focused too hard and heavy on listening to the door latch shut. Vera walks over to the mirror, as she is accustomed to, and begins to slip out of her dress, watching me oblige in the reflection of the room. Each button of my winter gray dress sparks energy as it is undone, allowing me to see the gigantic cleavage appear in the mirror across the room, which does the trick just enough for me.

And I turn away from my blood sister's (my reflection's) strip tease, sliding my plain gray dress off and feeling it fall to the floor at my feet. The world inside these hallowed walls, blessed by the poor in spirit, these inner ghosts who would look upon us are again treated to a sight so few have seen, that of a true Breast Queen, a goddess of macromastia in her bra, whose gigantic breasts push helplessly against the massive white fabric, above a waist curved sharply inward, to further display their sheer size and dimension.

As I begin to slide the straps down, I watch Vera Evans at the mirror, noticing her completely nude already, her widened hips exposed, with her fingers at both her nipples in manipulation, watching me slide my bra away from my breasts. When it happens, I watch her shake her head 'no' again, as I have seen many times over the years, to betray a soul of awe, and disbelief that renews itself to infinity.

I do not wear bras that pull my breasts up and push them out, but allow them to rest low and as bound in as possible, so that their naked affect is always a shock when Vera sees them. And every blouse I have, and every dress fits to conceal them as merely a bosom; a big, matronly upper half in my clothes, to divert attention away from them as two J cupped monsters that would surely frighten every mother and child at the mall, or at any mountain retreat. Their fascination, I suppose, lies in the fact that so much of my body weight is contained in them, and for a woman of my size, they are perhaps uniquely gargantuan. When I am naked, Vera tells me I could 'call in the horses' with them, whatever that means. And I do admit that I have come to love the heavy weight of them, which I feel now as I bend over, and slide my midnight blue underwear to the floor. *The way they hang,* Vera says sometimes, *the way they move, that perfect bell shape, flowing down and outward to the nipples.* She tells me that my breasts should be photographed at least once, so someday the world can see God's work on a woman's body. I share nothing of this opinion of hers, preferring my mother's Law of Modesty, which was *"keep 'em bound up and hidden."* And maybe this is why I feel such profound freedom when I undress, as if every time I am breaking a secret code passed down, and to look upon breasts of this size and magnitude exposed is to look at the latter day heart of lustful woman, to gaze at an uncovered treasure of the forbidden.

37

I sit on the bed, looking down at my breasts. Unmoved by what is normal to me, that I could smother someone to death with them, if they were bound so they could not move, and gagged so they could not bite. I glance up at Vera over at the mirror, who now studies her own face of ambiguity at the death of her friend, a confusion of sorrow and resignation, closing her eyes upon a sigh and a frown, rubbing both hands again across her breasts, down her waist, then around to the back of those great buttocks, that rival and exceed even the size of my own. Entranced, she turns and walks toward me as confidently as ever, the front of her body as hour-glassed as the back, big and rounded breast flesh in freedom above the strong, athletic waist, where the mildest muscle tone has been known to appear in the strain of passion.

I sit on the bed in dumbness, my senses heightened in fear, staring at the strong, grieving woman with the somber expression, waiting for my hair to be pulled on, or for my face to be slapped violently. But without laying a hand on me, she moves her breast directly to my face. "Put it in your mouth," she says. "No, don't touch it... just suck it..." and when I do, her brow wrinkles and her mouth opens in a look that is akin to pain and mild shock, her eyes closed in horrific grief and concentration, imagining herself at a flowered grave in the rain.

The rising wind of my own desire grown, I take one of them into my hand underneath, to get the strongest hold, and I suck her nipple hard enough to cause pain, which she breathes loudly, enduring it until I pop my lips free loudly, looking up at her for sublime approval, licking the tender area slightly. I put one hand to the big, fleshy buttocks, still holding the breast with the other, commencing her breast punishment again, then taking her buttocks into both hands, mashing and squeezing them while my head bobs at her breasts, yanking on them with severity in the sucking, popping my lips free again, this time to the sound of her voice in grunting.

"Turn around," I say. My voice is low. Almost whispery. Quiet. But determined enough to create pause, as she turns bewilderedly around. Immediately, with fire, I smack the naked skin of her right buttock once, watching her twitch once from the shock, then I hit the same spot once more with as much fire as I can from this position, watching her lower her head, hearing her breathe the deepest sigh, her voice deep and fully relaxed. I lean over to the creamy skin, reddened already by the two blows, sinking my teeth gently into the skin. Feeling her tense up. Licking the full buttock once, latching my lips to the red singed bottom, sucking the fat of her backside to where only a bruise can result, releasing the flesh in the loud popping noise, spanking the same delicious spot two very hard, ferocious whacks, then using my lips and tongue to numb the pain, pulling the irresistible flesh with one more hard sucking. Shaking my head back and forth vigorously, with fever, hearing my own voice go unquiet with muffled, low pitched moaning.

At this moment, Mother Vera, I am a Buttock Queen as thee! Needing to have my face at the South West of my mistress, as hungry as a lioness, to see thy bottom with this small bruise and burn! After this last, fervent lick, and the loud, popping release, I turn her back around, going immediately back to her breasts, sucking them with such ferocity as I am often accustomed, taught to me by my mother, when she told me to *"suck 'em like you mean it,"* which I was always inclined to do, whether soft or strong, to cause pleasure or pain, I worshipped her breasts in spirit and in the truth of my calling, as I do the big and heavy breasts of Mother Vera.

"Slide up to the bed," she says, as though she could not have held it in. I see her hand on her abdomen, just above her South East corner, watching me slide backward to the middle of the bed. Climbing on the bed after me, her eyes focused on both these heavy hangers, transfixed by the nipples as if they hid a message she could not deny. With me sitting, my legs straight outward, she climbs onto one of my legs, straddling herself at my thigh, not speaking, but just watching me take hold of the breast nearest to me, holding it up as before, pulling it in just once, amazed by the single hard twitch her body makes, her muscles now tensed and ready.

She does not slide her hips in humping against my leg. But resists any motion, watching me take her breasts into my mouth like a skin of warm milk, taking the nipple into my mouth as if there were milk to drink, leaving it in, nursing the phantom milk in firm gentleness, in gentle firmness, leaving my eyes closed just enough. Unaware of the grieving, growing anguish as she stares, hearing her groan quietly the name of God, as though what she is feeling cannot be waited for, nor can easily be endured upon its arrival. "Suck it," she says. A deep, lusty voice. "Like you're trying to get the milk. And don't stop. Please don't stop."

I open my eyes, seeing her looking down at the nipple pulled deep in my mouth, repeating for me to suck it, begging me at least once more, her groin straddled and pressed hard on my leg. I release the nipple in the requisite popping noise, realizing my error as she says "keep it in Baby. Please keep it in," calling the name of Heaven again as I take better hold of her breast, drinking what phantom milk there is in endless supply, my cheeks drawn in by the full motion of the drink, feeling her hand go down to the center of herself, sliding to her groin. "I'm going to have to cum Elizabeth," she says, her mind flashing to the attempted raping of Brenda Harrison upon her daughter. "I'm going to have to cum really deep," which prompts me to moan just once, moving my head up and down on the nipple. "Hold still Baby, she says. "Hold it still for Momma, suck the milk for me."

I fall into this last adjustment of hers, latching onto the nipple in pure, deep nursing, as she spreads herself open down below, her fingers at the place of this energy grown, the sound of this power coming from her voice in the pre-moan, energy built up from two points of contact, both clit and tit, then silence as she gauges the near explosion, saying the name of God aloud and with fierce determination while she starts to shake, as her whole lower half starts to slide back and forth on my leg with great ferocity, this energy rocking her hips mindlessly back and forth, her voice in a long, loud and continuous cry of both Agony and Ecstasy born, and released into the grieving air around me.

*C*ome forth, Barbara Jean. Arise to thy feet. Now step lively, lovely through the deep, Carolina rain wood. Thy body is fully formed, is it not? Thy face is aged to perfect beauty. Trudge slowly the miles from nowhere, to where it is you do not know. Brave the falling of the cold Autumn rain.

End of the world beauty travels the miles. Aged 20 years past a former life. Curves so full, so perfectly formed as to be magnificent. Breasts monumental in size and dimension. Waist fit and firm, curved inward as no other in feminine form upon the Earth, save but the daughter that was born from thee. A body rarely seen in the history of mankind, yet imagined through many a colored paint to canvas and paper. The body of the cat women, and the wonder women of old. Formed again by the spirits into reality, deep in the wet Autumn Forest Wood.

The Amazonian mother stumbles through the Carolina forest. Unafraid. Undeterred. Uncertain of all things but one. Burdened now by memories of a past life. Weighted down by the otherworldly calling. Strapped from head to toe by the lust of magic, the power of eroticism unbridled. The desperation of women and men unhindered. The grieving to cause pain unto death.

Walk these rainy, woodsy miles in the dark, Dear Mother. Do you know who you are? Art thou the rebirth of Eve, formed by the Hand of God? What woman on this earth can be compared to thee? Trudge though the Carolina forest, Dear Mother. Your hair is as black as the November night, your skin is smooth as ivory white. Every wicked mother and stepmother ever imagined, moves through the nighttime forest as thee. Remembering naught but the misery of the life you lived before. Remembering nothing of the woman who first bore thee, the Olympian breasted mountain woman, whose breasts you suckled in perversion as but a girl of twelve.

But not even your birth name do you remember, Dear Mother. Though you are Barbara Jean Coletti, in spirit and body, your mind is a jumble of wills. A chasm of emptiness. A reservoir of blind instinct driving you forward, your beauty anguished to a look of suffering, your countenance heavy burdened by a purpose. What is it that you know of yourself, Dear Mother? What form does thy body's memory of past suffering take in your mind? It is the younger likeness of thee, whose curviness is bequeathed from your own, whom you remember you once had a lust and a hatred for, of which ached your body to ruin night after night as she grew, until one day it spilt over into the evening day, into her first epic punishment in secret, when the leather bore down upon the skin of her back, to teach her that to be born is to be cursed, and to live is to suffer?

This is the prevailing flash of pain in thee, is it not? The agony of what you had to do, the burning you felt all the 20 years of your accursed adulthood, to exact punishment of the raven haired, heavy breasted bitch who split you open coming out of you. Do you remember why you hated her so? Do you remember why every particle of yourself was programmed, was taken over by the need to see her beg for mercy? To lay upon her screaming infant body, to smother it to death, only to be pushed over by a will so clearly not your own? To pinch the front of her when she was but a babe in the crib, to wake her up from peaceful slumber, so you could enjoy listening to the infant cry out in pain and fear? Do you remember the angry spankings to the toddler's little back side, the brutal pounding with the palm of your hands until her skin was black and blue? Do you remember the wooden spoon to the back of her thighs when she was twelve, the pressing of bed linen to her face until she could not breathe, her nights in the closet without food or water, her cold lockout in the pouring rain, and the bitter icy winters kept outside in the snow? Do you remember your mouth at her young breasts when she was but 13, after she was cursed with sin and blood? The way her young nipples felt in your mouth when you sucked them to red and bruising in the name of discipline? Do you remember the sound of her little voice beginning to cry, though you warned her not to, as you sucked her thirteen year old breasts to oblivion? Do you remember the feel of her backside, the tightness of her rectum, clamped hopelessly around your finger thrust up inside her, while you nursed her young breasts to bruising the color of blood? Do you remember the way she breathed, O Barbara Jean, when you placed your finger inside her bottom as you sat on your bed fully clothed, to maintain your pretense and delusion? Do you remember the way her body tensed itself as you began to suck on her breast, the last time in her youth, with your finger pushed surreptitiously in her bottom? Do you remember the way your 13 year old daughter breathed and shook, which frightened you into revelation, that the nature of this punishment was beyond inappropriate for thee, thou Lady of the Cloth, thou Lady of Church and Holy Scripture? Do you remember the six year hiatus, Dear Mother, when no such touching of your daughter was allowed? As you lay dying, boiling in midnight and morning lust, imagining the taste of the 16 year old's gigantic bosoms in your mouth? How many nights over those years, O Barbara Jean, did you rock yourself to a peaceful and untroubled sleep, imagining the pain as suffering, the bondage and discipline, the domination and submission you had repressed inside? How many of your nights were burdened, Dear Woman, by the image of your daughter bound nude, her hands behind her back, standing helpless in the middle of the floor? How many of your depressive nappings were interrupted by the sight of her in her pioneer skirt, her shirt open wide, flopping two heavy hung breasts wildly from side to side? O Barbara Jean, how many nights have you prayed, have you cried unto a place beyond these clouds of grieving, to be rescued from the burning of blue and black fire, to be rescued from the suffering of the Mother Line Curse, of things that were done to thee, and will most assuredly have to be done to your daughter!

Bring the Spirit of Defecation, Dear Mother of Straw! Woman On the Farm! As you remain in your bra, so as not to lure thine own epic and sensitive nipple to thee! How many harvests did you reap, how many have you sown, burdened by a lust so few women have known in full, but so many have been touched to fullness in part!

Ah, but there are none such as thee, Dear Mother, as you brave the rainy nighttime woods, driven forward by the lust of sadism, grateful that Creation has begun to restore the sanity of a human name to thee, that of whom you knew you bore in hatred, and raised in the fires of pain and suffering.

39

"This must be what we had been feeling," Vera says. "Brenda and Catherine Grace. Remember your shooting star? And I never told you this, but I dreamt that I saw the Spirit of Death itself."

"When?"

"About a month ago, back in October. Of course I didn't tell you because you would have been scared to death he was coming to get us."

"He is. Eventually. Maybe sooner than we think."

"What does that mean?"

I endeavor to leave her wondering. Opening the silver Mercedes door and getting inside. I so rarely see the inside of a car. My memory of them seems connected to the Curse of God over mankind, whether I am rolling to a hospital or a cemetery.

Vera does not bother to press me for an answer—an explanation for this round of gloom. Why ask a funnel cloud of its noisy, bleak disposition, its explosions of lightning and thunder; from whenceforth cometh its appetite for destruction and death?

I settle into this space of enjoyment, one of the few outside my mansion refuge. Rolling past the big, white statue and three tiered fountain out front, where harmonies pour down a crystal waterfall, from here to perpetuity. Atop the third tier of this fountain is the voluptuous Goddess of Music, unclothed above the waist, holding the small harp from where flows the gift of muse, to bathe the earth in song without words, which is the voice of God in beauty. She stands atop her crystal fountain, her head the height of the mansion itself, the base decorated by four swans in the waters below, who carry messages as to the four winds of the Earth. This monument to the angel that lives in me, to the voice of melody that burns the fires of Mozart, Beethoven, Tchaikovsky and Rossini as one in the modern day, across the landscape of the Twilight of Man, this statue alone glows white when the evening day has passed, and may be why more than one curious visitor has driven inside the gate before we started keeping it closed, some going the last mile up to the mansion itself, cruising the long, asphalt road past the prairie lawn of golf course green, boldly driving the left turn past the front of the house and turning around, rolling slowly again back past the mansion and the statue—the white stone wonder of this hidden, southern world.

Vera and I roll away from my touch of Heaven on Earth, past the open space of the Great Lawn, down the long asphalt road toward the brief stand of yellow and orange leaf maple trees on either side of the road, their leaves long since fallen away in the rain of November's arrival. Seven trees on either side, the gateway from the old world to the new one, where the lawn is unencumbered by a single tree, stretched to the mansion afar off and beyond. I watch the statue and mansion fade into the mirror on my side of the car, veiled behind the curtain of leaves swirled up in the wake of our passing.

There now approaches the House of Death. The old brick farmhouse. A good walking distance from the road. A house I once saw as the door of Paradise open. In quaint, plain, country, southern upper middle class striving, which is little more than a glorified holding place, while the Fates decide whether or not to exalt the tortured inhabitants therein.

"I was in there the other day. When you were at work."

"You didn't tell me that. I don't like you hanging around in that old house."

"How come?"

"Because we've got enough bad memories to last the rest of our lives. I wish you had let me tear that place down."

"Its too pretty. We have to keep it."

Vera breathes a deep sigh, which I ignore, gazing not at the big iron gate swinging open, the two big letters *A* and *L* drifting apart, and the words *Amherst Lake* they represent—but my attention is transfixed by the lovely brick farmhouse, as well as the property where the big equipment used to be. Gone are the concrete driveway and the gravel road where I took so many lonely walks with my husband before he died, and then with Vera when I was pregnant with Maria, in the days before our wedding in the blue marble Cathedral.

"I think I heard an evil spirit when I was in the old bedroom. I heard it rattling around in the kitchen. Then the footsteps came down the hall."

"Oh, no."

"What?"

"I knew if you kept hanging around in that house long enough…"

"You believe me, don't you?"

"Honey, I certainly believe you *think* you saw something. You know how your mind plays tricks on you sometimes."

As the car rolls past the towering open gate, and the two brick column supports they are hinged upon, I'm suddenly at a loss, as if knocked backwards from my path forward along the timeline. The car glides the rest of its journey as the gate closes behind us, until we come to the road, beyond which is still the deep, dense forest I once knew, when I used to ride this same road in desperation to the farmhouse. The prairie lawn was a cornfield then, stretching from nearby the house toward the horizon.

"So you're saying I'm crazy?"

"Of course I'm not saying that. How could you think such a thing."

"You said it was my mind playing tricks."

"Well, so what if it was Honey? The experience was still real. Probably activated by that house. I told you not to go back in it."

"It touched me."

"The house?"

"No," I say, stifling a giggle. "The spirit I heard when I was in the bedroom.

"What do you mean it touched you?"

"I tried not to let it bother me when I heard the noises. I stood there, but I could feel it come into the room. I haven't been that scared in years. Its an old spirit I've felt before. I turned to leave and it was all I could do to keep from running. And of course that old whispering started."

"Like what you heard in your old house that time? In the kitchen?"

"Exactly like it. And then I felt it brush against my hair."

"What did you do?"

"Screamed and got out as fast as I could."

"Well, even if it was an actual... *spirit*, it can't hurt you, can it? You just attract things like that. Artists are always telling ghost stories. Its probably something talented people just have to deal with. You've been sensing spirits your whole life anyway, haven't you?"

The rain on the windshield transports me backwards through this space in time, to when my mother threw me outside in a summer rainstorm. My twelve year old mind had flashed insane, I think, where I thought I saw a lion made out of pure rainfall in the front yard. The scriptures tell two tales in metaphor for the lion—polar opposites. One being the Root of David, the Lion of the tribe of Judah, which is Christ the Lord. The other being the Angel of Light, the false Christ, who is the power of the Antichrist, the ruler of the darkness of this world, which is the Devil, who himself walketh about as a roaring lion, seeking whom he may devour.

Accept for my music, and the prose and verses that I write, I have lived with the Devil in the walls of every house I have lived in, accept for inside the walls of my gray cottage, and the hallowed halls of our mansion home.

"This thing with Brenda has us all spooked anyway. I've dealt with violence and death a lot. But I've never heard of anything like this. I've heard of one husband who tried to burn his wife, but even then she survived. But a mother doing this to her daughter. And then killing herself?

Brenda never seemed that depressed to me, and I never thought she could even *slap* Catherine Grace. Let alone this."

"Poor Catherine," I say. "The pain she must have suffered. They say her face… her face was…"

"I know. I mean, we work in this field. We council people on the edge of suicide all the time. If she was feeling that badly about things…"

"There was nothing you could have done. It was meant to be."

"Does it bother you that she saw us?" she asks. "That she knows what we did?"

"It scared me a little at first. But now, its sort of a relief."

"Like you don't care who knows it, right?"

"I'm never going around those people much anyway. But what about you? Do you think she told anybody else?"

"I'm not ashamed of what we are."

"What are we?"

"Two people in love with one another. To me, that's all that matters."

Vera reaches over to take my hand, lifting it to her lips, touching it gently. The kiss floods warmth to the center of my body, radiating outward, to disperse away the fear and the cold.

40

The grieving gray countryside is awash with pain and misery. The brief winds are blown in from Melancholy Bay, splashing every forest and field with warning, while shrouding the lights of every passing car in mystery. Though I hardly ever leave the grounds of Amherst Lake, or my bedroom at St. Carmen in the Fields, I admit that I savor the loveliest feeling when we're speeding the highways. I cannot relate my joy as I soar into the sky with my mind. I watch every car as if it is a Golden Wheel, and sometimes I stare into a person's face from the safety of our car. I often feel brave enough to endure the reaction in a person's eyes when I stare. As long as Momma is here, their arrows have no power. Mother Vera is beautiful. Her love is beautiful.

What is better than watching the city limits dissolve into the countryside, until there is nothing left but grass and trees, and maybe a field of cows or horses? My brain often tries to tell me exactly how many I see, but I always ignore it. It is a part of my mind that troubles me, and I do not wish it to develop. For what purpose can it be, except to vex my fragile nerves? What can be said of God's blue sky on a warm summer afternoon, with angels as fluffy white clouds flying by? My heart is thrilled by the summertime fields of corn, where the horizon is touched by a rolling sea of green. But even in those Days of Heaven, when the joy of the Lord is unspeakable in the afternoon, I long for the mournful passing of Indian Summer, and the colorful death of melody displayed on the forest leaf canopy.

As I peer through the rainy mist, at the shimmering patches of color going by, I am reminded that if it is Autumn, the forests are my favorite things to see. The yellow trees call to my vision. There is a place in the Piedmont that I always remember, rounding a certain curve on Highway 40 towards Winston Salem, where the road overlooks a vast, rolling spread of trees, rising like the base of a mountain hill. Once I stared into the center of them, and I felt my awareness heighten, and my mind began to haze into a higher state, and it began to calculate the number of trees. But I quickly shook my head and surfaced from this drowning. It was as though I could suddenly see every individual tree, where before there had only been a forest of them. But I am lucky today, I suppose, that my mind is not calculating a single one of the thousands of raindrops against my window, nor the rhythm of the windshield blades into fiery melody and song.

41

"*Bitch!*"

The word rings in a voice I have not heard for a while. Making me jump like I've been stuck with a pin. I suddenly remember the nails dragged across my back (my husband), and the sharp stick of the straight pin in my buttocks and the backs of my thighs (my mother).

"Will you be alright? I have to go in. But you can stay out here if you want to."

As if awakened from one of my old musical trances, I stare at the hazy world outside the rainy car windows, the sea of parked cars and rainsoaked bodies moving about, all drifting as spirits of the dead, all shrouded in black, gray, and cloth of midnight blue.

"I'm alright," I say. Vera gathers her gray umbrella, opening the luxury car door into the infinity of rainfall. The shoulder length blonde hair flashes in stark contrast to the gray,that of the weeping world outside, and the dark gray cloth of her umbrella and full length coat, concealing the black mourning cloth underneath.

She braves the solemn weather, a soul adrift in the cold November wind, moved to where I sit inside waiting for her. She opens the door for me, and I step out in full melancholy splendor, hiding with her under the gray umbrella from the rain, and from the infinity of people. Two hearses, two black funeral chariots, sit undaunted one behind the other, near the church where their dead bodies lay.

Under grieving skies. Beside a blonde beauty, beneath the umbrella gray. I am a figure dressed in black. Moving like a shadow beside the woman in gray, adrift on a current of fear and grief, but one born from a far and distant place I have come from. Where I was born under this same cloud of sorrow and grief, and a fear greater than any of these tortured souls have ever known.

42

Take thy last stumble and fall, Dear Mother, in the rainy November woods of gray. These many days since the life was breathed back into thee, thou hast wandered the Autumn forest wood, guided by a force unseen. In grieving to find a place unknown. A place your eyes have never seen, nor hath your heart ever imagined it could be possible, in the days of the rightful life you knew. Knowing somehow that the culmination of years, the mountain peak of unrequited want and need lies just over the next horizon. In your heart pumping blood it rests, Dear Mother. The knowledge that you must continue through the lightning edge of the Pine Woods, moving past the edge of light, out into the rain and gray. This is the journey East, implanted in your blood when you were reborn.

Now, take this last, bold step to freedom, Dear Woman. Do you know your name, Barbara Jean? Do you know your daughter's name? It still rings every part of your mind and body. Your confused and vacant mind, knowing that this prairie field is where you belong, drowning in the cold, late afternoon mist of rain.

Her name rings in every part of your body and spirit. This fully formed, perfectly aged body, only an inch below six feet, perfect white feet taking steps into the prairie green untortured, legs rising long and lean, full hips widened to infinity. How is it possible, dear Mother, to have a girth of the hip so extraordinary? Bulging buttocks framed by the extra wideness of the upper thigh, for the strong, Amazonian curve of legend, hips not meant to be bound by naught but a woman's garment, lest you draw stares, awe and ridicule from all who survey. This, below a waist so obviously the source of my own, Dear Mother, shaped so remarkably alike in kind, but seasoned to a greater maturity; the fit, fleshy curve of middle age, flowing inward so far, to flare the burn of cosmic envy in the souls of men and women, to wish to be lost forever in the nature of its voluptuous flow, the middle part of the hourglass, the flaring of the Nova Curve in the heart of those so fortunate enough to see.

Walk, Dear Mother. Each unfettered step in greater dimness than the last, unencumbered by the weight above thy waist—undaunted by the pull, swing and wobble you felt on thy journey through the wooded countryside. The greater part of thine unclothed and naked splendor, bulbous and bell bottomed bombardiers, the top of the greatest hourglass of all time, evidence that thou wast conceived and created with a Divine purpose. To evidence this eminent Twilight of Man, to display upon the prairie green the power of womanhood exposed and wobbled, with two of the world's largest breasts, dangling disproportionate to thine curved and hip widened form, the truest sign of the times, that the lustful heart of woman is infinite, and will be uncovered at the end of the age, for all the world to see.

What is the sign of thy coming, Dear Mother? That mankind cannot cease from sin. And that beyond the mercy of God through Calvary, there is no hope for Redemption. That the time for petty judgment and hypocrisy is past, as we approach the fiery eve of Armageddon, and the Second Coming of our Lord and Savior from Heaven. These great breasts hang as mine, Dear Woman, nearly down to thy curved waist, in a key brighter even than the unknown song in J heard from mine, pitched somewhere up and beyond what need be expressed.

There is a lesser goddess that awaits thee, Mother Dear. Whose unclothed self you have not seen in a score of years, since they were much smaller than they are now. But the bosom this woman you know has grown, to dimensions that rival your own, since the days when thy grandchild was in her womb, and her breasts were heavy with milk long gone. Does your thirst ache your body, Dear Mother? What sweet and white nourishment for thyself doest thou burn in craving for? Can you taste the warm milk of her breasts in your imagination as you walk in the cold? Does it tickle the part of you down below, the center of your life and craving? Does the cold rain upon your hardened nipples harden another part of thee? Hath your awakening yet touched your greatest anomaly, Dear Mother, passed down to me only in part, hidden inside yourself as you walk, so that none could tell of this end of the world ability you possess, to grow thyself when in epic arousal, a clit to rival the smallest sizes of that which pertaineth to a man. Thou art a wonder of the post modern world. A Wonder Woman, to be sure. Called to deliver an end time generation from ignorance and innocence, and to slay the Dragon of

Hypocrisy with thy flaming sword, which burns hot with blue and black fire.

Go thee up, Dear Mother. Across the windswept prairie field of November, to the mansion of thy daughter beyond. Get thee to thy calling, Dear Mother. Drowning in the darkened rain.

43

*T*he line of funeral cars moves slow and desperate in the rainy afternoon. Vera and I, no, Vera and *me* are among the so-called principal mourners, in the Harrison funeral procession, the fifth car behind the two black hearses in a line of more than twenty, with Conrad Harrison and his new wife being up front, the first car being the engine of this Death Train. Brenda's mother and father are in the second car, followed by her two older sisters and their families. Behind these fine and semi luxury rides are we, chosen above every other member of the extended family and friend and prestige mourner, which are many. Conrad had wanted Vera to trail directly behind him to the burial site, but Brenda's mother would not have it, not bothering to hide her disdain while we were seated, loud whispering her son about how *"just because she's rich doesn't mean she should have my place in line... I don't care if she was her best friend, I'm her mother."* And I remember her husband (Brenda's father), leaning over and trying to calm her down. We were in the seat directly behind them when the truth was whispered, that *"who the Hell does that rich bitch think she is"* truth, from the heart and mind of cultured civility.

I wish I could be a comfort and protection for Momma Vera, out here among these wolves. But the truth is I'm just scared all the time. What people see as aloofness in me, as coldness, arrogance and conceit is really just a shyness I was born and bred into. A belt bred country girl, I am, masquerading as a woman of means at the funeral, gripping my new mother's hands to the point of exhaustion, when I had to stretch my fingers because they were getting sore from gripping Vera's hand so tight. I know that she was intrigued the entire hour of the funeral service, at the length and voracity with which I held her hand, betraying the nervousness and jumpiness I try to hide when I am in public. Though I have been told ad nauseam that I am *"the most beautiful woman anyone has ever seen,"* I cannot look people in the eye without extreme discomfort inside. I feel that my eyes are too big, my skin is too white, and my lips are too red, hearing my mother's voice laughing at me sometimes, telling me I look like a clown fish. I heard this many times growing up over the years, sometimes followed by a brutal slap or blow or just a plain old fashioned bop upside the head, ringing my ears or rattling my brain. *"Get your ugly, lazy ass back out to that field and chop those weeds right before I beat the skin off you,"* she would say, scaring me so bad I would have to go to the bathroom, but would have to suffer and hold it in while I went back outside to pull what few strands of grass that were still there. *"Fish faced slut,"* she would say, whacking my butt through my pioneer skirt as hard as she could while I was out the back door. It was like being hit with a bat, as she would put her whole self into it, the palm of her hand stinging my skin underneath the skirt. And even today, near the horizon of my forty first year birthday, her voice is still present when I am in public, to assure me that all claims to my beauty are false, and I am a fish faced clown to be mocked, stared at and ridiculed.

In the spirit of this violence, I ride the Death Train, this old hair pulling spirit of domination descended, flashing the Theatre of my Mind, forcing me to watch myself in the kitchen at Perpetuity when I was eighteen, before I had fully retreated to the world of sound and color. I stand in the kitchen in my dark green blouse and ground length skirt, before the tall and beautiful woman who is my mother, my head of fire, of lightning from her hands buried in my hair, pulling it hard enough to bend my head over and holding my throat with the other hand.

"Was that a look I just got from you," she says, which I respond to rather loudly, rather angrily over the tears that fall, enraged inside over being accused of giving her a look, which I most decidedly did not. *"Now, you get your ass to that field,"* she says, shaking my head once very hard on the word 'get,' *"before I put you so far underneath it they won't be able to plow you up."* She shoves me toward the kitchen door, sprung off the word 'plow, which in my teenage rebellion inside, I find a new balance and do not stumble, which incenses her, powering her to the hardest spank I have ever felt on my way out the door, to the music of the song *"Fished Faced Slut,"* which lurches my lower half forward, but to which I still refuse to stumble to her satisfaction.

I open the screen door in 18 year old defiance, letting the door slam shut behind me on its own. I am aware of the heat from her gaze, burning through the screen at me, watching me pick up the hoe and turn to walk toward the back porch steps. But I hear the squeak of the back screen door open, feeling the wind from it, knowing instinctively that I must not look back. But upon this step toward belated, reluctant obedience and freedom, upon this step I ride, feeling a punishment shove in my back as I start my first step off the porch, which activates my natural clumsiness, causing me to fly through space, the dirt ground rising up to catch my fall. I hold on to the garden hoe for dear life, the long, tall wooden stick, bringing it down to the ground with me as I fall flat on my stomach and breasts, my face slamming into the dirt an instant after. And before I can gather what few wits I have left, I feel the crashing of a mountain down upon my back, which drives my face into the dry dirt, to where I can taste the blood in my mouth as I struggle to catch a breath.

In this trauma of lost air, in the vacuum of my life on the farm, she flips me over on my back, ignoring the fear in my eyes, my mouth wide open to try and find the breath of life. Sitting on my stomach, she hauls back and slaps me with all her might at the temples, then she does this one time more, which flashes a bolt of purple light before my eyes. Then she puts her hand over my mouth and lays on top of me, while I kick helplessly through points of stabbing pain, from the bottom of my leg where the hoe blade has gashed it open, to my rib bones deeply bruised, to the fire in the pit of my stomach that will not allow me to catch a breath. My nose, though mercifully uncovered, is but a pinhole's worth of air traveling to my lungs, which I cannot feel as my mother and the house begin to lift and swirl around me. Against her own will, she stands up at the moment of truth, and it is as though the demon that siphoned the air from me is at once sent away. I can only turn to the side, thanking God while I cough from blessed air in my lungs, caring nothing for the grand burning in my cut, bleeding leg, nor the deep aching in my ribs and the pit of my stomach.

44

$\mathscr{I}$emerge from the Heart of Memory unscathed. Medicated from the cold vision by the warmth of the luxury car, and Mother Vera comfortably at my side.

Our funereal procession moves long and slow. Past the rain soaked forests and fields of November, on our way to Forest Lawn. It is a place all too familiar to Vera and myself, having already sent three souls back to God through here. As we creep along the rainy, windswept streets of this deserted town, I can feel the ghostly energy of Forest Lawn calling to me already, to remind me that my constant companion is Death, and the height and breadth of me is Fear and Despair. The rainsoaked windows cannot hide the truth from me, as the brake lights in one of Brenda's sister's cars flashes the warning. Through a shimmering mist of dark'ned gray, the Tombstones of Carolina beckon, stretching across the landscape of Forest Lawn Cemetery, marking the final resting places of bodies old and young—telling nothing of the secrets they guard until the end of time. Of secrets these men, women and children carried to their graves, and the Divine Secret, as to what manner of spirit came for their souls when their bodies died, and they were interred as the dead and buried.

While I watch such a royal and stately looking lot turn down the beautiful paved entrance road, I am already haunted by the ghost of Maria Peele, and the echo of the sorrow I knew when I left her in the ground. *Let me bury her in the garden*, I had begged Vera in the hospital, holding her hand and begging her once, slipping into a sob that came out on its own. How I had longed for her, to break the spell that I had lived in since I was born! Through Carmen Maria Peele, I would at last taste a life untouched by sorrow—to know a life where only happiness had been born and bred—a girl of privilege she would have been, learning the piano from the youngest age, hopefully a prodigy on the instrument that chose the two of us. But I think my second love would have overtaken her, yes, the sublime cello, wherein is contained the voice of the Mother Line Curse—the Modern Mother Daughter Dynamic which is queen, ruling every end-of-the-world family abomination in absolute power. Through Maria Peele, oh how I would have labored a smile, a laugh, and a kind word to ease her pain, to let Mother Vera speak words of revelation about the darkness of man, while I would have fought to be her rest from the truth, that this is the end of the age, and mankind is evil! Through my daughter, God would channel a blessing of laughter into my spirit, while I watched her grow tall in beauty, and strong in knowledge of the Spirit of God in power. Oh, how she would have carried my music to the masses, I think, playing my concertos with depth and understanding, named Maria Peele on the world stage, playing the music of Carmen Coletti on the eve of Armageddon!

All hail the second coming of the Lord, in the music of Carmen Coletti! But alas, such nonsense is not meant to be. No, Elizabeth. Gaze through the rainy windshield at thine own future Fate, across the field of Forest Lawn, and the gray stone and marble crosses in the rain. *"Those who turn their backs on Christ will die,"* is the word from the Lord I hear, when I feel myself drifting through this space of rain in our luxury car, turning with the line of cars in front of us, the seventh car in this dreary procession. Following the mother (Brenda), her daughter (Catherine Grace), the ex husband, the grandmother, the 1st older sister, and the 2nd older sister.

Forest Lawn over Pineview is the name that passes over the best friend, my loving companion, rolling so uncasually in the pouring rain. There is the Spirit of Death that roams this hallowed soil. Or perhaps this is ground unhallowed after all, bestowed little respect from the Lord himself compared to a Divine Calling, when he told some unknown and would be disciple *"let the dead bury the dead."* Yes, he came not to bring peace, thou lost and corrupt generation of vipers! The truth cuts down to the quick, and is sharper than any two edged sword!

We roll slowly but surely, in line with our funereal parade, performing our rolling march past the truth in concrete and marble, spread out in a field of grass colored golf course green, clearly visible through the shroud of gray descended all around us. The gravestone markers grow in rows parallel to the road we travel, so that all of the hundreds of graves are facing us when we peer at them through the rain. You can't judge a dead person by their gravestone. Is this true, dear Mozart? Thou wast buried in an umarked grave! How many of these finely manicured works of moribund repose, how many of these sleep stones can accurately gauge the loving heart and soul they hold place for! How many marble monuments can display the truth! O, what an unsolvable puzzle it is, to try and know whether the stone alter with the cross on top, marks the passing of a soul of goodness, or a soul of blackness unrepentant, and worthy of the everlasting Fires of Hell! There are none good, thus saith the Lord, for all have sinned and come short of the Glory of God!

Our line of cars rolls the rain soaked streets of Pineview, grieving for a reprieve from suffering! We are all riders on this Death Train, moving from the crib to the coffin! A victim of what was laid down upon us by the curse from the Garden of Antiquity! O Lord, protect us from thy coming Judgment! Lift us up from the mire of sin! Carry us to the mountain of repentance, to where thy redemption draweth nigh! God bless the lonely, lowly prophet, burdened with the truth in his or her heart, that greatest and most penultimate truth of our unblessed existence, that the only importance there is to this life, is where your soul goes when this life is over! There is the angel, I see, that guards the book of life! Pointing across the Poverty Field, the field of death and despair! O, woe unto them who have been given the Breath of Life! To be born is to be cursed, and to live is to suffer! And save for Elijah himself, who left the earthly plane in chariot of fire, even the Lord and Savior did not such a luxury partake, for we are all subject to the curse of sin, which is death! Except a man be born again, he cannot see the Kingdom of God! Of this final and greatest curse, deliver us, O Lord! Deliver us from the Second Death, which is eternal damnation from thee!

I see the few tents and new flower racks in the distances, scattered among the field of gravestones, that mark the departure, the passing of the bodies and souls of the damned. What few among these, after suffering the condemnation of earthly, physical death—what part of them were blessed of God through Christ, to receive the golden ticket to God's glory, and a reprieve from the second death, the separation of their soul forever from the glory of God? Who among us who ride the Death Train, who among us shines the light of God's glory? Who among us are skeleton faced already, to be judged evil by the Almighty himself, then be cast into the Lake of Fire and brimstone! Who among us can withstand the Power of God! Who among us is worthy to stand before Him! I take this ride of truth across the Poverty Field, riding along on the Death Train. Unafraid. Unwary of the great tent that awaits us. A sinner, I am. Saved by the Grace of God. Unafraid of the life that waits for me beyond the grave, but ironically, terrified of the life that awaits me in the Land of the living.

O, thou wicked and perverse generation! How can you escape damnation! My mind is blasted with this, as my mind shows me a waking vision through the rain soaked windshield when we park, of the fourth car in front of us suddenly blasted by fire streaked from above, causing it to explode mightily, shaking me to my foundation, rumbling the ground like an earthquake, filling the shimmering windshield with a flash of orange light, which is fire and smoke. I turn to Mother Vera in sheer terror, seeing her already out of the car in the spirit of helpless desperation, as the rainfall is suddenly lit up by streaks of fire raining down from the gray clouds, with the occasional big blast at the end of a trail of smoke to the pinewood forest nearby. And then, I hear another great explosion behind me, at the end of a gigantic trail of smoke, which blows another of the silver gray cars out of existence, turning it upside down into twisted and burned metal. And there are some cars which are rained upon by this fire, where the glass is broken, and the inside is lit up with fire, causing those who are alive and remain inside to open their doors screaming, one woman running through the rain, burning hot in liquid flame. She runs toward me in a scream that I can hear in my soul, even while the trees begin to burn nearby, and the trails of fire begin to fall to an infinity around us. Unable to move. Unable to breathe, unable to think no thought but *Lord, save me.*

I stare out the rainy window through the shimmering haze, seeing the woman on fire run toward me in rapid pace, agonizing aflame, opening the car door which I thought was locked, screaming at me to help her, with a hatred for me in her eyes, and a craving to see me burning with the same fire from Heaven, to see me burning in the liquid flames of Hell. She grabs my head, and I feel the heat of her death, I smell the charred ashes of her condemnation, and I begin to fight this demon woman, trying to push her away from me, beginning to scream Vera's name.

Then suddenly, I can draw no further breath for a scream, as I feel as though I have snapped awake from a nightmare with Vera's strong hand pressed over my mouth. Leaning inside the open car door, rain falling in, umbrella on the ground, with two fascinated children, a boy and a girl, staring at us through the rain soaked windshield, until their mother escorts them fearfully, and forcefully away.

I gaze wide eyed at the cold, tranquil Autumn rainstorm around me. With Momma Vera's hand still tightly over my mouth…

I tremble.

45

*W*ithout a word, Vera picks the umbrella up from the ground, then ushers me out of the car. She slides her arm around me with the patience of a nurse, escorting me through the rain toward the big tent, while I gaze apprehensively, in pure apprehension all around me. Although I can see clearly the evergreens of Forest Lawn Cemetery, and how they defy the deep Autumn with year round summer green—although I can definitely see them ruling this somber countryside in pristine, pastoral glory, in my memory, in my mind's eye they are all still on fire of Hell. My nerves have even transformed the soothing, familiar sound of the rainfall on the umbrella to the clamour of burning rocks and pebbles falling from the clouds, causing me to bristle against the image of our umbrella turning into a flaming torch. I feel the return of my characteristic expression, the look of a woman burdened by painful humiliation to be seen, and of shyness that borders on the pathological.

As Vera glides us to the green cloth covered chairs underneath the matching tent shelter, I am as nervous as a kitten, and the seconds marking our time here have slowed down like what I have not felt in years, as if the second hand of a ticking clock were being held still by a spirit. I await the passing of every minute as though it were an hour, sitting in the back row of immediate family mourners. Unwelcomed, I fear. Watching the two silver coffins be carried in one at a time, set down on the suspension straps above the burial pits, the places their empty shells must soon lie dead and buried in. With Vera beside me, holding my hand, I am able to focus a little better now, transfixed by the two caskets up front, and the backdrop of gravestones, of grass and evergreen trees beyond. Vera and I occupy the back row of chairs, with one of Brenda's sisters, the one closest to her age, who had always respected Vera as an important part of Brenda's life. Of every mourner, including Brenda's own mother, her sister Cindy had seemed the most broken up by the whole thing, and her tears and sorrow have flowed without ceasing. I have watched Vera too, struggle to hold it together, having to hold a tissue the entire time, her eyes red and damp all the time, while she is shrouded in a mist of sorrow.

"Blessed are the poor in spirit: for theirs is the kingdom of Heaven."

The sound of these words. Their quiet echo through our spirits is too much for Cindy Breckinrich, born Cindy Walker, and she says "Oh God," reacting to the wave of grief I feel flow through us all.

"Blessed are they that mourn: for they shall be comforted."

This second wave devastates the poor woman, I hear, as she descends into full sobbing, suffering great internal pain as what she is not accustomed. I watch Vera take her hand, and be the shoulder for her to literally lean on, while Vera still squeezes my hand tighter, as I hear her voice suffer one deep, grunting loss of dignity. Vera hold's Cindy's hand on one side, and my hand tightly on the other. Vera's deep suffering response brings a judging look from Brenda's oldest sister, who looks back at Vera with the quick, powerful once over glance of pure contempt. *Who the Hell do you think you are, blubbering at my sister and my niece's funeral...*

"Blessed are the meek: for they shall inherit the earth. Blessed are they which do hunger and thirst after righteousness: for they shall be filled. Blessed are the merciful: for they shall obtain mercy. Blessed are the pure in heart: for they shall see God. Blessed are the peacemakers: for they shall be called children of God. Blessed are they which are persecuted for righteousness' sake: for theirs is the Kingdom of Heaven. Blessed are ye, when men shall revile you, and persecute you, and shall say all manner of evil against you falsely, for my sake. Rejoice, and be exceeding glad: for great is your reward in Heaven."

As the pastor closes the book on this latest death and burial, Brenda's mother puts both hands over her face as if it where splashed with cold water, her breath taken away as she shakes her head, and begins to sob as if being beaten, knowing now that her daughter and granddaughter are gone, and this, by the sovereign will of the Most High. Brenda's father is splashed as well, sucking in a breath as she hugs his wife, sucking a breath like one who has emerged from underneath the water, drawing another quick and conspicuous breath of pure agony. This last wave of grief touches us all, through our tiny gathering under the tent, through the prestige mourners gathered around, through every tombstone, and every nearby forest and field beyond.

46

*T*wilight beckons our sojourn towards the mansion home. Away from the elegant suburban house of Brenda Harrison, where the medium sized gathering had descended like blackbirds on a field after a spring plow.

Do we have to go? I had cooed painfully as we drove to the house from the cemetery, enduring her gentle chastisement in response. *Honey, you know I have to be there*, Vera had said.

But why?

She was my best friend. You're just gonna have to be brave, Honey. Cyndi practically begged us to come.

I had turned to the rainy window and sighed loudly, hoping the sound of it would lash Vera away from this social spell she is under, which I despise when it happens. It didn't. She had driven us both unmercifully onward, towards the house of the dead woman and her dead daughter, to drag me out of the car and throw me into a suburban lion's den. It had been the most miserable two hours of my life.

I want to go home, is the theme that plays the Heart of Memory, as we had driven from the burial site to Grand Harwich Estates, where Brenda and Catherine Grace Harrison had lived and died. I remember cruising the upper middle class streets, unable to stop staring at each of the lovely gray cottages I could see through the rainy haze, noticing the conglomeration of Sunday cars in every driveway, wondering if this day feels any different or special to the people in these houses, but being infinitely glad that I would never know. In the Heart of Memory, I roll the streets of this town, past the upper middle class houses of splendor, so unenvious of each carefully manicured patch of grass and shrub and so-called flower garden. Feeling as though I could have never lived the social, community life that they take for granted, wondering how it is that they can be comfortable living so close together.

Perhaps, they are normal.

Better examples of humanity than I. For even the Lord himself was a social being, always placing himself in the midst of people, even though he paid the ultimate sacrifice for it. It seems that everywhere Jesus went, there was trouble. And he was the Son of the living God. Oh Lord, how much more trouble am I in, being made lower than the lowliest angel, imprisoned in a body of sinful flesh and blood! Vera's lack of mercy on me, it is a another lash to my back! Why won't she take pity on me, Lord, and drive me away from the streets of Brenda Harrison! The woman never liked me anyway, would she want me in her home today?

Vera cruises me unmercifully. Without mercy through the strains of a funeral march in my mind, coming of its own accord, to mark the misery of this lost hour in time. On the current of this somber phrase, we drift onward. Past the houses of hidden hypocrisy and isolated ill repute, these castles of kindling brick and wood. Along the gated streets of Grand Harwich Estates we roll, no longer a victim of the power that overwhelms those who enter here, who must succumb to the Spirit of Envy, causing the stress of hopeless longing and desire.

I think she sensed something years ago, Vera says, *when we buried your husband. She said, 'I want to be buried here. Somewhere in this beautiful place. Somewhere near that beautiful man,' she said. I looked right at her and said 'Amen.' Its one of the few times over the years when she was vulnerable. When she let me in. When I didn't feel like I had to walk on glass around her.*

She never liked me. She wasn't sorry for me when Chris died.

Please don't say that. Brenda loved you.

She loved Chris.

Well, Honey everything with breasts and a booboo loved Chris. A man that handsome, with that kind, shy personality? You two were birds of a feather. Brenda said you two were scary beautiful. She was always calling you the name of some famous Hollywood couple behind your back. Any tension you may have felt from her was... well... Elizabeth, your looks are intimidating.

As to what she means, I cannot abide. Not wanting to know whether what she says about my face is true, nor whether what my mother said is true instead, that I am the ugliest bitch in God's Creation. This, I heard in either the pitch of anger, or the key of mocking laughter. This laughter buries my self-worth under another layer of grief, as the palatial middle class home of Brenda Harrison appears around the next turn, causing my heart to flutter quietly again, while I take a deep breath of warrior's anticipation, to do battle with the souls of cultured civility.

Back and forth along the timeline. From the ride away from Brenda's house, to the ride I endured moving towards it. In the Heart of Memory, I suffer the loss of Vera's compassion for my shyness, as we roll the streets of this town. In Grand Harwich Estates, past the carefully manicured lawn of suburban dreams, then turning onto the black asphalt drive, where it seems that every kind and silver gray color of luxury car is already parked and waiting.

47

She was a lesbian, Cyndi says. *Brenda said that Catherine Grace was seeing a woman in Chapel Hill. But she was trying to hide it from everybody. From Brenda and apparently, from herself.*

Brenda never said anything to me, Vera says surreptitiously, sitting on the sofa beside me. The glass of white wine she holds is half empty. So too is my glass of grape juice, which I'm hardly interested in, taking every sip in fear that someone will see me and hear me gulping a swallow, even if they are standing across the room. Thank God they don't see me. I seem to possess the gift of invisibility, which kicks in after my initial appearance in a room. And God forbid that someone will push through the veil; the barrier that separates us one from another. It is one of my worst fears, that someone will actually talk to me, and ask me a question.

Luckily, I've already hugged and shook hands, so the family is used to me now. But there are so many strangers and friends of the family here that I saw at the funeral, all drinking and talking quietly in groups. Some of the family is walking around the house incessantly. Studying it, testing it, admiring the exquisitely tasteful, simple décor. And I see at least four lionesses from Brenda's Charity Brigade, her charity pride of nine, roaming lost and alone, scattered about the house in full busy, chatterbox repose, all giddy with inner delight that the Woman of Charity died by her own hand, and took her daughter with her. Their sorrow is as fleeting as the clouds of this November rainstorm, here for a steady, protracted endurance but for a long moment, but soon vanished as suddenly and as quickly as it came. The Four Winds of Southern Charity they are, blowing from room to room like visitors in a museum, from the elegant, carved bedroom suite in Cherry Wood, to the dollhouse bedroom of Catherine Grace, in which she had not slept in years, that mysterious shrine to a youth come and gone, a storage room of memories perfectly kept, with every plaque and trophy and ribbon won and given in high school and college, the white shelves packed full with textbooks and pictures of old girlfriends, cheerleading photos before she quit the squad, the royal, antique white mirror dresser, chest of drawers and bed carved in eloquent, so-called Italian Renaissance design, a headboard carved up to a flowing climax in the middle, with a low, matching footboard. A room from the imagination of overbearing, vicarious living mothers everywhere, chosen and created as the perfect girl's room though they themselves would never sleep in it themselves. A bedroom with a secret so devastating as to be apocalyptic, which is carried to their graves, so that not a single soul that ever touched their lives can know of what unbreakable bond this mother and daughter had shared—this, but a single time on her daughter's fifteenth birthday, hearkened from the many lengthy, mouth pressing kisses that lasted far too long when she was a girl and young teenager.

My mind shows me the daughter in the red and blue cheerleading shirt in the ninth grade, being followed up the stairs by her mother, all the way into the daughter's white renaissance bedroom. Sitting on the bed, calling the daughter to her side, telling her *I think every mother and daughter should have a secret. Something that is their own special bond, that they could never tell another living soul.* I see the blonde mother, in the spirit of what desperation can do to judgment; how boundaries crumble under the weight of generational pressures, leaning over to her healthy young cheerleader sitting on the bed, pressing the gentlest kiss upon her, but held in uncompromising length, then kissing the daughter's top lip and then the bottom, each again and again, eyes closed and fully engaged, not seeing her 15 year old daughter's eyes wide open. Not seeing the girl's braces when she giggles. Patiently waiting. Kissing the corners of her daughter's smile, smiling herself a bit. Locking eyes with the hapless young girl, so ignorant. So unaware. So epic in her lack of understanding, of how far and wide, and how deep this power affects a woman's body. So naïve. So unenlightened, at the source which fuels so much of Desperate Housewife Syndrome, and of what churns beneath cultured civility. Kissing her on the forehead. The cheek. The other cheek. Then back to her daughter's mouth, but this time, going in tongue first. Touching. Coaxing. Touching again, until the daughter's mouth is relaxed, opening just enough. Probing. Locking in the deep kiss, when the mother's tongue is deep within. Pressed deep inside her daughter's mouth. Tasting her daughter's lips and tongue.

The sweet. The mint of girlish youth. Drinking the innocence. Drawing it from her. Breathing it in through the nose. Ingesting it through the mouth. Woman is wayward. Siphon the life from her, Dear Lady. Drinking every last drop of this kiss, through motion and deep breathing through the nose. Pulling her daughter's tongue outward. Outward. Concentrating upon it, as the girl now opens her mouth. Letting the mother suck her tongue. Twitching when the mother's fingers slide under the red sweater to the nipples. Mid pubescence. A new energy in her body. Dear daughter, what dost thou know of this twitching! Already, your young body is devastated, and it has only just begun!

The mother lays her daughter down. Laying beside her, their legs off the side of the bed. Kissing her pretty daughter's neck. Gently kissing her ear. Standing up now, her daughter laying on the bed on her back. Close your eyes to this, young girl. Feel your mother's lovely hands up and down your thigh. Do you see the blonde headed woman, the woman who gave you life, do you see what she is doing? Where are your hands, girl, when her lips are kissing your inner thigh? Brave the fumbling of her fingers at the top of your underwear, Dear Girl. Yes. Feel the underwear cloth slide down and away. Open your eyes in brief, in disbelief of what you feel. Watch her stare at the blue cloth in somber defeat, as she slides it off your white legs, tossing it away.

Do her eyes bear mercy and compassion for thee, Dear Girl? They do not. Close your eyes, young girl. Do not watch her go to your thighs again. Brave each kiss up your inner thigh. Try not to lose your breath because of where it is this next kiss must happen. *Oh...my God! Oh, my God,* you say. After the lightning burns a vacuum, drawing the breath from you. *Oh, my God,* is the second declaration, of what pleasure you had not thought possible! Of what your 15 year old mind had not surmised for thee! Small town girl, thy mother is a charity queen. *Oh my God,* is the third declaration, to announce the coming of impending doom, the arrival of the first hurricane at this shore. You look down, unable to resist, seeing her blonde head down between your thighs, her hands locked around them. Holding them in place. The image, the sucking pressure down below, these coalesce at your young breasts, at your heart and lungs, from your brain to your bowels, to bring the fourth and final *Oh, my God* to life, which makes you grab your mother's head with both hands, turning to the side and screaming once more, holding still now, your face twisted to an ugly grimace. Straining. Your body spasming a seizure. Releasing the last of the energy in a long breath. A groan when God's name is again at the edge, but is locked inside unspoken.

Now, young girl. Feel the kisses in your inner thigh again. With the woman who has killed you. Now, Daughter. Suffer the lust of thy mother spilled over. Suffer the climbing. The quick crawl she does up to your face. Yes, Girl. You will taste the sin of this endtime perversion. Do not feign reluctance. Do not pretend a loss of desire. Kiss her like you mean it. Put both your hands to your mother's head, as she lifts her skirt of midnight blue, sliding the underwear of this selfsame cloth down and away. Her shoes are on the floor, so appropriately black. Lying dead on the carpet at her feet. The top of her stockings are tight in lace beauty at her thighs. Her buttocks are white in the daytime dark. What is this you feel, Girl, the squeezing of the front of herself against yours. The squeezing that becomes writhing. The rocking of her body, the squeaking of your elegant bed. Who is this woman on top of you, Girl? Did you know her thinness was capable of such strength? Lay there, Daughter. Legs up and open. Listen to her lose control of her voice. Her breathing. Listen to her say *'no'* as it happens.

Now, feel the mighty jerking her body makes. Listen to the epic grunt, the deep grunt that repeats itself in each spasmodic tremble. You know that it is the quiet overflow of years, the flood of energy built up from a decade of kisses under pretense; a containment field split open by the sight of your ninth grade body in that cheerleading uniform. A decade of built up energy released, and poured quietly, and secretly onto thee.

Before she came, Dear Daughter, did you feel her body stop moving? Did you hear her voice grunt in a breathy tone, the name of the same God you called out to? The single *"Oh, God."* So much heavier, with so much more power even than your own? Calling to him as a warrior woman in the throes of blood lust, in the midst of a conquering and a kill? What did you think was happening, Young Girl, when she stopped moving and said *"Oh... God,"* with such confidence, inner rage and contempt? What did you think of it, Dear Girl, when your mother's body began the single, convulsive shakes? What did you learn of this part of a Witch's Crown, daughter, of this orgasm achieved by a mother upon her daughter?

Breathe, Dear Daughter. But shed no tears in this flame. Rest, Dear Girl. In the burning of blue and black fire.

In the Heart of Memory. In the mist of a bygone gathering of souls. I am compelled to stand up from the gray sofa, ready for Vera's initial shock when she looks up at me. *I'm just going upstairs*, I say. Not staying to answer any questions or try to read the confusion in her expression. I leave her to her conversations about Brenda and money and this house— the true source of this odd collection of folks anyway, much moreso than the mother and daughter who left it behind. Grape juice drink still in hand, I drift across the living room invisible, a ghost seen only by she who knows me, drawn up the carpeted staircase toward the upstairs hall, suddenly visible now to everyone in the livingroom, who all seem determined to catch a glimpse of the pioneer ghost in modern times climbing the staircase in full fair skinned, dark haired melancholy gloom.

Desperation looms, roaming the crowded room. Spirits of repressed lust and envy—the inescapable pull of the suburban landscape, the craving to escape its money bred mediocrity. The irrepressible instinct they feel when they look at me. Vera's girlfriend, Vera's live in lover, Vera's crazy bitch; that life insurance widow who made a fortune in the stock market—that fat breasted frump, with the dumpity dump, with tits so heavy they make her slump. *Who the Hell does she think she is, walking around here like she owns the place... oh yeah, that's right... she practically does own the place. Because what Vera owns, she owns, I'll bet.* I can feel the heavy jealously, the caustic contempt and covetousness. Aimed at my spirit from their own, as I climb to the top of the staircase, escaping to the upstairs hall.

Fate has decided to be kind, allowing this moment to be deserted, as I creep timidly down the hall Vera has described to me many times. Telling me so often over the years that I should see the white furniture in Catherine Grace Harrison's old room. I peek first into the master bedroom, where Matrimony had lived and died here. Wanting to walk inside, to see what I look like in Brenda's dresser mirror. The King sized sleigh bed rules the court of dark wood night stands and dressers. Exquisitely searched for and found are the wide bottomed heavy lamps, in league with the floor length curtains draped at every window. The simple elegance touches the country girl in me, the accursed woman that was born in the dirt, before the days of Hope and Prosperity.

I continue the short trip down the hall, past the bathroom, laundry room and two other bedrooms, until I am at the Door of Secrets. The doorway to revelation. I step from the empty hall, away from the clatter of men and women's voices below, moving into the space that I myself have known. The space where I lived and died on the little dirt farm, where atrocities are done in the name of Love and Discipline, behind the veil of the unknown.

Brenda! Catherine Grace! Beloved mother and daughter—where have you gone! On which wind of eternity have you flown! Oh, what horrors I have felt in my spirit concerning Catherine Grace and thee! In thine letter, I hear the declaration of death, thine concession of rebirth, that you knew you must take the hand of Christ, before you swallow the pills and a glass of wine! This, you knew before you died, with contempt in your heart of Charity! Oh, but what dark wind hath blown through the Carolinas, Dear Woman, to take thy daughter from thee! How cruel was her birth, how impossible was her death! To suffer the burning of the flames I myself burned in, so that the two of you hath corrupted yourselves as I! Then to leave this world in a flame of fire and pain, to close her eyes in the bewilderment of loss, in pure regret for having been born. Oh, but such dark regret on this side of the grave, what Paradise it still may be! Catherine Grace, my heart aches for thee! Hast thy soul been touched by the blood of the Lamb, by the blood from the accursed tree? Hath thy dark soul been washed clean, or Cartherine Grace, Dear Woman, art thou still tormented in this flame! Dost thou see thine mother afar off, in Abraham's Bosom, with this great gulf affixed, the eternal divide laid betwixt thee! I feel no relief in my spirit for thee, O Catherine, only sorrow, when I think of your burning departure, as you lay dying, wondering where it is that your beloved mother could have gone!

O Catherine, Catherine Grace, there is no hope for thee beyond this life, except by the grace of God through Christ! Of thine eternal fate, O

Catherine, I pray that I do not know, that I do not see the end of your game played. The end of your race run, where you chose not to believe—to reject the Messiah as the Son of the living God—to reject his death at Calvary, to reject his resurrection from the tomb! Despise thy earned trip through the humanities—loathe your doctoral papers! *The Christianity Myth: Christ and Secular Humanism*, it was called. They said it was inspired! You spoke so glowingly of Christ as a teacher, yet you mocked his claim as the Son of God. *"The day that mankind realizes that God is within,"* you said, *"is the day his final and best evolution will begin."* 'The Christianity Myth,' you called it! *"Christ as God is mankind's greatest problem,"* you said! *"A great teacher, greatly deluded,"* you said! *"Human reason is the path to fulfillment. Rejection of Christ as God is the beginning of wisdom,"* you said! Whether you believed it is immaterial, Dear Girl, you created it for academic attention—you rode it to academic immortality! The title alone assured that they would not forget your name at Chapel Hill. Catherine Grace Harrison—thy name is not forgotten! Catherine Grace! Your niceness was insignificant! Your success of no import! Your intellect? To none effect! Ever learning, never coming to the knowledge of the truth! *"That Baptist prison,"* you called your Mother's church—cry out to thy Mother, accursed soul, that she may dip her finger in the river nearby, and cool thy parched tongue, for thou art tormented in this flame!

49

I am pulled forward along the timeline. From the afternoon gathering of wayward souls and speculation, all wondering what is to come of Brenda's beautiful brick home, worth at least half a million dollars, which is the main reason they had all shown up anyway. A house full of scary intellectuals from Brenda's family—high school teachers and college professors—not to try and find out how and why Brenda committed this mother-daughter suicide, but to confirm the unbelievable details about ownership of the house. "It's a half million dollar house," Vera says. "I can understand their concern. But Brenda's will left everything to Catherine Grace. And besides that, the house isn't in Brenda's name. Its in mine. So they can't touch it."

From this rainy twilight I'm in, traveling back towards our mansion home. I am again pulled to Grand Harwich Estates, to where I had drifted to the upper room. On my way back down the stairs, from the tragic spirit of the Modern Mother Daughter Dynamic, I am stopped again by a glimpse of the master bedroom, with the elegant sleigh bed and Brownwood nightstands and dressers. I just have to step inside this beautiful but simple bedroom, where understated elegance is carved and contoured into every corner of this furniture. Appearing as though Tranquility and Hopefulness might prosper around it. How was it then, that two relationships were destroyed here, with the mother at the top corner of this triangle? The first being the slow death of a marriage, where this king sized mahogany bed bore witness to the infinite fights over lovemaking and moneymaking, the formation of problems all too common to man, where the spirits of Marital Discord and Chaos come to live.

This accursed sleigh bed. So smooth to the touch. So pleasing to the eyes. This graceful, luxurious last stop, which saw the second and third sides of the triangle fall just over a week ago. When the corners called Brenda and Catherine Grace imploded here, devastated by the influx of poison, a curse from somewhere far backward of them, beholden to an unknown prophecy in the stars, that assured them of this demise, having tried to have their part of the forbidden without consequences or remorse, or the fearful looking over their shoulders for whatever it is that is overdue. This accursed king sized bed, which saw the fulfillment of a dark destiny, when the mother tried to resurrect the spirit of Mother Daughter Perversion, and press it down with a kiss, and feel it with a fervent rub and grind.

I turn upon the elegant hopelessness left behind, hoping to go back downstairs and convince my new mother that its time to go. But then appears in the doorway an older, meaner looking version of Brenda Harrison herself. The oldest of the three girls, the three women Brenda Harrison, Cyndi Breckinridge, and Betty McCauley. Betty Walker. The twelfth grade teacher, and the most impressed by her youngest sister's flight of upper middle class luck, and the academic heights her capable young niece had achieved.

"Hello. I thought I saw you come up here a few minutes ago. Do you mind if I talk to you about something?"

The types of Fear are many. And uniquely distinguished. Among these is the Fear of Humiliation, which settles inside me like a wave, flowing from the center of my chest where my heart was stabbed by her sudden appearance, spreading to my lungs and past the pit of my stomach. I open my mouth to speak but nothing comes out, and I can only smile with as much friendliness as I can, while I struggle to maintain a steady breath, and a wine glass of grape juice on the edge of a visible tremble.

She stares at me for several seconds. Through the loss of cultured civility, as the pleasantness in her expression fades in the excruciating silence. No, it is not a nightmare, Carmen. There is no dream to wake up from.

"Has Vera said anything to you about what she plans to do with the house?"

By now, I can only tuck my lips in and breath through my nose, shaking my head no, knowing that for the moment, speech would be impossible without stuttering. Why God, did you let this happen to me? Is this a punishment from my time on the dirt farm? When my mother's perversion was queen? When I did only what I had to do to survive? Why didn't you stop me, Lord, when I got up from the sofa to walk across the room? Why did you let me climb those stairs, in this house full of people?

She is unable to hold her eyes at mine, and I see the contempt flow from her expression on its own, as she glances at my long hair, following it down past my shoulders, then a quick and powerful look at the way my dress bulges so big and heavy at the top, above a waist that appears to be even smaller than her own.

"Honey, I asked you a question," she says, stepping towards me in the energy of frustration, which I can only respond to with wall-eyed silence, and a wine glass of grape juice that is now over the edge of that visible tremble.

"Not everybody can afford to play games with money, Elizabeth, is it? You and Vera are both like nothing I've ever heard talk of. People just don't become life insurance widows, and then grow it to 60 million dollars overnight. I don't really know how you got your money and I don't care. But what I do care about is this house and... why are you trembling?"

She asks the question with the irritation of a teacher out of patience. Speech is now impossible for me. I couldn't talk now if I wanted to. All I can do is imagine this grape juice knocked out of my hand and having my hair pulled and my faced slapped. The fear in my body has risen to a level I've not felt on this side of a nightmare in a long time, to the level of near physical pain. With ill will, she takes the glass out of my hand, sniffing it as if it were vinegar.

"Let me help you with this," she says, taking the glass to her lips for a sip. The look on her face is a quiet, mocking contempt.

"My husband says I drink too much." She swirls the glass, placing it gently on the table. *"You don't drink do you?"*

I shake my head no. Lips tucked in. Eyes widened.

"Why is it always the same? The same stupid, uneducated people who get lucky. While the rest of us slave our fingers to the bone, and barely make enough to get by."

She turns her stare away from my glass. Looking through me as if I were the same. Incredibly, she goes to the bedroom door and closes it. Walking back towards me. Why didn't I just push past her when I had the chance and run? How did this happen to me?

"If you don't tell me the truth about what you and Vera are going to do with this house, then so help me God... I'm going to slap the taste out of your mouth."

A sudden thump at the bedroom door evokes a scream from me. A quick, thunderous pounding at the door, making Betty turn as fast as lightning, the terror of guilty secrets uncovered. The unlocked door swings open, a lovely, white hand gripped around the golden doorknob. In the ease of slow motion, my salvation steps inside, so appropriately cloaked in black dress cloth.

"Elizabeth, go downstairs and wait for me."

Feeling strongholds crumble and fall, I take this flight to freedom, walking past her respectfully, lips still tucked in, not daring to look her in the eye. The door closes behind me, so that only by the Spirit, am I able to see Vera walk toward the 49 year old school teacher, raise her hand, and slap her like a bolt of lightning across the face, evoking a sickening yelp from the shocked woman, who stumbles to the side from the blow, both hands over her face—staring at Vera in awe and disbelief.

Sometimes, there *is* thunder in a November rain.

50

Can a person love someone so much that it causes physical pain? Mine is a mixture of Love and Fear, as I hold Vera's hand. Rubbing it gently, looking out the twilight window as we drive.

"Every time I think I've seen everything," she says. "I'm sorry you had to deal with that, Elizabeth. You said you wanted to go home, didn't you? Maybe I should've listened to you."

As we slip forward in time, splashing the rain to get home, all I can do is lift her hand to my lips and close my eyes, pressing a kiss to the back of her hand, and then again and again, allowing my tongue to slip through on the third kiss, but hidden by my lips. I dry the damp skin, gently rubbing the kiss away. What feeling I had for my husband, what desire I had for my mother are coalesced as one power now, to ache my body from head to toe at Vera's touch. The smell of her perfume, the smooth caress of any part of her skin to mine.

"You better take it easy on me.," she says. "Unless you want me to stop this car."

And what if I do Miss Vera! Oh, how you could rise to the challenge, I know, to handle yourself upon me! What you don't know won't hurt you as you drive, My Dear, as the spirit of who I am is awakened within! The spirit of this, moving at the place beneath your hand in my lap! You rub my thigh over my black coat, and its all I can do to not close my eyes and hold my head back in rapture!

"There's something special I've been wanting us to do," she says. "I think maybe its time now. I'll tell you about it when we get home."

Listen to me, Mother Vera. And I'll tell you about it right now! Pull this luxury death ride over! Undo your seatbelt—swim across to my side of the river! Slide over here, take a clump of my hair into your hand and yank my head backward. Lay the kiss down upon me in punishment! Kiss me, O Vera, until the spirit has taken over me! Run your hand up my black stocking leg, until you find the shore of white! Move your hand, Lady Vera, until you touch the center of me, but not releasing the kiss so that I can draw a breath! Lady Vera! Have no mercy on me!

Vera braves the treacherous roads, driving with one hand on the wheel, and the other in my lap over my black coat, rubbing both thighs up, down and across, back and forth with such promise, with such power and passion, to give pause to my expectation. Vera! Rescue me from desire! Raise your hand, and spank the top of my thighs over the coat! In the throes of this image, which burns the Theatre of My Mind, I kiss the back of her hand again while she drives, placing her thumb in position. Then I wrap my lips and tongue around it, giving her this warm and gentle fellatio of the thumb. Sucking up and down the length of it, with the image of the car stopped now ablaze inside, with us lost in the passion of a kiss. Vera is a one handed driver now. Breathing more than one trembling sigh. Allowing me to hear the overflow from her voice in the deep, woman's moan, while I work her thumb as if it were another part of her anatomy. Kissing it. Licking it wet, then sucking her thumb dry. At last releasing it in a soft kissing sound. Drying her thumb with my hands. Rubbing her hand gently again.

Can a person love someone so much, that it causes them physical pain? The fear in my desire hath dissipated, and what it leaves behind is only love, and the lust of passion, powerful enough to cause pain in my mind, body and spirit.

"I better take my hand, Honey," she says. "You're gonna get us both in trouble."

In the pouring twilight rain, Vera is again a two handed diver. Whirling us safely along the rain soaked streets of this town. Moving us forward along this part of the timeline. Towards the mansion home at *Amherst Lake*, across the great open field of grass, in the middle of the prairie green. The trees on this part of our journey are more familiar now. The red, orange and yellow trees of Bear Trap Road, their leaves half gone in the month of Thanksgiving, under the clouds that hide the Forest Moon.

And suddenly, I can see the half dead forest trees through the rainy windshield, lit up by a flash of blue light from all around us. Then the light flashes again gently through the clouds, spreading across the bottom of the sky like tiny rivers of energy, followed by a low, booming rumble from the clouds, rolling across the twilight countryside like the voice of eschatology.

"Momma did you see that? Those rivers of lightning?"

"I saw something. But..."

"It's the first time in my life I've ever heard it."

"What?"

"Think about it. Have you ever heard thunder in a November rain? That lightning went across half the sky. Did you see it?"

"Well, Honey how could I miss it?"

"No, I mean did you really see it? Did you see those rivers of lightning spreading out all over the clouds? It spread out over the whole sky."

I am lucky at least, that she saw as much of it as she did. Because I know what skepticism burdens her silence, and what concerns about my sanity are at the tip of her tongue.

"I know you think I didn't really see it Momma but I did. You were looking through the windshield, right?"

"Yes."

"Well, I saw mine out this window. I went across the whole field and back over those woods."

"I believe you. I saw part of it too, remember?"

But all she sees now is the back of my head, because I am turned towards my passenger window with my eyes wide open, gazing through the dark'ned rain, at the twilight crop field we're passing by, and the silhouette of trees in the distance.

"Look! Look!"

Framed by the passenger window, a single bolt of lightning winds across the bottom of the clouds from beyond the trees, spreading out into an infinity of smaller bolts of a lightning tree, that lights up the twilight countryside as bright as the rapture of noonday.

"Did you see it that time? I told you! I told you!"

"Calm down, Honey, I saw it."

"I *knew* it."

"Knew what?"

I have to hold on to the response, that *something weird is going to happen*, keeping it held quietly in check, while I look excitedly (or is it apprehensively?) out the window. Forgetting now that we are at the end of this part of our journey through grief, nearby the entranceway to *Amherst Lake* and the mansion home on the prairie green.

We roll past the last of the forest groves and woods easily seen from this long, country road, where the darkened landscape opens up into a field of grass that stretches to an eternity, which I now recognize as the far edge of my own property. "We're almost home," I say aloud, but without a thought as to whether Vera heard me. Saying it to myself really. Talking to myself, like I am so accustomed to doing when Momma is not around.

"You're workin' me up," she says quietly, rubbing my thigh down to my knee. "Somethin' special tonight," she says. "Somethin' different."

The prairie field soon vanishes behind the forest groves of home, that mark the front border of our property near the entranceway, hiding the great front lawn from the road, obscuring the far off mansion and the tall statue fountain from view. I feel the car slow us down, turning us into the short asphalt driveway, moving us past the open gate into another world. In my side view mirror, I see the lighted gate closing upon another flash of lightning, but this one producing not a single bolt that I can see, lighting the sky above *Amherst Lake* in full, but not the same noonday brightness to the countryside as before. While the brick farmhouse behind us is cloaked in the coming dark, our mansion shines like a beacon of hope in the distance. The statue fountain glows ivory in the twilight rain.

High above the mansion, in the evening day, two separate networks of lightning spread out at the bottom of the rainclouds again, evoking the glory of the Divine in earthly matters, leaving us both in shock and awe at the rare and hidden beauty of such phenomena. Lightning unlike anything I've ever seen before, that does not strike, but *flows*, from a single point of origin, spread out into many rivers and tributaries, as if many jagged lines of light are painted in electricity on a canvas of storm clouds. And remarkably, though we are not more than a mile away, only once have they made a sound, as if the sky has told us already what good or terrible thing it has to say, and dare not speak of it one moment more, from here to the Apocalypse and beyond.

We roll the long road home. Past the open field to our left, then past the gray cottage on our right, which rests in front of the only grove of trees anywhere near the mansion. We make the left turn in front of the Great Southern Palace of beige earth stone, fourteen windows wide from end to end, the house three stories high in the center, but the roof still hardly as tall as our statue fountain goddess out front. We take the final, blessed turn left, our lights flashing across the bricks and windows, inviting us to leave the cares of this dark world behind, and come inside out of the cold, dreary rain.

We disembark our rolling chariot in the storm, both of us hardly able to stand the wait between here and the night's perversion. Holding hands beneath our umbrella, we take the steady incline of stairs to the grand entranceway, both of us shocked to see that what lies beneath the columns and shelter is not a bundle of white boxes, but a bundle of white curves, balled up in the fetal position near the door, so obviously a nude, fair skinned woman, naked as the day she was born, and so cold to the touch that Vera wonders whether or not she is dead.

The Heart of Charity beats warm in Vera's chest, as she immediately takes her coat off and lays it down across the woman's curled up body, from her shoulders down to her feet. Vera opens the tall, white front door quickly, then she tells me to help her stretch the woman's legs out, which I do, noticing long, white legs full of scars that seem so tragically familiar to me, but of a memory too far off for me to recollect. *She smells like the woods* is the thought that flashes my brain, as Vera turns the woman over on her back, her face suddenly lit up by a flash of lightning; a face which floods my body with the fear of the ages, making me jump away from her as I scream once in pure fright, my hand over my mouth in something beyond shock and disbelief.

51

*I*n the early evening rain and lightning. I back away from the sight I see, which may as well be a six foot cobra with raised hood and red eyes. Vera calls my name, in pure bewilderment, and genuine lack of understanding.

Vera! Have you not known me! Am I not the soul of fear? As you too would be, if you knew of the serpent you caress, and invite into your home!

"Elizabeth, be strong. I need your *help.*"

Never in my life, have I had such a profound lack of compassion. But I can only back away slowly, shaking my head in the same, slow rhythm, hair starting to get wet in the drowning rainfall.

"Elizabeth, Honey. *Please.*"

Vera stands up from the sleeping woman, stretched out on her back under the sheltered entranceway, the sleeping or comatose thing I see. Vera begins to walk toward me as if she were approaching a runaway dog she had cornered but did not want to scare.

"I know you're nervous around people, Honey. But Momma needs your help. I need you to help me carry her inside."

Already at the top of the brick steps, I begin to climb down, careful not to fall and break my clumsy neck, like the comatose thing might do if it could wake up and get its hands on me.

"Elizabeth, you're going to put a *stop* to this," she says, rather sharply. "You get over here and do as I ask."

Unable to speak, I stand at the top of the brick staircase, a safe distance away from what I see. Vera moves deliberately towards me, determined to confront me at last, and possibly grab me by the head and shake me awake from this latest insanity. I stand still in the rain, just in case she means me no harm, as Vera grabs my wrist with force, and begins to pull me back towards the sleeping woman.

"Please," I say. Stuttering out another, and then another. Vera does not speak. She only grabs and pulls. Her natural strength is remarkable for a woman, as I find it impossible to break free. But the sight of the sleeping woman's face again, trips the switch and flips the bitch in my brain, and I take full control of myself as a woman, who is free to make her own choices in life. I open my scared mouth and let anger rise up and have its way.

"I'm not touching her," I say, twisting my arm away from Mother Vera in the rarest show of strength I've ever done.

"This time," Vera says, grabbing me again, "you're going to do what I tell you."

But when anger mixes with fear in the body, the combination is explosive, as Vera learns why mental patients and wild animals have to be handled with care. I pull and twist and punch against her chest and arm with the force of fighting, as that is exactly what I'm doing. I'm fighting to be free. I'm fighting to live. I'm fighting to not be forced to touch an uncaged white tiger if I don't want to. Knowing that only her best and most violent show of strength could stop me, Vera releases me in the rain, and watches me take the steps in pure luck of retreat, it being a miracle that I make it down the brick steps without falling.

I run past the glowing statue that watches our scene with foreknowledge, splashing into the wet grass, where the full clumsiness of my nature takes over, and I slip trying to sprint across the grass, falling, splashing into a noisy, wet heap on the twilight lawn. Feeling a cold, white hand grab my ankle when I'm on the ground, making me scream *"No!"* all of my anger having morphed into fear and terror again.

I scramble up to my feet again, powered by the prickling energy on my skin, as I run in the strength and speed of two types of fear, the Fear of the Supernatural and the Fear of Death.

52

*I*n my gray cottage. In my refuge from the rainstorm, I pace the floor in revelation. Understanding now, but all too late, what the blazing of a fireball across the sky could mean, and what the touch of a ghost in an old house can mean. In my heart, in my spirit, I had always believed she was dead. Driven into the woods by nightmares and dreamscapes, visions so terrifying, Divine delusions so dreadful that she could not stay in the farmhouse that hot, humid summer night, but felt that she had to run to the safety of the Carolina woods, running down the dirt road from these terrors, crossing the paved street and into the deep summer forest beyond. I remember that she had been searched for briefly, then put on the books as missing, which she has been for 20 years since then. Since I was a 21 year old woman. Abandoned. Left alone to live and die in fear. And I have always trusted my instincts, the spirits that give me knowledge, that tell me in dreams and visions every deep and dark truth in my little world, and glimpses of it in the outer world, to the deepest regions of the cosmos and beyond. Though her body was never found, I was always confident that I knew what happened. That I knew she was a victim of Divine Judgment, which came to take her away from the sufferings of this life, on the night she had envisioned the walls of our house drenched in blood. On the eve of the sharpened axe blade, and what it was going to do to my body.

Yes, I know that she was going to kill me. And maybe guilt visited her already feeble sanity, a grief that had driven her to madness, guilt and grief coalesced into her mind as certain death for her, which she ran from that night. Running miles deep into a moonlit forest, running far beyond her body's endurance, a heart already stressed by supernatural terror, which had begun to slow down in agony in her chest, until it stopped in the midst of a breath hard to take. She had cried out to Heaven once more, to a God that had turned his back on her in this life, and she had fallen straight over in her white night gown, gazing at the blackness of the forest floor, at last slipping away from the earthly plane in gratitude, from the Fear of Death and Hell forever. When I think of the nightmares and dark visions I've suffered over the years because of her, I wonder if we shouldn't just go get the shovel now and bash her over the head, and bury her back in the ground she came crawling out of.

This time, I don't care if Vera thinks I'm crazy or not, I *ain't* goin' back in that house. I'm not going in there. Vera doesn't know the fullness thereof. Of the nightmares I had to endure; being held down on my back in sleeps so deep there was no hope of ever waking up, being carried across the front yard and down the dirt road, across the paved road and rapidly through the darken'd woods for what seemed like two miles, seeing the big, naked backside of a dead woman laying face down on the forest floor, her head turned just enough so that I can see her dead eyes looking at me in the dark. Then I had to endure the fear response every time, the influx of fear that caused physical pain, turning and running through the woods away from what I've seen, in tragic slow motion, with no way under God's Sun and Moon to find my way out again. In the weeks after she left me, how many nights did I endure this—and again and again over the years— but seeing the naked woman's body in various forms of decomposition, until the body was nothing but skeleton bone being walked upon, nudged and ignored by wolves and bears and deer, even crawled upon by black serpents and every manner of creeping thing. These were not so much dreams as they were journeys, my spirit pulled into the astral flow, and projected across time and space in *reality*. These dreams were always the same, down to every detail, even my begging of God to have mercy and let me please wake up, which he most certainly did not, according to his infinite wisdom. *Accept thy calling*, I had heard at times, and also *control the fear*, and *driven by depression, inspired by fear*. The smiling face of her bones has followed me into the morning light too many times for me to remember, until I learned that waking up in a scream wasn't even necessary anymore, ending about seven years after she disappeared. I was 28 years old when my last vision came and went, when I saw a leafy green brush overgrown in the place where her lovely bones were laid to rest.

And these steps along this part of the timeline are marked in groups of seven, as a fervent sign to me, that this is of Divine origin, dreaming of her the first seven years of my marriage. And not dreaming of her bones again until seven years after I buried Maria in the ground. And then, I counted seven dreams this month, on seven different nights, showing me first the reappearance of her bones from the brush pulled and dug away by animals, having laid there undisturbed in the forest undergrowth for twenty years, it seemed, these bones unlovely, and unremembered by history.

The second dream in this fantasy, this Suite for Cello and Orchestra, shows me her bones again, but in the condition of newness, not yet dry and corrupted by time, with every piece of flesh taken away quickly by the woods, leaving her smiling, skeleton face exposed, along with the outstretched bones of her left arm reaching forward, where her body had sought to crawl when it fell. I see your lovely bones, Dear Mother, laid down in the Carolina Woods, braving every light and dark, every heat and cold, every rain and snow and falling of the leaves, until your flesh concedes the prophecy, that it is to the dust thou has returned. All that is left are your bones picked clean, washed clean in the flow of Time itself, and left as your only grave marker on the Carolina forest floor. These bones lie bleached in the Autumn mist, in the cold, wet rains of Indian Summer's passing, partially covered by the fallen leaves from above, and the yearly death of the southern forest leaf canopy. I see your bones in the snowy days of winter, when the dead leaves have rotted away, and their blanket of brown is replaced by the icy blanket of snowy white, to touch your feet and leg bones, and the Divine architecture of your ribcage, lying partially uncovered in the ice and snow. I see the truth in the Spring, Dear Woman, when the rains return to replenish the ground around you, and the flowers have redecorated the deep woods solitude of your grave above the soil. What is it that even the lovely bluebird doth know, Dear Mother, which is compelled to light upon these bones uncorrupted, in the southern Carolina Woods of Spring? And the bluebird hath returned without fear, in the warm and windy Summer rain, which I see blowing all about your skeleton in the deep woods Summer brush, every tree alive with the message of what is to come, and the inevitability of its arrival.

The third dream of this Woman of the Woods, is the departure of the bones that lie, covered now in every muscle and sinew, painfully red and freshly formed, with the agonizing appearance of life thereabouts but laid dormant in the woods of deep Autumn, below the colorful death of green, before the falling of the forest leaf canopy. Sleep well, thou accursed thing, that every nerve in the body is not alive with warning, that this state of being is a touch of Hell on Earth! Every red and raw muscle and stretchy thing pulled tight and ready, not meant for the eyes of man to see! But even in this rawness, this horribly unfinished place in time, already I can see the likeness of a woman, the shape of which is already formed to perfection, the precursor to what beauty there is likely to be. Woman of the Woods, laid bare for every anger and Devil to see. Thou art bone of my bone, and flesh of my flesh, for I know that I am what was formed from thee!

But now, here is the fourth dream, the fourth movement of our Suite for Cello and Orchestra, where I am in a blowing and wavy Summer woods again, so plush and green in the daytime dark, as rich and green as a tropical paradise, but still as familiar as the southern Carolina forest I know it is. And I am privy again to these lovely feet, but this time covered with the delicate, silky white skin, perfectly pink with life at the bottom. My eyes follow the contours of thine uncorrupted feet made new, up the smooth caress of ivory skin upon thine leg, to the epic hips widened upon the grassy woodland soil, made more prominent by the dramatic segue, the foray to the inland waist curve, narrow as any woman of our size could hope for, but with substance and power still—this figure eight curve continuing upward to the strong back, replete with scars crisscrossed faintly upon my soul's memory, in league with those upon the beautiful legs and thighs, and the occasional wisp of these upon the buttocks. I gaze the beauty of the fairest skin, as ivory cream barely touched by the color of life—even the skin of thine lovely face, the face of a mountain beauty I once knew, though aged to a score of years beyond what I knew. How is it that thou wast asleep in the forest, Dear Woman, lain uncorrupted in twenty passings of winter ice and cold? Asleep in thy above ground tomb, Mother Dear, through the revolution of the Heavenly Sphere, until the twentieth trip around the sun? What is the significance, Mother—what is this sign of thy coming? I beg of thee, Woman of the Woods—do not open your eyes to look at me! O thou accursed Woman of the Woods, I pray for you to have mercy on me!

And to the fifth dream I now suffer, my vision agaze again upon the outstretched arm of such silken white, touched further by the color of life, in a deep shade of ivory crème. I am forced to look upon the smooth and pristine hand, the hand that reached for life twenty years ago. Waiting, I am, for the spark of terror there must be when I see it, the unearthly fear I must endure. Oh Heavenly father, I beseech thee! Answer this prayer of thy lowly servant, that I may not see this impossibility! Oh Lord, let this cup pass from me, that the witch of my youth may not return, to finish the torment she had intended for me before she was taken by these woods! Oh Lord, do not let these eyes open again—do not let her bring Hell back to me, even if only in my dreams! What feeble comfort is the green of these Paradise Woods, as I am shown the skin of her lovely outstretched hand! And there it is! I saw it! Oh God, please do not lash me again! Please don't let it happen again, my Lord. Oh God! I see it again! The finger of her outstretched hand on the carpet of grass and summer leaves! I see her fingers twitch! I see them curl up into a fist, Oh God! This Woman of the woods that breathes the sound I hear, Oh Lord. I hear the ghostly echo of a phantasmal breath. This, Oh Lord, the longest breath ever drawn in the history of man! Show me not, Oh Lord, this woman pushing herself over in the forest upon her back. Oh, my God, what is it that I am forced to see! I see the woman turned over hard to her back, to expose the two greatest breasts ever formed in the world, bobbled naturally, gigantically to her sides, the look of epic, breathless terror on her face, grieving to exhale, to push out the poison breath of life, so that she may draw another and live. I watch the woman push this breath from her lungs, hearing the high pitch squeak from her throat as another breath rushes in, her head back, her eyes wide open in terror! Gazing to the top of these forest trees plush and green, looking to the sky hardly visible beyond, for a reprieve from this end of the world pain and suffering. Show me not, O Lord, the Woman of the Woods, Our Lady of the Breasts, writhing in what has not been since the beginning of time, in beauty that was formed by the Hand of Thee, Oh God! Let me turn and run from what I see! Let me flee thy wrath to come!

And now I suffer the sixth dream, Oh Lord, where I am again pulled fast through these dreary summertime woods, to the place so familiar to me, to the place from which you will not let me run! The place where you will not set me free! I am unprivileged to see the beautiful woman seated, leaning on her hands as if she is raising up from her side, her head down, her long, black hair nearly covering her face and down to the forest floor itself. She takes every breath as a solemn oath, breathed in deep commitment to replenish her body for what must be done. A woman of strength and power, whose muscles are new and ready to push beyond the veil of helplessness and lack of Hope, beyond the barrier of despair and darkness. I see the Amazonian lean over hard upon her hands, to steady herself for the pushing, the clawing, the desperate pressing against, to push herself forward from Death into Life. In the blowing wind of Summer, in the swirling breath of Forest Green, I watch the woman's muscles tense to Warrior's Beauty, in the trembling of effort in pain, as she hops just a bit, sliding her legs quickly to where she is on her knees. Then she throws her head back, her eyes closed, her beautiful mouth open, breathing the wind in the forest, knowing that there is a tear in the Veil of Shadows, and the next tension in her muscles will allow her to rip a place in the barrier, and step through the Wall of Eternity, to her appointed place in Creation, in the latter day flow of time and history. Her muscles tremble again, amidst the softness of the Great Breasts hung low beneath her, and she puts her white foot forward, resting briefly on one knee. Then she pushes one last time, rising in the forest, leaning the goddess form clumsily forward, moving her feet to catch the weight of step number one. Upon this step she rests in triumphant upright stance, raising her head back, turning her face skyward, to dream of a time when these steps will come without the agony of Hell in her legs and feet, when the breath in her lungs does not burn, and when the light in her eyes does not send a sword to her brain. This forest creature takes another step and crumbles to her knees, and I must endure the sound of a banshee in anger, howling in pain and suffering. It is a lonely, epic voice. The lamentation of Hell on Earth. The Woman of Beauty on her knees in the plush, Carolina Woods, howling in the travail of rebirth.

And now, I am transported again across the forest floor, in the Seventh Dream of Eschatology, the dream of the end of the world. But I am granted the mercy of rest, so that the cello may flow romantic, weaving in and out of the orchestral flow, to mark the space of Paradise lost I see, the empty space of forest underbrush, where I saw the bones of a dead woman live and breathe.

53

In the dark'ned cabin of dreams. Away from the piano of improvisation, I sit at the desk of contemplation. Having already begun to write in full, the Suite for Cello and Orchestra in F Major, where the cello must sing *Seven Songs of the Carolina Wood*s. Sitting unrelaxed, I am, unable to stop looking at the tall statue glowing in the rain, imagining once that I saw her hand move at the harp, but quickly dismissing this as foolishness and fantasy. *Sometimes I really do see things*, I had said to myself. The statue makes me uneasy all of a sudden, making me give in to a flash of nervousness. I turn my desk light on, so that I can see my reflection in the window, so that my blood sister can keep me company. These songs for cello and orchestra, I must commit to the bars of music, knowing already that it will be the last composition I intend to write for an orchestra, as if I had any say in the matter. But my soul has grown weary of music, and my spirit exhausted from rhythm and melody. *A retirement from what*, I'm inclined to ask? Retirement from laughter and pain. So what is left of me to put on paper, but the mindless scribbling of madness reworked and revisited, the same songs rewritten nearly two thousand times, until I am beginning to know in my heart that the House of Melody I have built can hold no more bricks, and no more furniture within.

54

The Earth is under a curse. And every inhabitant therin. And we are all prisoners of the forces of Fate and Destiny, sent to guard the mouth of Eden with a flaming sword. What happiness there is in a life is as fleeting as the first glint of sunlight over a morning mountain ridge, and as feeble as that same warmth of bright sunlight on a snowy winter's noonday. And although the problems that plague every human life are common to man, these curses are tailored to every individual under the sun, and displayed uniquely from person to person. The problems that I face have emerged in end of the world uniqueness, I'm sure, sent to me first as a warning this month, in the seven part dream I remember.

These Seven Songs for Cello and Orchestra, they are as follows: Beginning as Song No. 1 in E flat Major, called *The Grave.* Song No. 2 in the same lively but serious tone and key, called *The Bones.* Song No. 3 in G minor is called *Muscle and Sinew.* Song No. 4 in B flat is called *Skin.* Song No. 5 in D is called *The Breath of Life.* Song No. 6 in F Major is called *Rise and Walk*, while Song No. 7 in A Major closes in the cello's andante, visited briefly by the piano's colorful tears in crying, to sing a melody called *The Empty Tomb.* These are the Seven Songs for Cello and Orchestra, The Woman in the Woods, where the piano lends its whispering voice in secret, over her empty grave and tomb. And although agitation and distraction are a steady drip, drip, dripping onto the pages of my notebook, I press on by inspiration alone, the hallmark of my composition, as I can hardly bear to write any other way, despising to manufacture a single phrase of music.

I am distracted though, or perhaps driven, by the fact that I have not seen Vera leave that house in an hour to come and see how I'm doing. What about me? What about how I feel? Oh, the things we think we know about other people's needs! But in the long and short run of it, we truly understand nothing! And this that I sense about that stranger in our house, what I believe has happened—how can I make Vera understand? I know she already thinks I belong on the third floor of Martin County Memorial, where so many of them too have seen ghosts and earth comets that no one else has seen. But how many of them have even imagined, let alone say out loud, what I believe with all my heart has happened to me alone in the universe, and has been revealed to me by the Spirit of God!

Is it really her?

But how?

Have I really been deceived all these years? The woman I saw, the scars on her legs. The long, black hair. The beautiful, somber face. The gigantic bulge at the bosom, underneath the coat Vera laid on top of her. The tallness, the strength in her sleeping body, the tight, curved waistline I saw. The pale, white skin—every nerve, every cell in my body had cried out for me to run! But truthfully, do I need to be afraid, even if it is her? To be sure, her whereabouts for the last twenty years was not the soil of the forest floor! If not, where did she go? Where has she been living? What has she been doing? Where did she run to that Summer's night, when the crowravens sought to kill her, and devour her flesh down to the bone? Did she receive the reward she had sown? Did she receive the judgment that she had meant for me, her body laid down in the woodsy brush, protected by a curse until now? All that is between me and an answer to this is a look into her eyes, whether that face is aged to fifty years or no. And I'll know it in a glance, if I see those pale, witch eyes that stare. Not the subtle, autumn gray of Mother Vera's, but the cold, winter gray of Mother Barbara. The eyes of Barbara Jean Coletti.

These eyes now look back at me, in the mirror of her bedroom.

55

*M*y pencil scratches the lines and dots of its own accord, while my mind and will are lost in the Heart of Memory. Where I am in the kitchen of my 19th year after church, suffering the burden of her anger, because I accidentally returned a boy's fervent gaze in church. Yes, there are homes where such trivialities are not trivial at all, and can be the source of solemn conflict and crisis. This crisis rises for me in full, as Barbara Jean Coletti stands over me tall and strong, accusing me of thinking I am beautiful, and wanting to do things with that boy I saw. And I can remember that he was good looking, though not handsome, but his looks were made better by a certain shyness he attempted to overcome by necessity, having to look back at me until I looked up at him. And when I did, the southern farm boy humbleness in his expression caught my attention for just one second too long.

I stand in the kitchen of memory, feeling the strong, wicked slap on my face which rings my ears. Then I am forced to make that walk, that quick death march to her room, while she locks both the front and the back door, and pulls closed every shade and curtain.

In my mother's room, there is descended a darker shade of blue, to give such lovely contrast to my spirit, which is the color of ashen gray regret. She has been mad so many times before, so many untold hundreds of times, in the three thousand days since I was ten. But from the walk home from church, to our time in the kitchen of judgment, I have never seen, have never felt this level of anger before. The mere thought of it, the mere echo from the first wind of it, is as the leading edge of early autumn fury, when the swirling bands of death blow hundreds of miles across. I can feel the warning breezes, the bursts of wind that leave no doubt, and I can see the loud and foam filled crashing of the waves in the ocean, the thrashing of the Sea, the waves of the crashing, sounding sea.

Of these winds and waves that move ashore, I am ill prepared, as the door of the bedroom blows open, and my mother steps in so calmly, and closes the door again behind her. *Take your clothes off,* she says. *Every stitch.* Which I do without resistance, in the countenance of one with a contrite heart, and the manner of a daughter with a broken spirit. She stands there, here, watching me take my clothes off with a steadiness too slow and deliberate. *Hurry up,* she says, *stockings first.* She watches me bend over in my bra and underwear, breasts spilling over in the old bra too small. Each black leg stocking is made quick, unceremonious work of, pulled down by me and tossed carelessly to the floor. *Wait*, she says. *Clean that mess you made—fold that dress, that slip. Those stockings. Place those shoes.* This, I do. Still in my tight, white bra and big white underwear cloth, pulled waist high, stretched tight and concealing across hips in sizeable contrast to the youthful waist, every baby-fatted inch as bloated as a bowl of bread dough on a hot stove.

Now, come here to me, I hear, which I do so willingly, head lowered in false modesty, exploded away in a flash of blue light from a monstrous slap to my face, dispersing the last of any pretence I may have built up. *Now take your bra off. And save the tears, Honey, 'cause you gon' need it.* She takes the bra from me and lays it on her dresser. *Fold your underwear down. I didn't say take 'em down! Pull 'em back up you dumb bitch!* The word *bitch* is played on the beat, as is the pulling of my hair, which sends a hot iron's heat to my skull. *I said fold 'em down. Fold the top down to your hips. Just like that.* I stand here stupidly. Breasts hanging free and freakishly big for my frame. Waist exposed now, so the impossible curve can exaggerate my thighs more than they already had been. The false modesty I had is being replaced now. By shame. And this hath worketh itself to a greater notion, until my shame facedness hath achieved red faced embarrassment.

Mother turns to the mirror, and begins to make steady work of the many buttons on her dress of navy cloth, until the silken white slip is exposed. I am careful to watch attentively, absorbing every detail of the beautiful woman sliding the navy dress off her white shoulders, lowering it just enough for her to step out of, tossing it un-neatly to the bed. Still in the slip—which can hardly conceal the girth of the hip, or the birth of the impressive nip I see—she bends over to the boot just over her calf, and zips it down, sliding it away from her sheer stocking foot. And she does the same to the other, placing the black boots neatly out of my sight beside the dresser.

A woman of at least five feet 10 inches in her bare feet, climbing above the six foot barrier in her two inch heeled boots and Sunday shoes. Her beauty is extreme. But marred by a perpetual frown, one born from nearly forty years of heartbreak, pain and suffering. Her depression is as complete as the cloud cover of a rainy day, which she does not work to conceal from me in the house, as my beatings have become increasingly evident of, and less inclined to mercy and compassion.

She stands up from the placing of her boots away, her back to me now, crossing her arms, raising her slip up like a curtain over a stage show, showing to me what God meant by the knowledge of good and evil, which is the uncovering of her backside, bound up in the tight, white underwear, as much a wonder of the hidden world as has ever existed. Her ass is a triple threat, if there can be such a thing, having the perfect shape, width and depth, which I see when she turns to the bed to place the slip away. When viewed from the side, the effect is what artists and butt fetishists around the world have aspired to for centuries, having the classic bubble outward far enough to call attention, which is mostly hidden in the pioneer skirts and dresses she has discovered. The stockings are pulled tight by the little suspenders, attached to the garter belt pulled high over the tops of her snow white underwear.

She goes back to the mirror, her backside toward me, allowing me to see the incredible width, of the likes that have rarely been seen by the public, most unaware that a woman of such beauty and fitness can have a set of hips to achieve such amazing girth and spread, bubbled from the side view, upside down heart shaped and spread out to infinity from the back. And this is joined so perfectly to the inward slope, climbing to the waist so fleshy and fit at the same time, so that the effect is both athletic and soft, as curvaceous as any woman ever born would ever need to be. The effect of her buttocks exposed, even inside the big underwear, is irresistible. As the panty cloth cannot hide the wide shape at the bottom, nor its smooth flow to the top of the heart upside down. Bodies like this, I know, are the ancient source of mankind's lust for all things feminine, causing the flash of images to the brain, and their lingering imprint on the soul.

I watch the beautiful woman at the mirror unhooking the stockings and garter, sliding the garter belt away, then rolling down the sheer brown stocking to below the knee, sliding it down her calf and away from the reluctant foot. This, she repeats upon the other leg, until the stocking is gone as its sister in crime, both tossed un-neatly on the bed with the rest of who we are. At the mirror again, she rolls the top of her underwear down, showing that waist in full, and the soft, hula-girlness at the bottom of it. Then I watch her do what I myself have never even imagined. She turns the panty fabric up from the bottom on both sides, exposing half of each great buttock, her entire lower body now framed by the minimal white cloth shown.

She turns to me, allowing me to see that her front is tightly and barely covered by the white cloth tucked in, giving her a more powerful stance, a more battle ready presence, her body covered only by the cloth cinched to bikini size, and her enormous breasts held tight in the industrial strength bra. Her breast cleavage is forever. As is the size of the mountains that made it happen.

56

*C*ome here to me.

I take the quiet, tense step forward. Feeling the lightning spark go to my groin when she grabs both my nipples in her hand gently, but taking a firm, strong hold. Then the spark of pleasure is instantly transformed to a spark of bee sting heat, piercing into my breasts from both nipples. She twists them without mercy, until I have to bend over on the edge of the scream. And she drives me like a biker woman on the open road. Revving the pain up to cruising power, pulling and twisting hard enough to bring forth the scream she has so skillfully created.

Put your hands down. Put 'em down! she says, holding them at the edge of agony. *So you want to play with boys. You want to put one of these in a boy's mouth, don't you?*

The words *no, I swear*, find their way out somehow. Feeble, in the midst of a screaming, sobbing fit.

I have felt many pains along the way. Sampled many dishes of it. But the taste of this is unbearable, to say the least, as she twists again the front of my breasts until I know to put my arms to my sides and shake with effort to try and keep my mouth shut. But the pain and hopelessness in my voice has already taken affect, causing the front of her to awaken inside, to flow an epic pleasure into her body that brings a quick pause, and her wondering how such a thing is possible. Only the echoes of this have touched her body in the past, even when my nipples were bitten when I was 13. Even when the wooden spoon striped welts in them. But the fullness thereof, the echoes of this are the loudest inside her that they have ever been, resounding to make her understand the possibilities of perversion, and the depths of deviance and depravity. It is the sound of my voice. The sound of my suffering. The sight of it that has fluttered her heart, and flustered the heart of pleasure in her body.

Take off your underwear, she says, relishing the great hang and swing of my breasts as I lean over, sliding my underwear down and away, folding them in the nude, placing them neatly on the bed. She turns on the cushion of a deep breath, gliding casually back to the dresser, opening the top drawer, pulling the wooden hairbrush from its silken hiding place. As I watch, as I listen to the wooden brush click softly onto the dresser, I am reminded that the types of fear are many, and uniquely distinguished. Without even looking at me, she ignores my sudden bout of quiet, determined pleading, even asking her to let me go and cook her favorite dinner, to show her that I have repented. But this part of my voice falls on deaf ears, the part which calmly asks for mercy. She instead obeys the voice of her inner calling, and goes to her closet, reaching into the tiny space of it, emerging with what causes me to ask her in the name of the Lord to forgive me—in a quiet, somber wailing—while she tosses the coiled, black whip onto the bed, where it lays in the power of serpentine, filled with unearthly pain and terror.

Without another word, her face burdened by the frown, the frustration of her failed life; the death of her husband before I was born, the years of poverty on the farm, the suicide of her best friend, the growth and surviving of her little bitch of a daughter—who is the clumsiest, stupidest waste of space in God's Creation—all of this is burdened upon her face in a sorrow condensed, and coalesced into a look of painful despair and defeat. The path of her life chosen, chosen for her by predestination. And this is her only medicine, her only reprieve from the suffering in her mind and body.

With her stockings, she binds my wrists tightly together. Then, to the brown wood bedpost, which is as tall as my chin. And then she takes my bra from where it is folded on the bed, and binds my legs tightly at the ankles. At this moment, I am too numb with false hope and disbelief to be afraid. As if something in my brain has kicked in to medicate my body from the fear I should feel. But when she picks up the coiled leather whip, a black handle with two feet of leather attached, the same fear I had when I saw the hairbrush starts in my chest, and floods into the pit of my stomach and beyond.

I have been beaten with belts so many times over the years, even with the buckles once in a while. But this leather, I have never seen before, and

I wonder how many years she has held this in secret, and how many years she has waited to lay it across my back in grieving.

In the quiet of eternity. In a space warped outside of time. I suddenly feel a flash of heat spread across my back, hearing a loud pop and snapping sound. The heat disperses itself into my lungs as pressure, to take my breath away, then to send it back through in a shriek for the ages. It is a scream of defiance, a refusal to surrender to the hot sting of what I just felt on my back. And even before this energy is done, I feel another lash attached to the first one, which breaks this scream at once, into one of Holy Fear and Submission. The world *please* is repeated over and over in this scream, until I realize that I am not going to pull free from the bedpost, nor from the tragedy of this whipping on my skin. And the third lash of the whip on my back changes the tone of my screams, tearing the flesh, tearing out of me the Death Scream—the long, deep woman's scream—which lasts until there is no more breath left to scream. The hopeless pulling against the bedpost is morphed to a hopeless trembling, and struggling to breathe—flailing against each subsequent fire burn to my back, done with deliberation and full strength, amidst her fervent grunting from the effect. This continues with every ounce of strength in her body, until my skin is welted and torn from my shoulders to my thighs, with her not allowing me to slump down until the *fifty seventh* lash has come and gone. The end of her wrath—the last, planned flash of the whip—they both have come to meet the last of my endurance of this part of the passion, as I have finally lost my ability to stand. I slump over, my hands tied tightly at the top of the bedpost, bleeding from the many open wounds, sensing the assuagement of her for now—blood lust obeyed and conquered, by a lash for every year her husband has been dead, for every year she was plunged into poverty, and for every year of my miserable life.

In the Heart of Memory. In the isolated house by the dirt road. I see what is left of the girl of nineteen. Standing at her mother's bedroom mirror, crying quietly, her back bruised and bloody. Her strong, stern mother having knelt down beside her, tirelessly checking the girl's bra tied around her legs at the ankles. In the Heart of Memory, I feel the fabric of my bra, binding my legs together so that I cannot run, nor lunge against the second and the third part of this truth I must endure. Having been drug from the bloody ordeal at the bed, and lifted upright against the dresser, to get a good look at the Death of Melody, and the rebirth of it in blue and black fire.

57

*S*ounds coalesce. To form words in the air around me. And these words activate my mind, to make me understand that with the Hairbrush of Legend, she intends to *split the skin* on my backside, as if it had not already happened in part from the whip. But most of the flames I feel on my skin are at my back, which I have not yet seen, but knowing that the cuts on my arms and legs must be the precursor of what is there, crisscrossed over my back from top to bottom. And my bottom is truly the bottom line, the canvas to paint the second part of the bloody truth. Oh, how many generations along the timeline hath paralleled, in some form or another with thee!

She puts one hand around the front of my waist tight, to anchor me for what needs to be, which begins when the sound of her voice forms these words:

If you pass out, I'm going to beat you again.

I have already felt the burn of this brushwood many times, so I know whenceforth of what she hath spoken. In the mirror, I see her stern concentration, her arm held firm across the front of my waist, her hair pinned up and away from her grim, beautiful expression. Gazing hard at the back of me, she raises her arm as far back as is possible, her face anguished from the effort, and brings her arm toward this side of the pendulum swing, slamming the hairbrush hard against my already bloody skin, a pain renewed for this part of the punishment, a fire that causes my loud and low pitched woman's screaming to return again.

And these blows to my big bottom continue in rapid succession, my mind counting them of its own will, while she struggles to hold me still while I scream. The pain is such that I cannot control myself, not caring at all if the brushwood hits my hand anymore. But she wastes no energy talking, or screaming for me to move my hand. She merely takes up the stocking that was ill advisedly cut away, and binds my wrists together again, down in front of my body.

I glimpse the face of the damned. In the mirror, I see the trauma registered on my face, fear and bewilderment, colored by the depth of despair. Behind the traumatized face in the mirror, I see the face of Wrath and Beauty rekindled, the beauty of Truth and Judgment, raising her arm again to the back of the pendulum swing. When the woman in the mirror brings her arm down again, I feel the return of acid, lightning pain to by bruised, bloody skin, causing me to focus my eyes upon the woman in the mirror, screaming in as much defiance as it is defeat. The last few scores of hits, she concentrates on a single spot, until the last of over three hundred hits slams to the lump raised on my backside. The screams have quieted down to a frustrated, rebellious sobbing, which she already knows I cannot stop, nor could I ever be expected to; even though her requisite *hush up* comes my way, while she lays the brush back onto the dresser.

Crying, sobbing with the ease and ability of a little girl. She does not tell me to hush again. At least, not with words. She steps close behind me, pressing the bra hard against my back, which makes me draw a cold breath in through my teeth, from the echo of raw agony. The scratchy, rough bra fabric is without mercy on the cuts and open wounds. She presses herself calmly. Lovingly behind me. Kissing the side of my head and my face. Waiting patiently for my tears to subside, for the last of the jerks and sobs to pass through. In her eyes is the calm of uneasy acceptance—the coming to terms with the inevitable, as one surrenders to a dark destiny—one that she has spent a lifetime running from and pushing against, having finally given in to its solemn will and purpose of being; to envelop her in darkness, to tap into a soul of deviance, and channel through her body and into our daytime darkened room.

Telling me to scrunch down a little, until she can lean over my shoulder from the back. Taking one of my big, long breasts up into her mouth from over my shoulder. Sucking it with purpose, her voice moaning once of it own accord. Sucking it as though starving for the feel of it. Swirling the spit formed in her mouth as drink. Releasing the breast in a loud kiss, letting it fall free on its own. Standing me up straight again. Cupping both breasts in both her hands. Massaging them. Pressing her groin to the sores on my bottom, pushing me against the dresser with enough force to creak it loudly in the quiet. Taking my nipples into her hands, twisting them hard enough to hear me howl, unable to push back against her because of the soreness in my back. I can only stand still and endure the pain. Trembling. Letting it out in my voice.

She pulls her fingers away from my nipples. A hard, biting pull. Her face twisted by an inner burden too heavy to bear. I see her surrender to it at last, leaning down towards my legs behind me, her bra heavily stained with blood. Squatting down, looking down at my legs and feet. I feel her fingers at my ankles fumbling, scratching to make work of the bra fabric tied. At long last, at her patience and leisure, I feel my bra loosen from around my ankles, releasing the blood flow back to my aching feet. She calmly rises up, taking the hairbrush up again from the dresser. Surely, I will not be beaten again.

She places the bristles of the brush into one of the gigantic cups of my bra. Wrapping it carefully inside, then places the bundle inside the other cup, and skillfully does the same. Sticking out from the crudely wrapped bundle of cloth is the smooth, rounded wooden brush handle. Then, as if I am not even here to judge, she wraps her beautiful lips around the handle as if it were a popsicle. She savors the taste of aged wood, I suppose—the years of sorrow in dried, invisible lotion soap and perfume—closing her eyes once, holding her head back, holding her newest and grandest weapon at her bosom.

Leaving her underwear in its proper place, she opens her legs just enough, and places the soft bundle of cloth, closing it in between her legs tight, so that the handle sticks out straight in front of her. I see her looking down at it, but she does not look in the mirror, holding it with one hand, getting behind me again so I can only see her head and shoulders. She licks a heavy glisten of spit into her hand, then I see her look down again at what she is doing. Of the feeling I have, when her finger goes into my backside, of this, I cannot tell. I only know that it is on the barest edge of pain. A pressure that I find familiar, revisited from when I was twelve.

I was twelve, when this spirit came unto me. I was twelve, when this cold and dark spirit hath come. Seven years it hath waited, until the autumn of my nineteenth year. And this spirit is joined by another, but one perhaps I have not felt before, where it pertains to pleasure. With one hand, she memorizes the front of my body, which sends a chill and a spark to infinity. As to this feeling her hands hath wrought, of this, I cannot tell.

And the Seven Year Spirit enters me from behind. Splitting me from the outside in, to cause a quick, pathetic shriek to leap from my throat into the room. And this pushing, this tearing slides forever up into me from behind, joined by the biting pain at my ear, from where her teeth have taken hold, and the gruff calling of God's name from deep within her. In the mirror, I see two strangers. One, a woman of great beauty and power. The other, a younger woman of straw. Devastation and Defeat, at the end of a long road of hope, on the verge of the road to nowhere.

I am drawn away from the women accursed. The two lonely souls I see, and set adrift on the long, dirt road, which is the road beside our house, I see. Where my attention is gathered, adrift among the leaves of every dying autumn tree nearby. At the end of this road is despair and disillusionment, where all hope for what is normal had died, where the future is a wasteland, an infinity of nothing between sorrow and happiness, where the colors of the future have faded to darkness and ashen gray regret. Along this road I walk, to take hands with my Lord and Savior in spirit, of which is the only hope left, for every lost and lonely soul under Heaven. But in the Valley of the Shadow of Death, I cannot find the Spirit of him who walks with me, and I hear a long and plaintiff wail, from inside

245

the house I have drifted from. And although I try to run from the house in this valley, to find my Lord and Savior again, I am transported through the Walls of Secret, back to my place in front of the mirror, where I can again feel the splitting pain pushing into my rectum from behind, and I see the woman's reflection in the mirror behind me, the look of awe and fear on her face, shaking her head 'no,' then suddenly calling the name of *God and Holy Jesus* to *please have mercy*, as twenty years of repressed lust suddenly explodes into her body.

I am held tight in the storm, to witness the devastation, and the screaming siren of a woman in great travail. Her body rocks and slams violently into me for many long seconds, to the rise and fall of two separate and distinct screams, flown out of her body on their own, to release the spirits of Deviance and Depravity into the room. She grabs me by the neck and around my waist, pinning my arm, suffering each convulsive wave in moaning and sobbing, the sound of grief unveiled, which is the voice of lamentation, where there is only weeping and gnashing of teeth.

In the aftermath of trauma. In the burning of blue and black fire. I stand at the mirror calmly. Soothed by the same spirit that hath overtaken the woman of straw. The calm of uneasy acceptance, which wells up in eyes of red and defeat, flowing down my face in a slow and steady stream. She holds onto me for what life there is left to siphon, her entire body alive with a continuous trembling, a quiet, steady shaking that lasts all of a full minute, then beyond to a full minute more. And for a third minute, she stands before she can move. Breathing. Recovering. Wondering what manner of life or afterlife this is.

Words coalesce. To form meaning in the mind. And of these she speaks, I obey. Pushing my tongue into her mouth. This, at the end of the age. On the eve of the Second Coming of Christ the Lord.

$\mathcal{V}$era Evans stares in disbelief. In awe of the power of Creation. The power of feminine beauty. Curves bequeathed from the Garden of Eden. A woman in her 40's or 50's thereabouts. The truth of which seems to shift from moment to moment. The sliding spectrum of modern, mature sensuality. The peak of it, forty seven to fifty seven, thereabouts. Of this, Vera cannot tell. The woman lies on the sofa nude, covered in a cushy, cloud gray linen. A fascinating trip it turned out to be, from the coat to the comforter. Frustration manifested at the rainy open door, when the brunette kook screamed and ran away. With every ounce of hospice strength born,

Vera had lifted up the sleeping woman lying under the gray coat, carrying her in both arms, cradling her into the mansion, across the grand living room. Leaning down in strained, sore muscles, gently plopping the beautiful, sleeping woman onto the sofa. Standing up in back pain, blame and bewilderment.

Why did she run? How could she let her silly fears get in the way of her helping this poor woman? This, amidst another flash of lightning and rolling thunder in a November rain. Deep, regular breaths, she had thought. Hurrying to a linen closet down the hall. *I should take her to the hospital,* she thinks. Hurrying the gray comforter from the linen closet, back to the mysterious stranger. Back to the task at hand. Stopped cold by the beauty in the woman's face. The eyebrows, naturally arched. The sculpted nose, the creamy, white skin. The full, pink lips. Jet back hair, long and wet, grown to the length of her back. The look of health and vigor, held captive in a deep and abiding sleep. What trauma hath induced this sleep? What drama hath introduced this sleeping beauty?

In the safety of her own home. Safe from uncaring eyes of robotic care. Vera is free to let pretense fade. To allow herself to contemplate reality. To consider a beauty unlike any she has ever seen, save one other she thinks about. Letting her eyes gauge the rise in the comforter, laying over this woman. The bulge that was in the coat at the woman's chest. The echo of what she thought she saw when the woman was outside, curled up in the fetal position. Waiting to be born. On the sofa, Vera had boldly removed the coat. Unable to look away. Tossing the coat to the side, down to the other end of the sofa. Whispering, *My God.* Gauging the fullness thereof. Seeing the rarest sight of feminine Creation. The macrocosm of the breast mystique. The macromastia. Gigantomastia. As formed in perfection upon a woman. Amazonian strength, uncovered. Monumental, bulbous breasts, larger than what many would believe was possible. One supported by the back of the sofa. The other laid to the side. Both of tremendous size and weight, with large, pale brown areolas and nipples, perfectly placed at the front of the great globes, the great globules laid still. A sight people would pay money to see. A memory burned into their brains for all time. Obviously the source of so much of the dead weight this woman was, when she was brought inside. How on earth, how in God's Creation can they be? By what power do they live? In this woman's former life, how did she conceal them in her clothes? She must be civilized, she's too beautiful not to be. Sensuality aged. Seasoned to what is perfect. What is good. A waist similar in shape as one other that Vera knows, but in middle-aged thickness, accentuating the deep, inward curve. A genital uncovered by hair of any kind, lips formed smooth as pink ivory.

What manner of woman is this, where the hair of her privacy does not grow! Nor is there any under the woman's arms or upon even an inch of her long, silky smooth legs. Your eyes are drawn to the hips, Vera May, are they not! Swallow at the girth of them, even wider than the woman's shoulders—what manner of buttocks will hips like these reveal! What is that at the woman's private, Ms. Evans! It is unmistakable, is it not! A tiny fold of skin—in protrusion from her vagina! And what, Oh Vera, is the shape of this anomaly? It is as the tiny version, unawakened, of that which pertaineth to a man! It is a thing of extraordinary beauty, is it not! Is it indeed what it appears—this tiny fold of skin in protrusion, from the genital of this beautiful woman, this lovely and extraordinary creature of the woods!

Vera covers the woman. Letting the truth of Creation vanish from her eyes. Watching the comforter rise and fall. Deep, regular breaths.

Vera Evans stares in disbelief. At the beauty of feminine power. Masculine strength bound up in curves, gigantic breasts, hips widened. Face softened. Strong hands, smoothed by the kiss of Estros. An earth goddess manifested. A goddess of the woods. Of the hunt. Whose presence was foretold by the earth comet. Whose life sparks new energy in the November clouds, spreading across the sky above the Great Lawn again, from the middle of the field of grass, down to the distant and abandoned farmhouse, and to the Autumn Pine forest beyond. A figure not seen since the sunrise of Creation. Since the tree of the knowledge of good and evil. This figure, even more hourglassed, more extraordinary than her own. A figure reminiscent of one other she has seen, touched and kissed. The taller, heavier version of the same. The bigger example, of the shape Vera's wife and daughter possesses.

How can it be, Mother Vera, that this older woman is the striking image of one you know and love, whose face and body are younger versions of the same? Mother Vera, be not burdened! Think nothing of the flash of revelation you see in the November clouds—over the spirit of the one you love as a little girl!

See her in the wisp of memory, Mother Vera, having been thrown out of her little farmhouse in the Carolina country. See the little girl of 12 years old, having been told *you will never be allowed to go to school again!* This, at the end of her fifth grade year! See the little girl in the summer lightning storm, on the porch in a violent, rainy wind, a vile and windy rain. Look up through the little girl's eyes, Mother Vera, at the woman behind the screen door. Staring. Glaring down at the little girl of straw. *Get off my porch,* says the tall and beautiful woman. Watch the little girl turn and face the pouring rain, Mother Vera. Watch the little girl take the impossible step, the cold step into the summer rain and wind. Watch her turn once more toward the house, gazing at the beautiful woman behind the screen door, who looks on without mercy. *Get off my porch*, is her quiet refrain, spoken to the little girl with a look only. The girl turns back to the rain, to take the next step, until she is fully exposed, away from the safety of her mother's porch. Then a third and final step to the ground, to the unnaturalness of it all, leaving shelter to go into the rain. Watch the little girl flinch at sights and sounds that only she can see, forming from the raindrops pouring down, and leaping at her in the flashes of lightning and thunder. Watch the little girl, Mother Vera, be given mercy by a Divine thought placed, to run around the side of the house to the back yard. Watch her cold, wet little fingers fumble with the hook latch on the rickety old shed, popping it open and hurrying inside from the gust of wind, and the sheets of rain coming at her from the empty crop field beyond. She waits breathlessly for their arrival, inside the cold, dank shed. Hearing the massive splashing of new rain thrown at her in the feed shed, amidst a blast of thunder nearby, and the rolling boom of a thousand cannons across the countryside.

Now, watch the tall, beautiful woman. See her turn in the daytime dark of this summer storm. Gliding through her tiny house of poverty like a ghost. A spirit of desperation. Disillusionment. Despair. Through the tiny living room. Through the kitchen devoid of life. Absent of joy. To the back door, opening it with deliberation. With anticipation of what is there. With expectation of the little drowned dog on the back porch in disobedience. Waiting to get her wet hair grabbed. Waiting to have the skin on her back bloodied with the punishment stick gathered. Waiting to be thrown off the back porch into a mud puddle. Waiting to hear the back door slammed behind her.

The beautiful woman opens the back door. Seeing nothing. Save the infinity of rainfall, the empty back porch, and the flashes of summer lightning. Intrigued, but hardly worried. Wondering if the dog was smart enough to seek shelter. Not in the woods. Not under the back porch. Not in the henhouse. The smart little bitch is in the shed.

Eyes of winter gray. Gazing through the back screen door. Marveling the fervent sheets of rain. Watching them splash against the roof, and the door of the feed shed. Placing the punishment stick against the wall by the kitchen counter. Stroking it once. Imagining it stained with blood. Having no desire at all to taste the rain today. No desire to walk out in the storm, to do what must be done.

Let the child be. Let her hide and tremble in the storm. Let it come and go as it has before. Let her wait for the coming night.

No.

Who the Hell does she think she is?

Hiding. Mocking. Claiming victory in her spirit of defiance. For a disobedient tone. For a sluggish response to duty. The shed. She's in the shed.

Take up thy rod, accursed woman! Obey thy calling! This is as unto God, that if thou beatest a child with a rod, she shall not die! This is not that same merciful day, when she huffed and puffed at thee, when she learned she would never go to school again! This is not that merciful day, when she was allowed back into the house after a rest from the rain! When she was taken back in after dark and dried off, and placed in a cushion bed of dreams. No, Dear Woman. This is not that day. Take up thy rod of discipline. Obey thy calling! Flinch, Mountain Girl. At the lightning strike from the clouds, to above the woods that lie beyond the back cropfield. Flinch, accursed woman. Terrified of the voice of God. Terrified of the grave. Terrified of eternal damnation. The reward for them who disobey a Divine Calling.

Take up thy wooden sword, Mountain Girl. Throw open the back door in power. Walk down the back porch steps in the drowning rain! March to the beat of these drums of lamentation. This Funeral March for a Mother and Daughter. Splash your black shoes through the black mud towards the shed. Pity for her sake, that she chose not to hide therein!

Rich Woman of Charity! See the rainfall from another place along the timeline! See the beautiful farm widow stroll through the summer storm, carrying her punishment stick. Letting the waters drown her. Letting the raindrops prick her skin with icy cold. Raindrops from high above the earth, falling to each predestined place underneath the clouds. See the woman's somber expression turn sour, as she glides closer and closer to the wooden shed. Drenched. Soaked from head to toe already. Reaching up to take hold of the wet wood. Swinging the door open in the storm.

See the beautiful woman vanish so briefly, behind the open door. Reaching inside the shed. Now, see her emerge again. Dragging the little girl by the hair. Sliding her out into the mud. Raising the punishment stick. The far side of the pendulum swing. Bringing the stick down onto the fallen little girl's back. Her buttocks. Her bare thighs and her dress. Holding her wet hair tight. Beating her legs, buttocks and back in rapid succession. Trying to break her shinbone. Trying to crack a rib. Holding her by the hair. Unrelenting. Unrepentant. Trying to draw blood.

Listen, Mother Vera. Hear the scream in the noisy rainfall. A scream of fear and pain. Watch the little girl in the mud. Cowering there, in the fetal position. Screaming while the stick breaks the blood free. Her head. Her back. Her thighs. Now watch the mother. Standing up in the storm. Frustrated. Defeated. Unable to break the curled up girl's spirit. Hearing the defiance in the wet screams. Watch her yank the girl to her feet. Dragging her hurriedly back to the house, going dripping wet inside. The two of them. Watch the mother take the name of God in vain—*get your clothes off—get your goddamned clothes off!* Ripping the little girl's clothes. Tearing them off her back until she is naked. See the mother go to her bedroom. Unbuttoning her blouse. Taking it off, leaving her skirt in place. Taking the bra off in quick succession. Gaze, Vera, at the breasts hung gigantic. Wobbling free as she walks to the closet. Reaching inside. Retrieving her dead husband's belt. See her walk back through the ghostly living room. To the kitchen of death.

The mountain woman grabs the naked little girl, and lays the folded leather belt across her skin, to place welts of less blood, across where the cuts from the punishment stick are laid. Watch the biggest breasts in this part of Creation swing. Hear the chiming of the bells, the great and fervent punishment swing. What does it do to your mind and body, Oh Mother Vera, to see the giant breasted woman topless in her skirt, scraping the blood from her daughter's naked skin? Cutting the daughter's white skin to blood. Dragging her by the arm from room to room in the storm. Burning a sun's energy worth of pain. Burning blue and black fire.

In the storm of the present day. On the eve of Armageddon. Vera looks away from the November lightning. Gazing down at the sleeping woman of the woods. Grieving to know where she has come from. Wishing to know where she has been. Turning briefly from the sleeping face of mystery. Walking to the other end of the sofa. Taking a mercy seat in repose.

Vera Evans stares in disbelief. Away from the Face of Beauty. Into the space of the twilight room.

59

*T*he nighttime November clouds flash their warning in desperation. In quiet grief to tell of what they have learned, of truths bestowed from the dawn of creation, to the twilight of humanity.

I am comfortable in the darkness of this evening day come and gone. Hiding at the big bay window of my guest house, every light inside turned off, so I can see out into the gentle nighttime rainfall. The bright light of the statue fountain is in mild conjunction with the soft lighting from the house, to display the hidden infinity of this mysterious rainfall. This is a melancholy storm. One of a dreamy, protracted endurance. This is a long and dreamy storm, seeming as though it might last forever. It is Autumn's final departure from the dark'ned landscape around us, and Winter's bitter, early arrival.

The melodies and memories inspired by her have faded. And now there's nothing left but me. A scared little mouse, content to be hiding in the dark, with the refrain *God, please help me* running through my mind on a loop. What I need is for someone to swat the seat of my fear and complacency, then drag me out of the darkness and into the light. Is this the light of Truth? Of Revelation? What is the so-called truth that I am hiding from? What is my devastation which awaits? What is the third part of this truth I must come to terms with? Sadly, or tragically, there are only two possibilities, and I don't know which one will devastate me the most.

The first, and the easiest, is the one that concerns my mind. My feeble sanity. Maybe, the years of grief have finally taken their toll. Maybe the same spirit that caused her to ask me of wisdom and white horses, maybe that same spirit of delusion and madness, that same spirit of dementia has finally come calling to collect. To take what is left of my rationality, which would likely be best for me, I think. I need to be strapped down and doped up anyway. So I won't be a danger to myself and anyone around me. What if one of these voices I hear tells me to do something drastic? Something that might cause harm to Vera, or to her mysterious stranger? What if I cannot ignore the voices any longer, that tell me to cut my wrists and my throat so that I can go to Heaven?

I can't do that. Because I'm too afraid to die, and I can't stand the thought of Vera grieving over my body and burying me in the ground. I have seen Death walking these grounds too many times. I may as well come to terms with it, I'm going to die soon. But I have prayed since I was a little girl, that God will let me die peacefully in my sleep, where an angel of the Lord will take me by the hand, and escort me beyond the glory of the cosmos, into the kingdom of Heaven.

Is the appearance of the Earth Comet a sign that I am going to die? Is this stranger a sign of my impending death? What I believe concerning her—am I insane? This is the easy answer. The one that truthfully, I am hoping for. Because insanity is a sickness, no? A disease? And sicknesses can be treated. I can be cured of the voices, the visions. The delusions of death and dismemberment, of every deer I see carrying a message from Heaven, of every buzzard and blackbird carrying a message from Hell. So what if buzzard hawks never miss an opportunity to circle my house and property high above, seemingly when I look toward Heaven for guidance? Do these buzzard hawks come to intercept my faith, to stifle my prayers, to make it harder for me to put my trust in God? So what if the words 'buzzard bait' flash in my mind when I look away, and go back from the balcony into my mansion room? I want my grand bedroom in my mansion now, but I can't have it. Because the Devil does not want me to have anything that is remotely good in this life, and were it not for the mercy of God, I would have died under the axe twenty years ago. So let me choose to believe that despite the mercy of God, much of what I think about the world is nonsense. Let me chose to believe that I am crazy.

Oh, God.

I'm not crazy.

Every fear I've ever had is justified. While God hath not given us the Spirit of Fear, there are some who are called to it, for one reason or another. Driven by depression, inspired by fear. The Seven Songs for Cello and Orchestra, these are operatic in their inspiration—Rossini at the end of the Age, tormented by fear and gloom. And though I have tried to believe I am crazy, though I have tried to hide in the refuge of lunacy, the substance of it has begun to fade like a breath in the cold, winter air.

No, I will not be allowed to take the easy road, and believe that the truth I must face is that I am ready for the psych ward. No. I am not. My mind is as sound as its ever been. My thoughts are as rational as they will ever be. So this is the devastation of a single choice, the destruction of false truth. Truth that came as an angel of light to trick me, appearing right because it was logical. The truth that says *'that woman in that house is not who you think it is. You're one crazy bitch.'*

No. That is not the truth. So this brings me a ticket to ride the Death Train. Cloaked in ashen gray regret. Because if I am sane, then yes, Mother, wisdom *can* be found in the carcass of a white horse, and the woman I saw in that house is a woman that I believe in my heart was lying in the woods dead for twenty years.

*F*inally, the Spectre of Expectation is adrift from the front door of the mansion. A cold, dark figure underneath her umbrella and carrying a black bag slung across her shoulder. The glow of the fountain barely lights her shortcut across the great lawn. I refuse to turn on a single light as she gets closer to my gray brick cottage. Crossing the asphalt road. Now crossing the small lawn of the gray house, finding her way to the smooth brick walkway. These are the steps of determination. The steps of conviction. I can see and barely hear, as the dark figure glides by the front windows towards the front door. The unlocked door swings open, and she stands there for a moment. Still wearing the long gray coat from the funeral. Finding my fearful gaze across the room, even before she steps inside. She bears the presence of a woman of substance, of TV reporting or politics or high administration. None of which she could be allowed to do, having not even achieved a high school diploma.

This charity woman, this volunteer queen lowers her umbrella, crossing the threshold into my strange little world, turning the living room light on, her gray coat and umbrella cloth both dripping with wet and weeping. Without a word, the coat, umbrella and black carry bag are placed in the front closet. The door to civility then clicks shut. Gently. She takes a step away from the coat closet, towards where I sit at my music desk.

Waiting.

"She should be in a hospital," Vera says. "But for some reason, I can't do it. Not yet. Her heart and her breathing are very strong. She'll be fine for now. As if... as if I knew what the Hell I was talking about."

The comment flows from the soul of disillusionment. Where one is confronted by their own insignificance in God's Creation.

"You've been a hospice nurse for twenty years. One look at her was all you needed. And speaking of twenty years..."

"No," she says, pointing at me, shaking her head, her face stern with warning.

"Yes," I say. In defiance uncharacteristic.

"Elizabeth, I swear. If you..."

I am ready for the anger I see. I see it in her strong hands. An open hand that she hangs in the air for a second too long. The open hand of discipline craved and denied. She blows a breath and turns away. Folding her arms. Looking to the ceiling and beyond it—saying *"God help me,"* just loud enough for me to hear. And I've been waiting for this day to come anyway, the day when I finally cross the line, and cause her to have to give in to the curse of who I am, a person to be slapped to within an inch of her life.

"I'm just going to say this one time. And pray to God I'm not crazy for even allowing myself to be pulled into this foolishness. You are not insane. You are a rational, extremely intelligent adult. I've been listening to you on these pianos for years and I still can hardly believe my ears. *Your* music. Music *you* wrote. So I know you're not *crazy.*"

She turns to look at me. Desperately.

"The woman in that house... is not who think it is."

"It *is.* I know it in my *spirit,* Momma, it is..."

"If you persist with this, Elizabeth, I swear to God and Jesus—"

"It is her—"

"It is *not!*"

The force of her anger clutches me inside my throat, making it suddenly harder for me to breathe. I open my mouth to speak, but nothing will come. All I know is that even if she crosses the line and grabs me, or hits me in anger, I know that she will never be able to drive this cataclysm from my mind and body.

A sudden, angry bewilderment takes over her as if she cannot fathom that any sane person could ever be convinced of what I'm thinking. Could never be coerced to believe that the Earth Sun is blue.

"You're going to sit there, and tell me with a straight face, that you believe that woman in that house is your *mother?"*

I wish I had the strength of others. That I could push through the barrier of fear and tension, and stand up to her. But while she stands over me fuming, the truth is, I am too afraid to speak.

"I have to put a stop to this," she says, her expression clouded by hopelessness. "Come with me," she says. Pulling me up by my upper arm, ignoring the pathetic, whining "no" flowing out on its own. It is the beginning of the end. The birth of a part of me that Vera has only suspected I am capable of. The beginning of the end, of our years of cultured civility. The breakdown of promises made but unspoken, as I begin to pull against her already, as if she is about to drag me to the edge of a cliff, or a highway filled with cars and trucks whizzing by. Vera's own state of mind is apparent; desperation caused by helplessness, frustration caused by fear, making her forget coats and umbrellas as she opens the door into the night—unable to simply say, *lets walk calmly over to the mansion and take one last look Honey.* No. She is as desperately afraid as I am. Me, terrified of the zombie laying asleep in the Great Hall. And Vera, terrified that she is on the edge of losing me to insanity.

61

*O*ut of the safety of my Music House. Into the trauma of nighttime rain. Our way enshrouded in country darkness, with the gray clouds barely visible above, still flashed blue every so often by the lightning built up inside them. Across the small lawn of the gray house, she hurries me. Across the concrete road, into the darken'd space of the Great Lawn. There is the glowing fountain I see, which is a beacon light of hope for my guardian, my mother, my wife.

My wife mother walks me so roughly along, to where I feel like I have to almost run to keep up, every raindrop now a warning on my face and hair, as the clouds above spit their cold warning into my eyes. Through my squinting eyes, in the periphery, I see the dark figure that holds me, pulling me along towards the lights of earthly progression, the unnatural lights of our amaranthine glow. And this selfsame statue fountain, while she guards the living waters as a ray of hope for Mother Vera, to me she is an Angel of Light—a demon risen from the depths of Hell, to mock me in the glow of tranquility, a warning light of impending doom and tragedy, having deceived the woman who takes care of me, so that she may drag me to the edge of the fiery pit, and throw me screaming into outer darkness.

Then suddenly, as clearly as is possible, I see the statue turn her head to look me in the eye, which pushes me down to the bottom of Fear, descending me into the violent fit Vera has prepared herself for. Taking the incredible hit to the face, and the blast of my voice around her into the Carolina night. She gathers herself expertly, grabbing my arms as best she can, holding me as I try to fall to the ground, soon tumbling down with me, falling directly on top of me in the heat of battle. Pressing herself to me, both of us clothed and soaked in new desperation—finally getting my arms pinned to where I cannot move them, while I imagine the statue climbing down and lunging at me unlit in the gray. Vera unleashes all of her strength. Holding me down. Listening to me scream a spit choked, tongue biting shriek of the damned. Moving her head away from my teeth, so I cannot draw blood from her face.

What does it do to your body, Mother Vera, to feel my squishy curves so tense with fear and rage in the storm? To hold me down on the wet ground, feeling the madness finally come and take me. You would like to put your hand over my mouth, wouldn't you? But if you let just one of my arms go for a second, you risk what I may do to your eyes with my fingers.

My claws. Take care, Mother Vera. Do not let me have space to give attack! Lay on top of me. Squeezing. Holding. Listening to the screams take every last breath I have. Hold me. Punish me, Dear Woman. Let the violence of this work its magic inside. It is the manifestation of the violence, and not the kind manufactured for pleasure! Oh, but what does my screaming underneath you, on this grand, nighttime property, what does it do to your mind and body! The strength it rises in you is greater than any I have felt from thee! *"You will come back,"* you say. Repeating it as my screams subside. "You *will* come back to me. You *will* come back. In the name of *God*, come back to me."

What is the perfect storm of stimulation? What is the release of water you feel! What is the lightning from your groin to your spine, Dear Lady, flashing up to cause your heart to flutter. I hear the release of this energy you have tried to hide from me, coming out of your voice in gruffness— *"come back to me,"* you say. And then I hear the grunt. A grunt in this perfect storm, Mother Vera. It is the Witch's Crown, is it not? The explosion of energy into your body, with no apparent cause or reason. Now, you release my arm out of necessity. Grabbing my head, my face with one hand. Breathing hard in my ear. Of this, none but the Goddess of the Harp hath seen. She saw the spirit form in the nighttime rain, Mother Vera. She saw it caress you upon your buttocks unbeknownst to you, and bestow unto you this River Queen, which you felt flow from inside you and take your breath away. Activated by the reality of violence, Dear Woman, and the power of my screams of insanity.

Through a mighty effort, you avoid the requisite after squeeze against me, still determined to rescue me from the abyss. With your groin still aching, in the aftermath of trauma, you lift me stumbling to my feet. This time escorting, and not dragging me to the nighttime mansion. While I stare at the statue wide eyed, unable to find the signs of life I saw and felt just a moment before.

We walk through the nighttime mist. Through the passing of Carolina fall into winter. Climbing the steps to the grand entranceway. Sheltered from the wet, weeping world of night. Both trembling. Suffering the aftermath of trauma. One, in grieving to see the return of rationality, the return of sanity to our midst. The other, in grieving to flee. To turn and run again from the white tiger outside of its cage. Supposedly asleep in our living room.

Inside the Great Music Hall, where the Bosendorfer's velvetine echo is Queen. Already, at the moment our threshold is crossed, I see a pale faced figure on the sofa. I receive another spark of terror. Fear itself. Flinching my body. Causing Vera to hold me tighter. Holding us still. Letting me plead my case in whining. Hearing "its not her, Baby. Your mother is dead, remember? God told you your mother is dead. You believe everything God says, right? Then you know this isn't Barbara Jean Coletti…"

The mention of that name. Bubbling my insides to water. I am a water creature all of a sudden. Feeling as though I may burst like a transparent water balloon, and splash into nothing on this hardwood floor. But Vera gathers me up. Gripping me tight as I walk around to where the undead lays sleeping. Yes, Vera—God told me she is dead in the woods. Oh, but what has he told me in my dreams as of late, concerning what I see on the couch in front of me! Can't you feel her otherworldly presence? Why won't you believe your own eyes, Vera, have you ever seen the likes of such a woman! How many untold and infinite actions and consequences— how many of them are activated by our breathing, our moving, by even the most insignificant step! Because I notice that upon my first step to the front of the sofa, the pale figure on the couch opens its mouth and pulls in the loudest, ghostliest breath I've ever heard, making me shriek one quick and powerful screech, turning away, with Vera there to catch me and hold on tight, hugging me in complete control. Telling me "I'm here. I'm right here. We'll get through this together."

Vera turns us toward the truth. Taking each step in league with my own. Believing in her heart that the woman who breathes is a stranger. That the truth will set me free. That this is the beginning of the end of suffering. That the first half of my life ends now, whereby the curse bestowed is lifted. That this stranger half dead with sleep is a Godsend— to achieve the psychotic break I have always needed. Vera inches me closer to the truth. The Revelation of the Divine Will in a life. The indication of mankind's nearness to annihilation. His proximity to devastation. The end of the Age of Redemption.

The woman breathes again, causing me to hold Vera tight in anticipation. But suddenly, I am as a passenger in a car on the rainy streets of Cataclysm, when the beautiful, mature woman flutters her eyes open, turning to gaze a pale, winter gray stare. Every ounce of strength I've ever had returns, in a wave of madness through my body, echoing into my Great Music Hall in a scream for the ages, while I tear away from Vera's hold on me, and tear through the livingroom in the speed and power of Fear itself. Breaking free from the haunting of spirits, from the calling forth of the dead, running back through the front door of the mansion, out into the raining, grieving cold—into the veil of a dark and fervent Autumn's night.

JONATHAN LOVEJOY

62

*T*he rains of November pass into oblivion. Swept up by the icy winds of Winter's early arrival, and the rise and fall of the Winter Moon. These waters are gathered again into the clouds, to rule the Christmas season in daytime darkness and gray. Through the Season of the Nativity, beyond the blessing of our Lord and Savior, the frozen rains are gathered into the new year, tossed upon the Carolina mountain winds, under the winter Mountain Moon. These are the frozen waters of discontent, carried along on the cold winds of wrath and God's judgment forlorn, held in Divine restraint for the passing of another trip around the sun. These crystals of grief and mourning are crashed and demolished one upon the other, high into the clouds of impending doom held at bay, until the cold sky winds can no longer sustain their time aloft. From the clouds of winter bereavement, the frozen waters of grief drift downward in crystal enchantment, falling to Earth in the forests, and the icy windblown fields of snowy white.

Vera has come under the power of grief and acceptance. The suffering realization, that where the will of man ends, God's will begins. Though she had tried again many times two months ago—even one month ago nearby Christmas—she finally understood that some things are better left alone, and that as surely as the snow, I am not going back into that house. The beauty of my southern mansion cries to me often, even to the necessity of a stroll. But they will find my bones in the prairie field, buried under a layer of ice, before I will ever set foot inside that place, as long as that woman is inside.

The woman has been a cold, gray mystery from the night she arrived. Hardly a word she has spoken, Vera tells me, since the first word she spoke, *Elizabeth*, which had made Vera's blood go as cold as the rains of that November night had been. Fear had pressed down on her common sense after that, making her call the paramedics, as much for the woman's health as to simply get her off the property, to see if the world could find a cure for what ails ya—that sickness being fear and confusion, as to who the Devil this woman is and where the Devil and Hell she came from. I can remember the red flashes of light from the ambulance getting closer, while I stood at the cottage window, with hardly a breath left in my body.

She's in perfect health, the Lady doctor had said, while Vera stood in the waiting room, comfortable in her farmer's wife's clothes, her tight jeans and tucked in sky blue collar shirt. Sitting helpless in the waking room, she had been, until cute compassion in Carolina blue scrubs had swirled out, smiling about the woman's perfect health (not even dehydration), and that the only thing she seemed to be able to remember was her name. *"Elizabeth,"* the doctor had said, which had only deepened the mystery for Vera, wondering how it is that the woman I had been describing to Vera for ten years suddenly showed up out of nowhere, naked on her doorstep, and the only word she spoke that night was my name.

That's quite a story, the Lady doctor had said, *almost as powerful that set of bosoms.*

I know, Vera had agreed. *I thought I knew what big breasts were.*

Me too, the doctor had said. *My mother is sort of big up top, but her body is big too, so its really no big deal. But my God. I've never seen anything like that in my life. If you don't hurry up and get her out of here, I promise you every male doctor in this hospital is gonna want to put his stethoscope between 'em. Know what I mean?"*

Vera had laughed. Such a genuine, refreshing burst of quiet laughter in the storm of grief. Staring at the doctor in something like quiet awe, that she would allow such a powerful truth to slip through. Vera had driven the woman home late that same night, not willing to leave her in the hospital unattended, anxious to get back home to me as well. *She seems very normal*, the doctor had said, *she just can't seem to remember who she is. I don't think Elizabeth is her name, though. Do you know who she might be talking about?*

No, Vera has said. Thoughtfully. *Let me just take her home. I'm sure her memory will come back.*

But this so-called failed memory had persisted. Even through the revelation from Sheriff Mary Ann Williams' office, that there are no fingerprint matches of this person. And no, Vera did not ask her to check birth records for a woman named Barbara Jean Daniels. Born somewhere in a Virginia mountain county about fifty seven years ago. Nor did she ask about records of marriages in Virginia about 40 years ago. Barbara Jean Daniels, to a Michael Coletti. Nor did she ask about missing persons reports from 20 years ago. On a woman named Barbara Jean Coletti. Sheriff Williams had told Vera that this woman, whoever she is, is like a ghost in the wind. *Don't know where she came from*, she said. *Don't know where in the world she's goin', either. You better keep a good eye on 'er*, she had said. Pledging to drive out here to 'check up on us' every now and then. In two months, the beautiful, lightskinned woman has driven out here one time, about a month ago on Christmas Eve. I saw her from the window, glad I wasn't anywhere near the house when her car arrived. What was it that Miss Sheriff Williams was looking for? Sheriff now, because her father Morgan was killed on the job. Does she think she can protect us? There is but one with that power, to lead us not into temptation. There is but one, who can deliver us from evil. You cannot help us, Miss Yellow Pretty Sheriff. To cause or prevent what may happen to us here, there is no power under the sun.

From the woman's dark and rainy arrival, over the graves of Brenda and Catherine Grace Harrison, nearby the cold of Thanksgiving Eve. Across the landscape of Christmas Eve, past the twilight barrier to Christmas night. Beyond the veil of New Years Eve, Vera's concern, her worries are gathered up in the swirl of Winter's unforgiving embrace, and sent across the snowy landscape to the four winds, where she can no longer grasp their heft and importance. Whether or not this woman is my mother, whether or not I believe it, these have faded like the memories of Brenda and Catherine Grace Harrison. Memories frozen by the arctic winds over the back prairie lawn, now buried in the sea of winter white.

In the ice and snow of Winter's grieving. Loneliness drifts from the front of the mansion, walking the asphalt road towards my cottage, to avoid the snowy shortcut past the statue on the Great White Lawn. Frigid, icy winds swirl the powdery snow at her feet. Her black boots are displayed in stark contrast to the field of snow, as well as the faded jeans, which hug her legs and hips impressively, in grand, country girl fashion. Through the window, I see the cold, bitter wind attack her icy stroll, making her zip her white, waist length jacket up to her chin.

Loneliness walks the frozen path, the chosen path in blonde beauty. Towards the thing that was special we were supposed to have done two months ago, when we were girls interrupted—by a woman of the bygone autumn woods and rain. In the ice and snow of winter's grieving. I see loneliness adrift, my unresisting heart aflutter. Closing my eyes from the spark of longing I feel, the pain of unrequited want and need. What feeling I had for my mother a lifetime ago has traversed the timeline to where I am, to deepen and strengthen my desire, my need to hear Vera's voice, my longing for her touch, my craving to feel her lips pressed against mine. On the wispy breath of feeling, I am carried from my place at the window, to the door of my cottage house, with only my gray, plain cloth dress over my skin. Of what needless concern is the bitter cold to me, as I drift the snowy walkway to my love, each step more heavily burdened than the one before. I take each step in the cold, bitter wind, unconcerned at the flakes of powdered snow that bite my legs and the top of my feet.

In the rushing, whirling Carolina winter, I fall onto my lovers neck with both arms embraced, feeling her grab me in woman's strength about the waist, lifting me up so slightly as I press my lips to hers, in the whirling and drifting flakes of snow. I hold on to her for what life there is to kiss from her, to drink from her in the long and deepened kiss, allowing her lips to slip around my tongue, twitching from a spark unseen, pushing it as deep into the blonde beauty's mouth as it can go, feeling the hum of the moan she tries to conceal, thanking providence for the feel of her arms wrapped around me, and her breath from her nostrils fleeting against my skin.

And in keeping with what we have learned over the years, she takes a firm hold of me and leans back, lifting me completely off the ground just enough; just long enough for me to feel carried aloft by the winter breeze, and drift back down to earth as a lonely flake of snow. I feel myself formed as a woman again in her arms, held so tight and strong, as I am lowered slowly back to the snowy walkway again. With not a word, for there are none that I dare speak to her, lest she vanish from my sight again, and leave me alone in the icy wilderness plain, to wonder where it is that my beloved could have gone.

I take my wife mother by the hand, not looking at her as I pull her along, crossing the threshold with her in great longing, and grieving for what love she may have to give. In the warmth of my gray brick cottage, in our tiny palace by the Crystal Wood, we do not spare one another's lips and tongue from the pressing, the licking, the deep, powerful sucking of wet, noisy kisses and moaning, until I am not fully aware of what my hands are doing to the zipper on her white coat, which is made of quick and powerful departure. After this, I tear at the bottom of her black sweater, pulling it over her lovely blonde head, greeting her lips with mine immediately, giving her not even a moment to catch a breath.

What breath there is to be had will come through her nose, I swear, as I lock my lips around her tongue, this time furiously, grunting a low, deep animal groan of fury. Her body responds with her hands gripping my buttons in power, ripping my gray dress open to the expense of buttons and cloth, ripping the dress away from one of my breasts wobbling country girl free, latching onto it in the hardest sucking pull of our lives, evoking a sharp, high pitch yelp from me, opening my eyes in time to see her face anguished over with desperation to receive what pleasures my breast may have to offer, which is nourishment for her spirit of desire, and the phantom milk for a hungry soul in grieving.

She releases the breast—returning to my ready lips and tongue, while I pay the buttons of her white collar shirt alike in kind, ripping her shirt open, then unlatching her belt and pants, tearing her shirt down from her shoulders and latching a kiss onto the creamy white of them, causing her to crumble under the weight of it with a louder moan, taking her shirt the rest of the way down and off, then pulling her pants down to expose her pink underwear cloth. I drop to my knees immediately for the zippers on her boots, unzipping them both, then taking them off one by one. Then her pants, her faded jeans are made easy work of, tossed away as I stand back up, my dress open down to the waist, her holding me tight in her white bra and un-matching pink underwear.

Then she slides my dress down from my shoulders, exposing the gargantuan, swinging breasts and nipples, grabbing me in a most bosomy hug, mashing our breasts together hard, the flesh squished up to a mighty cleavage against her bra, while she bestows another strong kiss on me, breathing, grunting from the energy built up and released from deep inside. She grabs both my fleshy buttocks, still hidden behind the underwear cloth, carrying me to the plush sofa nearby.

"I want you to sit on top of me," she says, taking her bra off, "so I can watch you when it happens," she says, sliding her pink underwear down and away. In full nakedness she stands, sliding my underwear away quickly, taking a last and quick taste of my other nipple, which twitches my body again. "So sensitive, aren't they," she says, tweaking them both once, making my entire body jerk once again from the lightning. Vera lays down on her back, guiding me as her bride down on top of her, where I slide onto where the center of these fires burn, both my gigantic breasts hanging free, obeying her sweet request of me, to place my own nipple into my mouth, and draw pleasure for her to see. She begs of me, to take this self service repeatedly, beseeching that I do it with passion, asking in desperate tone while I hold just one breast up to my mouth, pulling the nipple in deeply, hearing her lose control of the moan that was so pressed down in her body, hearing this moan tremble from the long, steady shaking I feel in her body, as it spasms from head to toe underneath me.

And when I open my eyes from this self pleasure, my body is as the tumbling, sliding of a mountain of snow in avalanche, triggered by the sight of her beautiful face twisted in the agony of reunion, shooting a single bolt of lightning through my body, stiffening me up as I straddle her, then sending waves of energy to every part of my spirit and beyond, while she sees my eyes roll back and my body shake, watching me from down and far away below.

64

We have all been abused in some way by others. It is the curse of sin. My mother would strip me naked when I was a little girl, then hold my head clamped between her legs and beat me like a dog. How many times over the years has the memory of this flashed me awake from a morning sleep? I lie here in respite, draped over the body of my guardian lady, in the warmth of my winter cottage. Breathing deeply on the edge of sleep, believing that she is watching us from the window of her bedroom in the mansion. The merest sliver, the vaguest hint of an echo, the slightest twinkling of this possibility snaps me awake like I've been poked with a hot knife. But sanity grants me mercy, allowing me to know that I am lying here on top of my Lady, safely protected from prying eyes out here in the country, too far away from the mansion for anybody to see into these windows without a pair of binoculars, which I don't think she has any access too.

Does she?

"Did you…"

I very nearly ask the question, almost disturbing Vera's sublime rest. Until I realize that yes, there are binoculars on this property, in the kitchen of this house. Safe from the prying hands of Miss Witchcraft.

"She's so soft spoken," Vera says.

The look I give her is a masterpiece of non-verbal communication.

"You wouldn't know," she says. "Because you won't give her a chance."

"Give her a chance to do what? To kill me?"

"She really is the sweetest, humblest person I've ever met besides you. Which is really strange, because she's tall and beautiful like all the supermodels. But without the supermodel attitude."

Tall and beautiful. Sweet and demure around other people. Sounds familiar.

I get up from my bed of blonde loveliness, my cushion of curves and cuteness uncovered, sliding back into my underwear.

"You're shaped just like her, you know. Same hips. Same small, curved waist. Same gigantic bosoms. Everything about her body reminds me of you. Her body parts are shaped just like yours. Only bigger."

The last thing I need to hear about is the naked body of a swamp demon. I resist breathing a sigh of strong irritation. Slipping back into my comfortable gray cloth dress. Going barefoot over to the white baby grand from the old farm house. In my vision, shades of color suddenly appear in the air above the piano wires, which I ignore as best I can, concentrating on the smooth, heavy bass notes that give life to the breezy forest of my memory, where the body of the woman in the woods lies sleeping in my dreams.

"Oh, boy," Vera says, still lying on the sofa, more comfortable naked than I am. "That one's special."

"Thank you."

"Did you just write that?"

Of course I did, wants to snap into the air like a whip, to nip a chip out of her skin. But I simply choose to let her question die rhetorically, concentrating on the orchestra come to life in the keys, as accompaniment to a cello that only I can hear, whose voice is also translated into this lovely grieving song. *The Breath of Life* is lonely and epic. A breezy lullaby for those in the Wilderness of Lost Hope, somewhere in the Valley of the Shadow of Death. At the melancholy keyboard, the wall of color captures Vera's voice and presence, to disperse it to where I can no longer tell if she is speaking. My cottage must surely dissolve away, I know, as it has done a thousand times before.

Around me is the source of melody in my spirit—neither the piano, nor the tranquility and solitude of wealth. But this is the summertime woods of Martin County, in the days after my mother's best friend lost her own battle with depression, by the remedy of pills and a glass of wine. I must spend as much time as I can away from the isolated farmhouse—to escape the visitation of death upon us, when the last hope we had of being normal was taken. *I don't want to hear anything else about Ms. Valerie,* she says, and I know not to mention her again. Today, in the summer of my 14th year, on a clear and balmy day in July, I am beckoned away from the lonely house, while mother is asleep in the bedroom. Since Valerie Kirkland died, it seems that mother sleeps almost all the time. Emerging from the room to eat or go to the bathroom, or to take a breath of fresh country air outside. Our harvest of watermelons has come and gone for another season. Our time in Mr. Shirley's old farmhouse secure for another year.

It seems that the closer I get to the woods beyond the empty melon field, the louder this song for piano and orchestra sings to me. *Rondo for a Sleeping Beauty*, this song is called, seeming to exist in 3D space, played in the piano's middle key, surrounded by the sound of a happy orchestra. But in the Heart of Memory, I see the happy melody dissolve into a mist, replaced by the somber voice of this winter cello I hear, the voice of depression which calls me from the house in the distance.

Thank God I can hear her. I have been lost a lot recently, in the strange flood of melodies that have called me from the walls and the woods, to the tune of wooden spoons and leather belts when I didn't answer. I have descended into pleading many times already over the months. Begging her to have mercy, telling her that maybe she should get my hearing checked, so I can hear her when she calls. Today, I turn and hurry away from the woods, back through the summer crop field of green, my old checkerboard cloth dress fluttering in the breeze, my long, black hair flowing in the wind. I am hardly apprehensive, this late summer afternoon, believing that it is time for me to peel potatoes for dinner.

I think that maybe, Mother and I will have a good time with one another today, though not a word will be spoken when we are eating. But hopes for the afternoon greeting are dashed upon a monstrous slap, which catches me in mid step and nearly knocks me over, which is saved only by her grabbing of a tuft of my hair with my ear, twisting it while she drags me into the house. The happy piano melody of my youth is drowned by the monstrous misery of future years, drowned in the music of middle age, played from the sea of winter white. From the breath of life which surrounds me, I see the 14 year old girl about to suffer a punishment of old, when she is stripped bare of clothing, and her legs are bound by her dead father's belt above the knee.

I see this waifish young girl, whose breasts are already too heavy for a lithe and elegant young frame, standing up but bent far over, her head trapped between her mother's legs, her buttocks being punished to red and spotted torment, the mother's big, strong hands possessed with power and toughness, from the lifetime of hard labor and turmoil. The years of this, the thirty some odd years of it, are pouring through strength in the woman's right arm, blazing power and heat to her hands in repeated whacks to her daughter's lower back and buttocks. And the pain is such that the little girl must push back against her mother's legs as hard as she can, burdened not just by the acid poured onto her lower back, but by that in her ears clamped as she tries to tear her head away.

But feeble strength must soon fade to weakness, as the girl gives in to the impossibility, the hard clamping of her mother's pioneer skirted legs around her head, and the hard clapping of her mother's hand against her skin. The woman stares down at her task, possessed, pounding away like a carpenter's hammer inspired, endeavoring to drive the truth home like the proverbial nail into wood. And the girl's screams have descended now, into that long, defeated wailing, as when weeping overtakes the soul in pain.

From somewhere in the distance, I hear the call of the lonely cello, morphing into the tone of a piano, diminishing the noise of violence and pain I see, until I can only hear *The Breath of Life* played on the piano, while the naked girl I see suffers in slow motion silence to me, her mother's face frozen in a display of controlled, merciless rage.

The call of this cello soon goes silent, and I can feel the return of my soul's orchestra, as it is played by the piano. As these piano notes display the closing voice, holding place where the orchestra would normally be, I see the mother and daughter begin to fade, as do the walls of poverty and disillusionment around them. My piano appears before me again in 3D space, the voice of an angel diminished to earthbound beauty, echoing in the clean, comfortable space that Vera and I are in.

65

*I*nside our cottage of dreams. Protected from the blinding wind and snow. I stand as a spirit catapulted from our reunion, my breasts hung low and exposed, with Mother Vera standing beside me in full, naked repose, holding my wrists together behind my back with one hand, while rubbing both my breasts feverishly with the other. Of this, she has learned how not to rub and squeeze for too long, lest she have to stop and hold me tight to keep me from falling over. As always, their profound sensitivity is paramount, to raise every nerve ending in my body to attention. My only relief, my only medicine for the pain of this plateau are her lips and tongue, which she provides only every few seconds or so to have mercy. The swing and wobble of my breasts from her rubbing and squeezing across them is almost more than I can easily endure, shaking my head often in denial, at how such profound pleasure can be possible. *"God and Holy Jesus,"* begins to penetrate the recesses of what rational thought I have left, which she can sense with expert ability.

Still holding my wrists together, she slides her hand down to the long, thin member strapped on, hanging down full in front of me, to lend powerful contrast to the curves they are strapped upon. The mere touch of this, the slightest movement of it against my groin sparks a twinge in my lower body which we both feel, making her understand now that I am ready. Vera helps me to understand of what needs she doth require—to have me over her knee in what she calls British Style, so that she can feel the palm of my hand, and then the back of a wooden hairbrush burn a bruise onto her bottom, part of what has burned in her for many weeks, since the passing of her best friend, and her best friend's daughter in fire.

In the cushioned comfort dining room, with plush towels over the high backed chair, I sit down with the motor of my body running, anguished inside to grieving that Vera will not rub my breasts and kiss me to the easy orgasm. Yes, for this I will make her suffer. In honor of the woman who raised me, for the phantom that lurks the mansion house nearby, I will burn Momma Vera's big bottom with fire.

Why must we do this in the cottage dining room? Why can't we go to the comfortable bed, to solace ourselves with loves? Because the myth of love without pain is dead. Vera understands that this agony is her required portion, what she has craved and put off these last nine weeks, distracted by the arrival of witchery born in the mud. In the mire of this secret perversion, Vera is burned, finally laying across my knee nearby the dining room table, laid naked across my lap, my phallic self tucked down between my legs in waiting.

Without mercy, without compromise, I raise my hand up toward the heavens, and bring it down hard to the skin of her naked backside, hearing her grunt once from the shock, feeling this travel through my phantom member to the core of who I am behind closed doors, making me close my eyes and hold my head back just once from the shudder we both feel deep inside. Again I raise my hand, in honor to our years of suffering and turmoil, in tribute to She Who Haunts My Memory, bringing the palm of my hand down to the same spot. Repeating this in slow, deliberate fashion seven times, on the same spot on her skin. I notice the poor woman having relaxed herself. Thinking that if she does not resist the pain that it will pass easily and harmlessly through. Oh, Vera. My lover! My mother! I will elicit a tormented scream from thee!

And I begin to incorporate a new tempo, to lay down the Barbara Jean rhythm to her skin, spanking her in the manner of a wayward child, to burn all hope of compassion and mercy away. A twinge of ecstasy unfamiliar, a brush of the sadistic, a taste of this forbidden fright rings a chime in my body, the power of causing pain, the pleasure received from the giving, the touch of breathless thrill from the switching around, the delightful sting in the palm of my calloused hands, hands made rough by the years of hard labor and pain. Of this pain, I sacrifice the palm of my hand to, to watch her begin to squirm and breathe, to watch the grown woman draped naked over my lap have to grab my leg with one hand and the chair leg with the other, to weather a storm she has not felt in many years—breathing, groaning, beginning to bellow like a Durham cattle in heat, wondering if she can suffer the greater part of the trauma to come.

But to give her a chance, the smallest breath of air, I switch to the unbruised side, and begin to wail the tar out of it anew, as if suddenly angered, slamming a hard string of clap slap slapping to her big bottom, to help her understand that playtime is over, and she is about to be brought to tears by what I'm going to do. "Take some deep breaths," I say. Listening to her oblige, gladly thankful for the rest between flames of fire.

My mother understood that a hand spanking can only go so far. A hand spanking is primarily perversion anyway. Born from the burning of blue and black fire—the fires of violence and deviance. Mostly good for the pain of humiliation it causes, especially when done over the top of a dress or a skirt or a pair of jeans. But the hand's patience wears thin, as the tolerance for pain subsides, and the fire upon the buttocks begins to bite back. My hand is burning good. Just enough to signal the end of this phase, and the beginning of a newer and a hotter part of Hell on Earth.

But I am the demon in this part of the Underworld, sent to cause unearthly suffering. By natural instinct, unnaturally gained from infancy through my 21st year, I reach down to the floor beside the chair, picking up the hairbrush from nearby her head, drawing further strength and energy from her nervous glance. She rubs my leg firmly, gripping it tighter, taking another deep, noisy breath. On the nearest, sorest side, I place the cold wood of my mother's hairbrush against Vera's buttock.

Oh, Dear Lady, how you stiffen against the wind! The cold, icy wind of Truth that touches your skin so gently, to such a forlorn and forsaken future! And I am shocked, by the loudness of the whacking wood on her skin, and the corresponding loudness of her fervent scream. "Oh my God," she says. "Oh, my *God* that hurts," which I don't doubt, when something whammed against the skin marks it the color of violence so quickly. Through the genuine shock, I push forward to a second blow, raising a white patch in the red skin, feeling the power of her second yell flutter my Heart, to call me to the required end of what must be, which is the beat this woman's buttocks to injury. "Relax your bottom," I tell her. Unable to sound any other way but sad. Defeated by the oppression of our lives, and the suppression of joy in our spirit. I bring the third blow down and around, onto the white patch raised, which causes her to squirm and scream again, shaking her head, moving around as if she might get up. But I hold her tight, telling her sharply, "you need to breathe and lay still. Lay still! Relax your bottom and don't move. Lie still and let the pain come out through your voice."

And this, she agrees to with the nod of her head, as I quickly bring the fourth and hardest blow to her skin, welted and deep red already. This is the loudest and most pitiful of the four screams, the one of acceptance and realization, that there is no salvation, and no deliverance from suffering. The fifth blow to her buttock is the beginning of a blister, and a powerful trembling scream and shaking of her head, and the word *please* echoed quickly at the end. "Relax your bottom," I say. Unmercifully.

The sixth. Seventh. Eighth. The ninth blow sees the end of a long and loud scream for mercy, and finally a reduction to sobbing, each new series of sobs begun by the word *please,* as I inspect the powerful, blistered welt raised, and the small, bloody cut on her bruised skin. But the beginning of injury is the way forward. Upon this hard and bloodied patch of skin I proceed. Revealing the hairbrush repeatedly on the blistered skin and around it. On the other buttock. On the backs of her thighs. Continuously for several minutes, marveling at the ferocity of tears and wailing that can pour from the spirit of a woman in pain.

She has taken to kicking her legs to endure the agony, the pain of a backside with patches of burned, white skin inside deep red and blue bruises, with one bleeding, L-shaped cut that I pound every so often with the most strength I have left, which seems to shatter all her remaining control every time, to start a new barrage of gruff, pathetic wails and screams. The screams soon morph out completely, replaced only by the long, banshee noise of eternal torment, which draws the spirits in from far and wide, to see how it is that a grown woman is made to suffer as a child over her mother's knee, to see this woman tortured, until she is brought down to nothing.

When the third part of this century is passed. When the threshold of three hundred is crossed and left behind, I am now sickened with regret for what I have done, as I gauge the manner of welts, dark bruises and blood on her skin, and every inch of suffering caused by the blue and black fire.

66

The crying woman barely notices the hairbrush returned to the floor. Our quiet is disturbed only by the sound of her sniffing now, the thankfulness that the worst of this is over. I too, am glad. Caressing her back, and the parts of her legs and bottom not bruised to death. The L-shaped spot of red, the cut is painful to behold, reminding me of what I saw in the mirror many times over the years when I looked at my own naked hips in the mirror. The raised lump of skin nearby it is very hard to the touch, reminding me of what I have felt on my own backside, and on my mother's when I was nineteen, twenty and twenty one.

Every so often, the lust and depression would go deeper into the recesses of Barbara Jean's (my mother's) mind, until the pain was so great that despair was her only road back to sanity. And while there are some who take to drinking of pills or cutting, or even the open end of a gun barrel, my mother's remedy for the pain was corporal. And many times, she was simply too broken, too burdened under childhood regret and sorrow to be angry. It is those rare times when she would approach me with tenderness, the tenderness caused by a broken spirit, where her entire affect was pure misery.

She had appeared to me in my dreams one of these times, where I saw her entire being as a mist of sorrow. Often when she was under this burden, she needed to fuel the agony of her youth revisited, boldly guiding me through to the other side of our dynamic, which was her affinity for masochism. At least a dozen times in the last two years we were together, I was admonished to 'beat her like I meant it,' which I knew I had to do, if I wanted to avoid a terrible beating myself. These were awkward, intimate sessions. Often with us closed up in the tiny bathroom, with my father's hard, leather belt tight around her thighs, and her hands bound tight in front of her with stockings. I was commissioned, at these times, to 'wail the tar' out of her big backside (more ample than Vera's or my own), to beat her black and blue, until I had taken out all of my feeble rage on the skin of her behind. Sometimes, the tiny room would be alive with her screams as I stood behind her and twisted her nipples as hard as I could, afraid that if I showed mercy, it would go bad for me. Whether I was slapping her in the face, twisting her ear or pulling her hair. Whether I was twisting the skin on her sides or choking her with the belt. Whether I was whipping her with this same belt, or was on top of her biting her breasts, or welting her skin with a paddle, a cane or birch rod, I always did it with as much controlled fury as I could—driven as much by fear as something deeply twisted. Even when pushing something deep into her rectum, I learned to do it without mercy. Standing behind her. The long banana fruit tucked between my legs, holding it secure by one hand. Slid far into her backside as she yelled a Baba Yaga shriek from the pain. Relaxing, both of us holding still, in the bedroom or the tiny bathroom in front of the sink. Rubbing herself feverishly in front, until the second shriek was from the agony of pleasure rather than pain. The wave of unendurable pleasure that shakes the fat of her backside when it happens. That convulses and trembles her body.

Lie down, Mother Vera. On the cold, unforgiving hardness of the dining room table. Take the final portion of the punishment you require. Here, there is no kissing. No caressing. No drinking from the nipple. Lie still on your back, Dear Mother. Open your legs wide, to receive the reward that is due. To receive your recompense overdue. Feel the length of that which pertaineth to a man. Feel it slide deep into the front of you, all the way up towards your womb. Open your eyes, Mother Vera. Gauge the look of satisfaction. The dominance, the control in my eyes. The sadism in my expression. Your desire is swollen around the phallus, Dear Woman. Though you are in too much pain from the paddling to squirm. To much discomfort to beg and moan. Relax, Mother Vera. Enjoy the visual. The contrast of these gigantic breasts—the deep, inward waist curve. The widened hips of a woman of forty one. The feminine form, sliding a big member up inside you. Holding it there.

Now, watch me take one of my breasts into my mouth. Not for your pleasure. But for mine. It sends a spark to my groin. Now, feel me slide it out of you. All the way out. Holding it with my hand, tapping it gently against your front. Of this, the moan does come, does it not? And along with it, the tell tale squirm. And now, the spittle. Yes. A long, vulgar spit fallen from my mouth. Down to the front of where it is we must go. I see your breathing, Mother Vera. You can't hide it from me. But I slide the tip of it back into yourfront. Is not what you want. Its not what we want.

Now, your greedy fingers fumble at it. Taking hold of it, putting the tip of it at your rectum. I know, Mother. And of this, I do. Pushing it in. The head of my perversion slips in. Out. Sliding so undecidely in. Our dinner is served, Dear Woman. Deviance is served hot, on the cold dining room table. Push it. Push it. Push it all the way in.

Your legs go up. Your eyes go closed. Your faced goes anguished. Your teeth go grit, from the pushed in spit in your bottom. The length of myself strapped on, stretched in. Every push and pull, every bang in and out, pushes you to another level of shock and disbelief. How is it that the pleasure of this act, Dear Woman, hath medicated every flash of pain away? Don't worry, Dear Woman. I know what to do. Feel the hard and fast pounding of this. Do you see my long, heavy breasts shake from the pounding of this? But I am in trouble. Because if I pound much longer, you're going to see me shake and tremble from it.

No. I will not let that happen yet. This, the frustrated stopping and starting again, Mother Vera. You wonder, where hath I learned such agonizing rhythm, such pleasure of torture given? To pound you up the rectum as if it were the other part of you? As if it were normal? Is this the great secret you have kept hidden even from yourself all these years? Is this because of what was done to you when your husband was killed? Is this because of the anal raping you suffered? Have you craved the feeling of this in your backside—the pressure that will not subside? The pressure that pushes hard against the sides, and slides up and down the tract of the forbidden?

And I can no longer hold it, Mother. Though I try to hold it back, watch my tits tremble. Watch my hips twitch and shake. Watch me reposition myself. Readjusting myself for balance. Every push I make into you, every slam into the back of you shoots a tingling into me now, and I can no longer stop the fevered pushing. I have to push it into you this hard. This fast. I have to slam it home. Because of what it has already done to me. I have to do this, despite whatever discomfort it does to thee.

But I don't know, do I, Mother Vera? I don't realize what the steady pounding is doing to you. I don't realize what feelings, what memories what desires, what fantasies it blazes onto the theater of your mind, do I? It is full on now, Mother. Because the lightning begs to shoot through my groin again. So now, brave the thought that has tormented you these last weeks, of the busen breasted, beautiful brunette banshee at the mansion house, standing naked over you as I, her clitoris stiff and swollen to the 5th degree [five inches], her end of the world face and body tensed into an orgasm that only she could endure. The image of this woman on top of me, pinning my arms as I scream is too much for you, inciting the wave you felt in your groin the night she arrived, and I hear you cry out to God from this raping, causing me to open my eyes in time to see the water gush from your front, in a clear, powerful jet stream, and then several times more as I hold myself still inside your rectum, each fountain of water corresponding to a quick, powerful scream.

*B*eauty walks the field of snow. Overwhelmed by the power of her calling, and the flood of a lifetime of memories born. Gazing across the prairie field, in awe of revelation energy. The burden of these last two months revealed. Beautiful lips of a mature, sensual woman. Partially open in the cold. Her breath drifting as a fog from lungs filled with life. With death.

Beauty gazes the field of winter white. Understanding the power of hatred. Breathing in the sigh, the breath of new life. Suffering the wave of relief. The release of a profound warmth from the top of her head, to the boots at the bottom of midnight blue. Eyes of winter gray. Piercing vision, misted by a well of sorrow and gratitude. Wobbly. The gray world around her in a swoon. Dropping to her knees in the snow. Enduring the wave of harsh, winter wind. Weighted down by a voice. A wailing, tragic voice of pleasure and pain. The voice of her blonde benefactor, hidden away in the gray cottage. Unhidden from ears of desperation. One of six senses in tow. The agony, the ecstasy of the forbidden.

Leave your room, her mind had said. Follow the woman to the gray house. Hide thyself behind the Great Rose Garden. Go into the forest grove nearby. Lurk. Press thyself against the walls of secret, until you feel it happen to their bodies. The feeling will devastate their bodies. The crying. The screaming. Their suffering will be great. Hear the blonde woman's cry for mercy. Receive her voice into your body. Into the soul of who you are. Of what you are.

Now, hurry away. Go thou to the open prairie field behind the mansion. See the rising, the resurrection of another voice in your mind. In your heart. It is the voice of a mountain girl. The child of an Hume and Evelyn Daniels. The voice of a little girl. Feel the touch of the little girl's icy hand at the small of your back. Now, see the scars. The blood of open welts on the little girl's back. Watch the winter welts heal. See the little girl who plays in the mountain snow. Suffer this revelation now, as you feel the icy snow on the little girl's cold hands. Feel the snow on your hands, Mountain Girl.

Beauty gazes the snowy wilderness plain. Blinking against the wind. Feeling the tears flow in the icy cold.

In your hazy vision, see the Mountain Girl grown. Grown into a young woman. Bound and gagged by Evelyn Daniels. Told that she will never marry. That Evelyn will see the young woman dead first. Bound. Gagged. Beaten for three days. The ropes. The ropes are too tight on the woman's wrists. Behind her back. The smell of blood and urine permeates the young woman's nostrils. There is no hope but to endure the beatings. To pray for mercy from the Almighty God.

Beauty surveys the field of snow. Lost in the vision of escape. The escaping of a young woman, in the fall of a winter's night. Escape into the arms of False Hope. The embrace of delusion and despair.

The young woman has a husband now. She is with child. From the Blue Ridge Mountains of Virginia. To the forests and fields of Eastern North Carolina. The woman is alive with hope. Loving her husband. Praying for a son for him to love.

But now, the young husband is dead. And the thing inside her begins to move. Doubling the woman over in pain. In the hospital, the thing pushes its way out of her. The woman's voice splits the air in screaming, as the child splits her body in two. The child comes into the world desolate.

In the isolated farmhouse, Desolation grows. A widow. And her daughter. A daughter that the widow hates. That she despises. Carmen. Angelina. Elizabeth. Coletti.

Now, breathe the breath of life, O Barbara Jean. Rendezvous to thine self again, Mother.

In the cold, winter wind.

The smell of death is sickly sweet. It permeates my nostrils in my dreams, and into the morning hour of summer. The snows of discontent, the icy winds of her resurrection are long gone, having already been taken up into the skies many months ago, where they coalesced into the clouds of Spring. And these fervent rains of renewal had watered the fertile ground, to bring forth the canopy and carpet of green, to color the forests and fields of our North Carolina summer. The heat of August rises into the hazy skies over the prairie green, where they are overtaken by cool winds that blow in secret, to conceal our colorful landscape in a slow, steady swirling of clouds that threaten high above, before they declare mercy, and let the rays of Summer sunlight through.

This is the ninth month of her arrival. Her time in our world has grown and developed itself to a tragic permanence. So much that Vera's judgment has seen fit to lapse again and again. Peaking back in July, in the cool of the evening day, underneath the crescent Prairie Moon. This was when I looked outside this bay window that faces our big mansion, and I saw Vera Evans, *arm in arm* with the woman who looks like Barbara Jean Coletti. Walking down the asphalt road, then across the Great Lawn towards the house. Death and Hell may as well have been outside my cottage that day, because that's how badly my nerves were shattered. But Vera had mercy, as Fate had touched what judgment she had left, and she had come into the house alone, while that woman waited politely outside. It didn't take long, before she came to her senses, and remembered who it was she was talking to.

She's such a beautiful person, Elizabeth. She wants to meet you so much.

I said no, I remember saying through clenched teeth. *You can beat me until there's no blood left in me but I will not see her.* When Vera sighed and looked at me with judging eyes, I had asked her *what's wrong with you?* And of course, she responded—

I was about to ask you the same thing. And then Vera had the nerve to say *she asked me to invite you to dinner. She cooked a very special meal.* I had put both my hands over my mouth, and stifled the most genuine laugh I'd felt in a long time. *She's been with us a long time now, Elizabeth. Don't you think I know her?* I've been with her for a lifetime, Mother Vera. Don't you think *I* know her?

The smell of Death is sickly sweet. It fills my lungs with dread and warning, as I try to kick in my morning bed, so that I can wake up from the dream of being smothered to death. The mercy of God intervenes, sending the angel to lift this phantom pillow from my face, sending the demon pressed down on me back into the shadows. I take this welcome breath of fresh air, sitting up in the bed as fast as I can, with one last fleeting taste of pillow linen in my mouth, and the whiff of Death itself in my nostrils.

Oh, how I wish I could spend time in the Rose Garden today, to breathe their sweet perfume, the scent of Hope and Life itself. But this will be the first summer since the mansion was finished three years ago, that I will not stroll the grounds to the very far edges, nor will I touch and care for the petal of a single rose flower. I only have a heart and mind for melody this summer. Trifles and chamber pieces, dominated by my piano, of course, including a piano quintet called *The Rose Garden,* where a cello makes a slow and dramatic walk alone, before being rejoined by the piano, two violins and double base. I entertain the finale to this 'Rose Quintet,' while I step outside the breezy front door to the walkway, the only place on this entire grand property I have the courage left to go.

Most likely, I'll circle around to the back of the house by the small forest grove, containing my little walk to the back patio, staring off towards the flowers of the blooming rose garden, where I have seen Vera and the woman walking together. Hiding behind the safety of the kitchen window, where I could watch Vera's adulterous rendezvous undisturbed. Have they kissed yet in the evening day? Has Vera squeezed a hug from the woman's gigantic breasts? This, I do not know. Have they pushed each other's kitty kats together and peed down each other's leg, while they each sucked one of the woman's big nipples? I don't know. What I do know is that Vera's claims of innocence during the woman's soothing, relaxing massages are likely not as innocent as she would lead me to believe. Yes, she's already admitted to giving the woman full bodied back massages, claiming she's never touched the rest of her, except for her thighs and legs. And feet. And arms. *I swear to you,* Vera said, that I've never touched her breasts or her bottom. And even when she said it, I conceded that she was lying, feeling totally sorry for her, that whatever she has done with this woman in the name of 'nursing,' she most certainly could not help, and I know that she will tell me the truth when she's ready.

And as I look across this little back lawn towards the Rose Garden and the North side, the near side of the mansion, I wonder whether or not this is another 'morning after' in Vera's bed chamber. I don't know what part of the woods this woman came from, or how she got here, but I would swear before God in Heaven on what I believe, that this extraordinarily beautiful, mature woman is the woman who gave birth to me forty one years ago. And because I know this woman better than I know myself, I knew that Vera was going to give in to her even before she did. She doesn't have to say anything because I know already. It is a byproduct of my insanity, that I see things. I know things.

And as hard as I try not to know it, the thought of them together burns inside my brain without ceasing, since about two months ago in July, when Vera told me that she wanted to meet me. The dinner they had that night had the atmosphere of a date, complete with glasses of red wine, which Vera takes before bed every night anyway, but which Barbara Jean Coletti never touched in her former life.

She didn't need the touch of alcohol that hot, humid summer afternoon.

I thought I told you I didn't want you leaving this house when I'm gone.

But I didn't, I say. Lying with conviction. With passion. *I swear to God and Jesus I didn't.*

You're always swearing lies to God and Jesus.

But I'm not lying.

I gave the woman in the taxi twenty dollars at the end of the road. Told her to wait for me while I walked back. I hid on the side of the house by the clothesline. I wasn't there five minutes before I saw you jiggling your big titties on the back porch, and wiggling your fat ass across the back yard towards those woods. And I watched you the whole time. I watched you disappear in the woods. Went in there to straddle a log, didn't you?

No, Momma.

Found a dirty magazine somewhere out there in the woods, didn't you? Saw a woman sucking on another woman's cock, I bet.

No, Maam. I wouldn't look at something like that even if I found it.

I bet. Was a naked woman alone on her stomach, with her hands underneath her with piss on the sheets...

No, Maam. Oh Lord Jesus, no.

You go out there to take your clothes off and pray to the Devil, don't you?

Momma...

It doesn't matter what you went there for. What matters is that you disobeyed me.

The types of Fear are many. And uniquely distinguished.

Now go to your room. And I don't want to see you again until tomorrow morning.

Yes Maam.

*E*ven at 16, I already know to turn and glide away on a current of the utmost respect. It lowers your chances of being beaten. Maybe If I give respect, I'll get it in return.

Or maybe not.

I walk now, 16 year old hips from the kitchen to the living room, hips bubbled and spread already under my country skirt, as tight and rounded as the buttocks of a white mare. These buttocks rest alone, underneath me, underneath Fear and Disillusionment, in the comfort cushioned chair of my bedroom.

I sit here. Lost in bewilderment and apprehension. Wondering how it is that I went from hope to despair so quickly. And I was blindsided by this one, which is not normal for me, usually being able to sense the rise and fall of tension in this house like a barometer. But this time I...

Oh.

This is one of those rare times. When her mood is adversely affected by her hatred for me. She is so proud of herself for having caught me going to the woods, that she can hardly contain her joy. So pleased for having found another reason to punish me. Even now, she sits at the kitchen table with her eyes shut, leaning against her closed hands, her beautiful lips pressed tight against them. Understanding that the only satisfaction in life is to perform thy calling. For whatever it is I have done by being born, by living in her house these 16 years, I am going to pay for it in tears and blood, and a healthy dose of fear and sorrow.

I sit here. Unable to lose myself in the melody that caused all this, that drew me from the house to the woods to find the full expression of it. A sprightly, and fully Rossinian piano concerto, as if the Crown Prince of Melody could have ever bothered himself with such pedantry, inspired though it may be. Pure rhythm and melody, colored by Mozartian winds, but lifted and supported by heavy basses, above where the most beautiful and unique piano melody expresses itself in laughter and pain. The piano sings Italian Opera in this piece, as if Bel Canto were unusual in my composition, which it most certainly is not. Not since I heard the overture to *The Barber of Seville* back when I was fourteen years old, which seemed to light up every Mozartian inspiration with something new, until already my concertos sound like inspired Rossini channeled through Mozartian form. But already, my piano concertos threaten to break down typical sonata form (where a single theme is introduced and then developed and resolved). Song-like melodies tend to disturb my composing so much, that I do very little developing of any phrase, but rather introduce many new themes in succession, so that the effect is irresistible for me to listen to in my head. My mind plays music like a live orchestra, perfectly balanced as I see fit, adding and removing instruments to achieve a desired affect. And often, this happens on its own, until the perfect scoring is there to express the melody. And I noticed that with this concerto, the Mozartian winds are more muted than usual, where the overall affect is smoother and heavier than both Mozart and early Rossini, but having their same fire of delightful rhythm and melody. Modern Classical music, if there really is such a thing, because there is truly nothing classical about most so-called modern music I've heard. Though at 16, what have I really heard, except what blares at me from inside my own head? What have I heard in life? What do I know? I know that tomorrow, I will eat like a pig, because tonight, I am going to bed without any supper.

In the Heart of Memory. In the fading light of a setting sun. In the fading light of a world beyond the sunset, I am resigned to a world of color and sound, where I have found the spirited piano concerto, to help sing and soothe my fears away. Though I do not know whether I will be beaten tonight, or tomorrow or three days from now, the Spirit of Fear becomes my most treasured companion, to add a spark of life to the finale to this concerto, which is a rondo for piano and orchestra like no other, with flashes of lightning that appear throughout the rolling thunder of rhythm and melody. Elizabeth disappears when music such as this is formed. My name is Carmen Coletti, in the spirit of Antonio Amadeus in the country. This is the Italian Girl in Carolina born, the peak of my youthful composition, where the strains of eschatology begin, and my end-of-the-world voice in music comes in. I lose myself in the world of color and sound, hearing the piece, seeing the piece again and again as the hours pass, committing itself to my memory without effort, only my ninth formal piano concerto, to join the many other single movements and fragments for piano and orchestra I have written.

My memory for music is exponential. Photographic to the last detail and beyond, so that I can access music I have composed years before, being able to see it for study and reference, oftentimes amazed at how feeble and primitive, or how monumentally powerful an old composition can be. Of the more than 1700 pieces I have scratched to life [age 41], I can clearly see that over 400 of them might be remembered forever, distributed across every known genre, perhaps even considered great works across the landscape of classical music. Concerto form dominates the structure of my composition, even to writing a sonata for a solo instrument, as the orchestra I hear is often transcribed into whatever song they sing.

Oh, how I long for a piano to play! Or even a clumsy cello to tame! But I satisfy this urge to play in pure composition [at 16], writing very small and precise amateur, unlearned notation, to guarantee space in which to write, making sure she buys me plenty of notebooks to write in. Bible verses and poetry, she believes—with the occasional nonsensical dots and dashes, written in such a way as to make her eyes glass over with confusion, kept in these same few notebooks handy for when she is nosy, daring not to write a single word about her or myself that she can understand, my favorite decoy being my notebook where every verse in the New Testament where Christ the Lord is speaking I have written and archived for my protection. The notebooks that contain my music are hidden underneath and behind my dresser, sometimes for weeks until I can find the perfect window in time to crawl through, where I can reach underneath the house to where my music is wrapped in three layers of black plastic bags, underneath the floor of my bedroom.

I sit in the comfortable armchair, above where the melodies are hidden in the color of night, in the fall of darkness across the forests and fields of night. I am lucky that she hardly ever steps foot in my bedroom, leaving me alone to listen to my radio well into the night before bed. For what could it possibly matter what I was doing anyway, being that it is in the throes of hunger, having had to smell her baking ham and boiling collard greens and baking sweet potatoes for my benefit. Oh, how I wish to God she would come into the room with a compassion plate, so that at least I can ease the torture of this hunger before I am beaten!

The hours slow down to a crawl. Where I am forced to await the arrival of the giant planet from beyond, sent by God to devastate my world to oblivion. The arrival of Truth and Cataclysm. My mind assigns every sound to a slow motion dream, as I listen to her mill around the kitchen, cooking and eating the dinner she knows I can't have. An eternity later, the clanging of dishes is loud in and around the sink, as she has even taken to the after dinner chores herself. Every footstep is a sublime reckoning. Drifting ice cold warning through the walls that separate us, as she goes about her comfortable, complacent country routine, which is a favorite TV show, then a journey back and forth across the floor, every pass making me hold my breath, until finally I hear the noisy bathing water begin. The tension and fear lose their hold on my body, and I close my eyes in a grand sigh of relief, knowing that she is about to forget about me for at least another hour. Every splash of water is a divine reprieve, pushing me further and further away from fear and dread, believing now in God's mercy, and the arrival of a Divine Reprieve. My punishment is to go to bed without supper, which I will do gladly, even though suddenly I am more hungry and thirsty than ever. But I know better than to even think about touching the doorknob, or whispering a word loud enough for her to hear.

And when finally, the last of the bathwater is come and gone, and the last kitchen footstep is taken, and the last trek past the outside of my door is done, when her bedroom door clicks shut past the ten o' clock hour, I thank God for the flash of so-called good luck, that I will not have to go to bed with my entire body itching from welts, and spots of blood on the inside of my nightgown. I spend the entire night in the world of sound and color, observing the lightning storm fashioned as a concerto, seeing it in my dreams through the night, believing it to be the beginnings of something special in my music, which can produce apprehension, and can call forth the spirits of Fear and Dread. I commune with the spirits of Rhythm and Melody through the night, at a piano in the woods beyond the crop field, breezing effortlessly through the opening allegro, then the Italian andante, then at last the rondo brilliante, where I can hear the end of the age echoed around me, from an orchestra I cannot see, but whose playing is more perfect than which might be possible. I hear the Players of Orchestra's Light, the Orchestra's Light Players, blazing away after my piano is finished, even though I suddenly cannot see the forest around me anymore, and I'm finding it very hard to breathe. At once, my tranquil scene goes dark, and my breath is taken, though the conclusion to my concerto blazes itself out in a final blast of energy.

In the sudden darkness around me, I am held immobile on my back, wishing to call out to my phantom players to help me, from the demon spirit that seeks to push the breath from my lungs and will not let me breathe in. And I suddenly cry out to God in my soul, as my body begins to burn from lack of air, being granted mercy when the weight on top of me begins to shift, allowing one to turn my head under the pillow just enough to catch a precious breath, and a glimpse of the summer morning light in my bedroom. The heavy weight on top of me lifts suddenly, then the smothering pillow is tossed away, to reveal the sight of my mother sitting on top of me nude in my morning bed, my arms pinned underneath the covers. She sits there for a moment, bent over slightly, her breasts wobbling as she shifts her weight, pinning my arms motionless under her strong legs and the bed sheet over me. The look on her face is somber and serpentine, her eyes glistening winter gray in the morning light.

Even in the midst of a screaming trauma, I am acutely aware that this woman's beauty is as uncompromising as her need for punishment; as overwhelming as a hurricane at sea. Her black hair is pinned up from her face of perfect features, enhanced by the color of her eyes, which are pale gray and piercing. The long, pearl white neck rises elegantly above strong, creamy white shoulders, from which arms of great feminine strength and power are grown. And hung from the front of this powerful chest are the Olympus Mons, two of the world's greatest breasts, formed as the macrocosm of God's intention for the feminine form, his glory exaggerated upon a woman, which would cause only awe and wonder. Breasts that can only be described as gargantuan, the Busen, the Olympian, breasts hung down and around, where areolas and nipples are placed perfectly out front, to give the classic nursing breast form, breasts that draw energy from deep inside any who might observe them, because of the gigantic size; the classic, wineskin shape, and the large nipples in front that stare. This earth goddess, this fallen angel looks away from me for but a moment, reaching behind her on the bed, showing a roll of duct tape to me. She rips a piece from the roll, tearing it with her teeth, then quickly presses it over my mouth, securing it, saying *so you want to play nasty in the woods*, tossing the roll of tape to the side. *I don't want to play nasty in the woods*, is the pathetic sound I make muffled under the tape, while she slides forward onto my body. She takes one of her gigantic breasts in her hand, guiding the nipple, the center of life, the nourishment of her deviant mind, guiding it to my nose. And I feel the rest of the warm, heavy flesh fall and press to my face, while she holds me down tight under the cover.

I am a figure shrouded in white, in the burial cloth of my 16th year, pressed to smothering by the breast that once suckled me to life, which will now suckle the breath of life from me. With every particle of strength, I try to turn over, to pull my arms out from under the sheet, but to no avail. I can only jerk and kick under the sheet, and shake my head under my mother's great breast, as she lies nude and straddled heavy on top of me. As to the feeling that permeates to her soul, as to the veil of water that spreads through the sheet to my nightgown, as to the depth of feeling channeled to her body from mine, of this, I do not know. As to the fervent pressing of herself down upon the watered sheet, of this, I do not know. *Pulled it out of me,* she says. *Pissy little bitch. Pulled the piss out of me. Witch.* And my soul cries out to God again, to grant me a reprieve from Death. My nostrils breathe in the cool breath of life, which this most certainly is, knowing that I was a second from drifting, then perhaps only a few minutes from death.

In the Heart of Memory. From the breathless waking dream I emerge, finding myself outside my gray brick house, staring at the Great Rose Garden nearby, and at the window of her bedroom, in the mansion a good distance away.

*T*he lazy days of August loom heavy over our mansion home, and the entire property of *Amherst Lake*, beneath the hazy skies over the prairie green.

Wash yourself, Mother had said, when the smothering punishment was done. *Wash these sheets, and go hang 'em on the line.* She told me this under the umbrella of shame, which she had tried to hide from me, climbing off me slowly, still fully nude, that Amazonian body exposed, the incredible backside turned to me as she walked defeatedly out of the room. I am a quarter of a century removed from that day. The same day she

315

noticed me at the clothesline hanging out these same sheets, and became enraged at what she saw that had blossomed in me, that I was the younger version of herself nearly grown. I remember the look on her face when she burst from the screen door, nearly running across the porch and down the steps to the back yard, as if she were chasing a wayward dog from muddying her clean linen. I am totally bewildered as she runs toward me, watching her haul her big, beautiful hand back as she takes the last steps toward me. The slap I received that day, at that moment—was a benchmark. A checkpoint along the road of truth. She brings her hand from the far end of the pendulum swing, down and around, slapping me with a boxer's might, rattling what few brains I have, startling me with a flash of lavender light to my brain, which proceeds to send me flying to the side, stumbling, struggling to stay on my feet. I gather my balance and my wits, turning quickly to look at her in a hurt, angry bewilderment, allowing the 'what did you hit me for' shock to overcome my being, while the tear rolls down my face to her satisfaction. She takes a deep breath, relaxing her angry expression to a satisfied calm (on the edge of being pleased with herself), then turning to leave me there in confusion and emotional devastation, holding my face, looking after her for even the slightest hint of an explanation—getting only the loud clack of the screen door shut when she goes back into the house.

The soft clack of my sliding screen door obscures my lonely vision, so that clarity is only an illusion. The Rose Quintet has come and gone, waiting in the archives for me to find it and write it down. There are enough trifles in my imagination to keep me writing for the rest of my life. I think that later this afternoon, when the sun slides down toward the western gate, I'll see what this piece sounds like on the piano. But I'll only play the piano part as it exists in my mind, and let the string quartet languish alone, (two violins, cello and double base with no viola), invisible in the space around me and the piano. I miss the smooth, velvety sound from the piano in the mansion, and the concert house echo present in the big livingroom around it. It seems that every sound is carried and echoed throughout the grand, American Gothic, even those of my own footsteps on the tile and hardwood floors. I imagine that the low heels of whatever shoes *she* is wearing echo the same reverb of fascination. And no, Mother Vera, I will not play the piano in that house for her. Not now. Not ever. I may as well admit it to myself. To just go ahead and come to terms with what I know.

Things have changed.

In every life, there are emotional routines. Balances and counterbalances, rituals that are created of their own accord, so that we don't ever realize it is a routine until it is broken. And for Vera and me, there have been patterns developed between us over the years, and across the passing of every season. The summer months were once beyond special for me, as I could be coaxed off these grounds for some long trip or another. Whether it be the swaying palm trees and crystal blue waters of Key West, and a stroll along the soft, powdery white sand beaches, or to northern Arizona, to see what the Colorado River supposedly hath done to the ground all by itself. (No, it did not). Grand Canyon National Park calls to me every summer, until I think the *Grand Canyon Sonata* will have to finally be written, probably this October I'll bet, in the heat of Indian Summer. And I know that writing about my summer trip in three part song is the closest I'll get to it this year. Because things have changed. And the sad part about it is she thinks I'm stupid. And maybe I am, but I'm still not brain dead enough to not know that even though they may not have touched from the waist down, the two of them are carrying on one of the hottest titty relationships in the world outside of a maternity ward. Nipple to nipple, tit to tit, I know what I know, and breast sucking is it. I know because the heat that once blazed between us is not quite there anymore, unless waist down touching is involved. How can I compete with the gigantic breasts of such a beautiful older woman?

For ten years, Vera has been the older woman to me. Forty eight to my forty one, just old enough to brush the edges of the modern Mother Daughter Dynamic, as I am much younger than forty one in how I feel. I'm too doggone scared of everything to take care of myself. And where people are concerned? Out of the question. But this woman is easily ten years older than Vera. Ten years taller and stronger in her maturity, made more irresistible by the quiet strength, and the humble, elegant demurity. There is a queen-like power to this woman's presence, which I know has pulled Vera in like the Sun's gravity and burned her up— down to the core of her mind, body and spirit.

There are patterns in life, yes. Routines. By these, we measure what changes have come, whether they be good. Or whether they be evil.

ve.

She says her name is Eve.

Typical.

And what else would it be? Barbara Jean? Would she be stupid enough to take the mask off to her benefactor? If Vera suspected for one second that this woman was really my mother, feathers would fly in that house like black and white hens in a coop. Fur would fly like black and white cats on Halloween. Because as passionate, as compassionate as Vera is about nursing those in need, I have seen her doubled over in pain enough from what she knows about my childhood, I have seen her cry enough over baby

Carmen Coletti to know that Vera hates my mother. But the thing I don't understand is how, why can she not sense that the woman in the house is Barbara Jean Coletti? Why else would she be on this property? Where did she come from, how did she wind up on our doorstep (instead of anywhere else in the world)? Naked in a pouring November rain? It is one of the only times I've seen her overwhelmed by denial, which in my heart I know is pure *delusion,* caused by the state of mind that strange woman has placed her in. And though it was not until seven months into her arrival, back in July, that I saw her again for the first time, she had ceased being a stranger to me long before, a condition solidified and justified, by my quick dash to my binoculars when I saw them coming down the steps, and get into Vera's silver luxury car.

The look on the woman's beautiful face, on Mother's beautiful face is sheer delight, the bliss of having every promise, every desire of your heart fulfilled. Pleasures and luxuries she was denied in her former life, now suddenly bestowed upon her without effort, having become the Royal Visitor, the elegant Lady of the Manor, but still finding a way to cover herself in gray and midnight cloth every chance she gets. She dresses like a teacher. Like a private girl's school teacher, in tight gray and navy skirts and blouses of every color, that have no hope of hiding the macromastian bosom. She is the image of any actress or model seen so rarely in real life, causing one to stop and look again, to make sure that the person was really as beautiful as they appeared. And it seems that here lately, just since July, there has been a steady line of cars on and off this property, with women and girls and ladies getting out and looking around, a bunch of people I have never seen before; some stopping and looking at the tall statue fountain, adjusting their little skirts over their little hips, looking around the massive property, staring over at the bay window of this little guest house, trying hopelessly to look inside. I always sit back just far enough from the window, binoculars trained, positioned so I know they can't see me. *My friends keep inviting everybody they know,* Vera had said, none of them admitting that the reason they're suddenly all coming around is the tall, lovely brunette with the piercing gray eyes and the biggest chest this side of God's Creation. *She's got you fooled Vera,* is what voice I hear now, while wide awake, watching the brunette get into the passenger seat of Silver Mercedes Luxury.

Eve! Where are you going! Where are you taking my new Mother!

This business of her actually leaving the property did not start until back on July 4th, when Vera tried to get me to go with them to watch a fireworks display. Was this fireworks incident her fullest arrival? Did every crackle of sparks and fire in the sky portend the birth of eschatology? As she sat and stared into the night sky, in awe of every flash and blast of sound and light, did she know that she was ready to begin to live, so that I could begin to die? When she took your hand under the fireworks, Mother Vera, what spark of delight or fear hath flown through thee! On the way home from the fireworks display, Mother Vera, what is it that she said to thee!

I did have a daughter, she says. *And I was a woman on a farm. That much I do know. But the only name I remember for myself is Eve. There was a woman I keep seeing on the farm with us… she called me Eve.*

It fits, Vera says. *Like you wouldn't believe. Its better than Liz, isn't it?*

I don't know. I'd gotten kind of used to it.

Eve, Vera says, shaking her head, gazing thoughtfully at the beams of light guiding them through the country dark. It couldn't be more perfect. Can you remember your daughter's name?

321

I have a feeling it's the key to everything. She might be looking for me right now, who knows? Who even knows if she's still alive?

Does the name 'Barbara Jean,' mean anything to you, Eve?

The look of determined, direct ignorance on her face is as brilliant as any non-verbal answer ever given.

I'm sorry, Vera says. *I shouldn't have asked you that. Please forgive me.*

No, its quite alright. Barbara Jean. Who is that?

Nobody. Trust me.

Vera shakes her head. Smiling. Feeling embarrassed for even entertaining the thought.

Vera, can I ask you for a favor?

Eve, Honey, you can ask me anything, she says. Stroking Eve's leg. A friendly, reassuring gesture. *Its something I've been wanting to ask for a long time. Would you... I don't really know how to say it.*

Just blurt it out, Baby.

Would you mind... would you mind giving me a massage?

The types of Fear are many. And uniquely distinguished. Among these is the Fear of Conflict. Which is only the long way around, to the Fear of Pain itself.

Something very clinical and proper, Eve says, *like what you might give a patient.*

Oh, Vera says. *Well, I have done massages before.*

When I saw the massage table... it was actually months ago when I saw it. I've been resisting the urge to ask you forever. I... feel kind of embarrassed.

Look, Eve. I told you. You can ask me anything, and I'll do it for you if I can.

Well, the reason why I was afraid to ask was... well, Elizabeth.

Elizabeth?

I know how close you are. And I wouldn't want to do anything she might find inappropriate.

Its just a massage, right?

Right, of course.

Well, who says she has to know about it?

You... you wouldn't feel strange about it?

I'm sort of taking care of you, aren't I?

Eve breathes a sigh. To try and blow a breath of sincerity. For her purposes. *I'd probably be dead without you.*

Vera tries, monumentally, not to stiffen when Eve touches her hand. And then the woman's hand pulls quickly, surreptitiously away. Then the woman folds her hands demurely in her lap, underneath that healthy, mountain jungle bosom. Looking away from Vera into the night ahead, and out of her passenger side window. Gazing thoughtfully into the nighttime countryside.

I'll be glad to give you a massage, Vera says. With conviction. Touching the woman's leg. Not pulling away when the woman takes her hand.

72

*I*n the world of Independence Day. Beneath the iridescent stars of night. Vera Evans rides the starlight trail. Arriving at the gate forever closer to the outside world. Her hand unsmoothly taken back. Having awkwardly turned the wheel with both hands. Though she only needs one. Vera Evans cruises the Wealthen Stream. Grieving for the Land of Plenty. Riding her new companion along. Gliding the cushion of uncomfortable silence. Sliding down the avenue of tension. Seeing my cottage light in the far off distance. Suddenly broken under the weight of this self-same tension. Pushing out words concerning the nighttime beauty of this property. Rising above it all is the Goddess of Music, the great statue of the woman holding the harp, which seems to stare across the distance of the darken'd lawn, into the windshield of the luxury car. Warning them. Warning Vera. Judging her. Admonishing them to ignore the flesh, but rather take heed to the spirit.

The luxury car breezes past the gray cottage in the dark. Unconcerned for the lonely soul who rests inside. The pathetic soul who walks alone. The car takes the left turn, to the smooth roll in front of the mansion, where the mighty columns loom tall from the bottom of the grand entranceway, climbing up towards the nighttime heavens, softly lit from the ground below. The woman named Eve gets out of the car, then takes the arm of her benefactor, kissing her on the cheek.

What was that for? the wealthy woman must ask, to maintain even the smallest part of her dignity.

I just needed to thank you. For everything.

The wealthy lady is disarmed. Unable to speak from behind the coy, but knowing smile. A smile, a sigh replete with frustration. With apprehension.

They are not ordinary women. The two of them. Taller. Hippier. Bustier. Prettier than most have ever seen. And what Vera's face may lack in perfect beauty, is supported by an extraordinary body, not skin and bones, but fit, firm and fleshy, so that to see her uncovered is to see a work of art, with her big breasts high and round, so fully supported as to not droop, but to still play a song in the key of F major. A waist medium thick, but curved, athletic and strong. Buttocks that bubble far out, with a modest, rounded spread besides. A woman at the bottom side of six feet in heels. Long, shapely legs. Always covered down to the strong calves.

But tonight, in her farmer's wife's jeans. Buttocks on display in them. White button down blouse tucked in. In perfect league with the elegant companion. Who has chosen to return to herself. To her plain dress of midnight blue fabric. Her favorite dress, given to her by her benefactor. In the heels, the fair skinned, mature beauty rises over six feet. Arms of strength. Long, powerful legs. Gigantic bottom hid in the dress fabric. Smallish, extremely curved waist hidden as well. End of the world breasts tucked away in the specially made bra. Fabric born from music in an unknown key, far above G major and beyond. Somewhere in the land of J. Breasts in Jubilee. Inside the regal, elegant livingroom space, the woman named Eve makes eye contact.

I'm going to go get ready, she says. *I'll meet you at the massage table.*

She slides both hands away from Vera's hand. Walking slow confidence and ease to the staircase. Turning. Going up the stairs. Refusing to even glance back toward the blonde woman. Listening instead to her footsteps echo toward the big kitchen.

Vera goes into the kitchen, where the sweet Merlot rests unhidden. From what seed is this so-called dry liquid grown? In what, inside the human heart, is it required? Vera pours the dark red liquid into the wine glass. Sipping. Closing her eyes, holding her head back. Upward. After the sigh, swallowing the rest quickly. Then, a second glass. Swallowing it quickly.

The blonde woman returns the red wine to its cabinet place. Unhidden. Brushing the strands of blonde hair from her eyes. Walking out of the kitchen. Clip clopping black heels across the tiles to the alternate staircase.

On her journey to the upper room.

73

*I*n her bedroom, Vera tucks her lips, braving forward through the pretense. Just a massage, she reassures herself over and over. Gathering the banana scented oil, and the big white towels from the towel closet down the hall. Gathering a prayer or two, that the only part of this woman's skin she'll see is her back. That old massage room. Abandoned by her and the other woman who lives in the house. A long time ago. The woman who has refused to step foot inside here for seven months.

Vera takes the towels and the oils and her feeble knowledge of massage technique to the small room at the end of the hall. And uncomfortable, uninviting little space. Clinical. Utilitarian. As intimate as a doctor's office. Vera pulls the curtain across the cathedral shaped window. Listening to the guest bedroom door open and close. Bare footsteps on the cold, summer hardwood. Large, white towels folded. Banana oil ready. She takes a deep breath in time with her newest patient's arrival. Wearing the plush, white bathrobe Vera hath given her. Wearing a broad, demure smile. White teeth gleaming. Breaking the icy tension of fear.

You sure you want to do it in this room, Honey? Its so drab and dank in here.

Its just fine for me, she says. *I don't mind at all.*

Vera takes one last look around the clean, clinical space. Conceding that this table, brilliantly, has wheels.

Help me roll this table out of here, Vera says. Unlocking the wheels on the high end, high priced table, rolling it away from the oppressive little space. Toward the space of comfort. To her new Gray Palace.

As they turn the massage table from the hall to the bedroom, Vera braves the spirits of anticipation and delight that flash through. While the woman called Eve looks at the crystal chandelier above. Then the four corners of the high canopy bed. Seeming to be awestruck. In genuine amazement at the bed's gothic, dark wood beauty. As well as the plush, gray chairs and small sofa nearby. A room fit to live and die in.

The table rests now, where it was surely meant to be. Vera locks the wheels down tight. Breathing the sigh of tension dissipated. Ready to oblige.

You can take your robe off now, Honey, she says. Partially ignoring the woman's strange, undeniable attraction to these surroundings, who seems distracted into a haze by the dark wood canopy bed. *I know*, Vera says. *The bed goes too far.*

It goes just far enough, Eve says. Shaking her head 'no' just once. Stroking a post of darken'd wood.

Gently.

74

Pretense is undone with the motion of a hand. Swiped across the front of her robe. Looking down, Eve unties her belt, then slides the robe off her shoulders and away from her hips, tossing it to the bed. Vera feels a lightning spark of pure awe. Zapped from her mind to her heart, then to the center of her body.

The possibilities of extreme femininity are explored in Eve's body, from the back tapered in the classic V shape, curved outward again into the incredibly widened hips in the small black underwear cloth. And then, the woman reaches back and unlatches her black bra, sliding it away and tossing it to the bed, prompting the words *'Good Lord'* to slip out of Vera's mouth.

I know, Eve says. *But I'm so used to you now, there's no need to be embarrassed anymore.*

I guess not, Vera says, while the woman called Eve walks over to the table. The breasts gigantic and hung down to where even her waist is partially covered by them. Whether or not Vera is aware of her own mouth hanging open is a mystery.

Elizabeth…

The woman climbs unashamedly on the table, breasts hanging down, brushing the table, then bulging mountainously from underneath her like two great marshmallows, pushing to the sides of her body.

Only thing small about you is your waistline. This is one big…

White ass?

No, Vera laughs. *I wasn't gonna say that. But it is one big set of hips. There's more here to grab than one would imagine, I think. But then up here, your waist is so small. I think I'm a little jealous, really. Your waist is smaller than mine. But your hips are bigger. Reminds me of somebody else I know.*

Elizabeth?

Yes. Elizabeth.

Vera's hand takes hold of the hopeless underwear fabric, which hide nothing by way of true modesty, highlighting everything instead. Vera slides the underwear down and away. Walking over to the bed. Placing them neatly by the robe and the bra.

Why don't you get more comfortable yourself? Eve says.

Vera sees the white skinned, mature beauty on her stomach exposed. Raised up on her elbows, breasts in gargantuan cleavage. A bathing beauty. Staring at Vera with those piercing eyes, a look filled with the challenge of a dare unspoken. And of course, unable to back down, Vera bites her bottom lip a little, then lets it hang free in pretty woman confidence, undoing the buttons on her white shirt from top to bottom, pulling it off to expose the white t shirt underneath. Undoing the button on the front of her jeans, kicking her shoes off, crossing her arms to grab the white t— pulling it off in classic fashion. The F cupped flesh packed in her bra is just too big and too firm, too round and too robust for her to be shy, as she bends over and slides the jeans off from the white French cut underwear, then deliberately turning her back, her backside to the woman, laying her jeans on the bed, confident that her underwear shows off a tighter, more perfectly rounded version of the same.

Perfect, the woman says. Vera smiles without looking, taking too much time to arrange. Her clothes neatly beside the robe. She turns and switches hips of major consequence back over to her patient, comfortable enough to bring both hands down in a full whack to the woman's backside. Eve giggles delightedly. Resting her head.

My butt's big and round alright, Vera says. *Too big if you ask me, but that's the way I like it.*

Do you like spanking?

You're not asking for one, are you?

No, she giggles again. *Nothing like that. I just wondered because of what you just did. You seem very comfortable with it.*

I'm a breast and butt woman, what can I say. I've always noticed other women's big breasts and big behinds. Even more so after I got married. Go figure.

Is that what attracted you to Elizabeth?

Oddly enough, that had nothing to do with it.

Vera slides her oiled hands up the woman's big buttocks, shaking the flesh vigorously, hearing Eve relax with a deep grunt and sigh.

How's that?

Its too good, she says, sighing deeply again.

Vera wiggles the woman's fleshy buttocks in generosity, understanding the power of this fervent tranquility. Pushing her hands down upon the soft flesh, grabbing a handful in firm squeezing, repeating this over and over, eventually sliding her hands to the woman's small, soft and deeply curved waistline.

Until you came along, I thought I'd seen everything. Its amazing how similar your bodies are. Yours is the slightly bigger, stronger version of hers.

So she really is beautiful?

I guess you don't remember seeing her that night. You opened your eyes.

She was here? In the mansion?

The woman perks up enough to give Vera pause. To consider whether the third part of this truth need be revealed.

Elizabeth is... unique. And uniquely beautiful. That big painting of her at the top of the stairs. Its no exaggeration. And though you really do give her a run for her money, I'll have to say that based on every model and actress I've ever seen, in the movies, magazines, what have you, I think that she's got 'em all beat. I'd put her up against every so-called beauty pageant girl in the world. Of course, they'd want her to lose about twenty pounds of bosom and backside, but I think that would only diminish her beauty. As a total package, Elizabeth Peele is the most beautiful woman in the world. But believe me Honey, you give her some serious competition.

From head to toe. I'm looking forward to seeing you in full makeup and a formal evening gown.

Vera slides her hand from the familiar scars on the woman's back, past her waist, back to a slow, deliberate squeezing to her bottom.

Most woman would be scared to death to carry hips like this. They are magnificent. I don't like it when women are too skinny. My best friend was too skinny.

The woman who killed herself? Set her daughter on fire?

Yes.

Vera slides smoothly to the woman's back again. Pressing her thumbs down in gliding motion. Squeezing the woman's shoulders hard enough to cause such a welcomed pain. Then at last, Vera begins to trace the remarkable network of raised scars on the woman's back, suffering their depressive charge, and overwhelming sense of familiarity.

Larger than life, Vera says.

What's that?

You. Everything about you. Even here, on your back. There is a network of scars on your back that are either birthmarks..."

Or death marks.

Death marks. Well, like I said. Everything about you is larger than life. Your face. Your figure. Your voice. Your eyes. The way you carry yourself. The way we found you. Your memory loss. It only adds to the mystique of you. Who you are. Where you came from.

Vera watches the look on Eve's face descend. To a contemplative, depressive gloom.

I hope you won't mind Vera, but... I think I'd like to turn over.

Vera braves the spark of awe again, as the woman flips herself over as athletically as she can, the two gargantuans globbing like great globules of wonder. Vera stops to gaze—at a sight so few have ever had the privilege to see. She steps forward, with a somber sword to pretense, laying waste to it with a handful of breast flesh, squeezing them both fully, hearing the woman moan as if throbbing in slow, steady pain. Vera drizzles a small stream of the banana scented oil on one of the nipples. When she runs her thumb across the nipple just once, the woman's entire body twitches as if she'd been stuck by a pin.

I'm sorry, Eve says. Her sultry voice is low. Almost whispery.

Vera smiles. Brushing both thumbs against both nipples without mercy. Watching both areolas shrink. Feeling both nipples grow. Watching them swell to the size of grapes. Hearing the woman's inner suffering flow out through her voice. Vera looks down the length of Eve's astronomical, astral curves, to the smooth, hairless private part below. Even with the woman's legs closed, her greatest anomaly is apparent.

Vera goes back to woman's nipples, taking each one firmly in hand, pinching and pulling and tweaking them unmercifully, for many long seconds, looking back to the woman's private, to have her gravest suspicion confirmed.

Do you touch yourself? Vera says.

You don't know how bad I've wanted to.

You mean... since you've been here, you have not touched yourself at all?

A little, she says, *but I was never comfortable enough to finish.*

My Lord, Vera says. Staring at the tiniest echo of that which pertaineth to a man, protruding out and slightly upward from Eve's womanhood.

A sex goddess, Vera says. *I don't know whether you know this or not, but your breasts aren't the only thing you're packin' too much of.*

What do you mean?

Vera looks again at what many have speculated about and snickered about but have never really imagine could push through the veil of reality. *What is that?* Vera says, looking again at the maximum possibilities of female arousal. *Honey, do you know what happens to you down there when you're aroused?*

What? The woman says. Eyes closed. One hand on her abdomen, the other on top of Vera's hand at her breast.

Lets just say that everything on you is a specimen, Vera says. Kneeding both breasts again like so much dough. Looking at the beautiful woman's anguished face in something close to pity. *I think I just figured out why you're so tense,* she says, rubbing Eve's shoulders, neck and the sides of her face. Watching her breathing go erratic, her eyes still closed. Rubbing her shoulders and arms again, feeling the muscles grown tighter with tension. *I need you to stand up for me,* she says. Helping Eve sit up, and slide off the table to her feet. Vera turns the woman around, facing the massage table.

Lean back against me.

The wealthy woman's voice is soft. Almost whispery.

In her bra and underwear, pressed close behind the naked woman, Vera takes the woman's breasts into her hands. Squeezing them with all her might, feeling the bad tension finally begin to dissipate. To make room for the good tension to flow in. Vera takes the nipples into her hands again, not surprised by the woman's fervent twitching, the single shudder, the deep grunting that passes through. Whispering in the woman's ear. *You need to touch yourself. You need to let it happen.*

Vera releases the woman's breasts, wrapping her arms tightly around Eve, pinning both her arms to her body. *Let it happen,* she says. A deep, breathy tone, to whisper the spirit of tranquility to the Eve mind and body. Taking hold of Eve's wrist. Guiding her hand to herself down below. Holding it there. Waiting. Allowing the connection to be made. Feeling the woman slide her fingers to the proper place. Feeling the good tension in her body grow again. Pressing hard against the woman's bare backside, to give anchor and support. Readjusting her locked arms, so that the woman's great breasts fall free. Free to jiggle; to wiggle. To wobble as they please.

Vera holds the woman tight. Feeling her arm begin to move. *Yes*, Vera says. *Let it all out*. All of the frustration. The lost years. The pain of a lifetime unremembered. A reassuring voice delivered in softness and strength, for the woman to feel free to make as much noise as she needs to make. Hearing the woman respond to this, in the leading edge of the storm that must come ashore. The soft wailing of that rare explosion of power, the beginnings of the end of the world in her body.

Vera listens to the soft warning. The voice risen to the loudness of speaking, the wail of lamentation, the travail of inner suffering that must be. Vera marvels at the energy drawn in, coming together at this focal point in space. Holding this poor woman tight, her head pushed back against Vera's shoulder. Her voice at the edge of breakdown, where inner sorrow is released soon after. And by instinct, Vera steadies herself against the crashing of the wave, foretold by the rising of the howling voice of weeping, the strong pushing backward against her, and the feverish jerking of the woman's arm at the connecting wire below. And risen up from somewhere beyond her own will's horizon, Vera's sultry voice speaks to the heart of Eve's resurrection and life—

Cum on that cock...

And Vera braces against the mighty lurch of strength, which jerks Eve's entire body, stiffening her to immobility, as her weeping grows to a great cry to the heavens, and her body fills with otherworldly strength and convulsions of pure energy. Vera holds the woman tight, still pinning her arms, bolted against the Charge of the Light Brigade, displayed as two women who appear as in combat, one shaking in the burden of a Weeping Orgasm, the other in travail to hold her while the unendurable pleasure passes through.

After the Ride of the Valkyries. In the sorrow of guilt. Burdened by an ache at the center of her body, Vera returns to this evening's attire. Having helped the trembling, weeping woman to her own bedroom. Having sat with her at the edge of her comfort bed. Holding the white robed beauty as she cried in her arms.

Vera has returned to her room. Rolling the massage table to the far corner, somewhere near the sofa and a corner window, beneath the fine white bookshelves of book and song. Not quite out of sight. Not quite out of mind. Vera goes to her grand, private bath, carrying her bag of private desire. Slipping out of the pants alone, even the underwear besides. Sliding into the extension of herself tonight. The thin red line of hot and fire. Attaching the long, thin phallus hanging down. Strapping the leather up tightly against herself. Nearly shuddering from the feeling, as she tucks the phallus far back between her legs. Pulling her jeans back up. Zipping. Buttoning. Walking uncomfortably. In somber discomfort down the long hall. Past the great portrait of her daughter wife. Shuddering the strange feelings between her legs as she walks. Hearing the Sapphic. The echo that exposes. That judges her in every footstep she hears. Past the grand piano void of sound. Having not been played for the better part of a year.

Under the stars of Independence Night. On the anniversary evening of the sundown of humanity. Vera walks in the strength of inner craving. Her mind on fire with memory from just moments ago. The faint lights of her daughter wife's cottage beckoning, just a few long steps away. The feel of the beautiful woman's breasts in her hands. The smell of pure mint on her breath. The fleshy, squishy feel of the woman's buttocks. Pushed back against Vera's groin, as if to punish her with further temptation, for having ventured thus far. The feminine strength, the power in the woman's muscles to match her own. The great soul of weeping brought forth. The rare sound of a full grown woman in the throes of deep sobbing. Pleasure, relief so intense as to induce weeping. The feel of the woman's body in spasms, in jerking and trembling, in the shaking brought on as the quaking of the earth itself, from the buildup of years of pressure, slipped into a sudden, violent release. Feeling the shockwaves pour through the woman's body as she screams. Fighting the warrior's power in her Amazonian muscles and curves. Power combined with the beauty of nature. To echo the first daughters of Eden. Those that walked the Earth in the body of woman. Muscles touched by strength from the other side of Creation. Of that power which pertaineth to a man.

Vera walks the asphalt road of dreams. Crossing onto the nighttime cottage lawn. Frustration walks in blonde beauty, stepping onto the concrete walkway to the front door. Having to ring the lovely C major tone. Waking me up from the beginnings of another troubled sleep. I know in my heart, that it is my love, having finally come back to me. I slide out of the bed, onto a cushion of false hope, hurrying to the door which must remain locked now, unlike before a certain being drifted in from the woods and the prairie.

I open the door to my blonde companion, my angel of mercy sent in love, so glad that she has finally come to visit me. But no sooner than the door is open than I see my blonde lover in somber expression, crossing the threshold to me in a bitterness I cannot understand, latching her lips onto mine in something like rage and fury. Seeming to suck the life and breath from me.

The hard, unkind kiss ends, and she reaches down and lifts me up, her arms wrapped around my legs under my buttocks. Walking me without a word to the bedroom. Throwing me violently backward onto the bed, slamming hard on top of me. Latching the deep, sucking kiss back onto me until I can't breathe. Then she tears at the buttons of my white cotton nightgown, reaching inside and pulling my breast out to wobbling, pulling the nipple into her mouth to quell a starving instinct, bellowing once in a deep, gruff call to this kill. Shaking her head vigorously. While her lips are clamped to this painful nursing at my breast, I feel her fumbling with her jeans down below, until they are open, and she slides them down below her hips. Sliding up to my face, her expression overcome with lack of mercy and compassion.

I feel her hand at my private, probing, pushing in. Then the same hand moves away, taking hold of her violent self strapped on, finding me with it. Until I feel the tip of it slide pressure inside, followed by a grunt from her as if it were part of her physical body. Then she pushes forward, watching me hold my head back and grit my teeth from the pressure. The look in her eyes is the madness of hunger satisfied. Slamming it up into me one thrust at a time, until he can find the rhythm of devastation, the magic touch of the soft leather against herself in the harness that will turn the rocket fire on. In frustration she pounds. Shifting position. Changing her tempo. Concerned with no pleasure but her own. Then I suddenly feel a strong pressure at my throat, as she clamps a hand around my neck, locking her lips to mine again. Daring me to try and breathe. I can only pull the breath in through my nostrils, as I know that even when the kiss ends, the breath through my mouth will be that of a woman being choked.

She moves her head to the side, so I can hear my suspicion confirmed, in the ghostly breath I try to breathe. And I feel her find the Road to Woodland, that switch turned on down below, which sees her thrusts go faster, feeling the member strapped on, brushing against herself more perfectly than she had hoped possible, until it seems that the deepest lust has coalesced and grown from deep inside her body, so that she can siphon the pleasure she needs from me.

Still holding my throat, to where I cannot swallow, feeling as though I may cough, she calls the name of God upon the down thrust, her hand slipping away from my throat as the high pitched animal bellowing comes out, while her body's rhythm continues to slam her against me on its own.

In the Aftermath of Trauma. Laid devastated underneath her, like a body pinned and crushed after a violent storm. Hardly able to draw a deep breath under the weight of her. Thankful when she grows tired of me, lifting herself up. Rolling over onto her back.

You been touchin' her.

In the periphery, I see her turn to look at me, somewhere between confusion and bewilderment. *And just what is that supposed to mean?*

Silence.

I'm not exactly sure where that came from, she says, sliding her jeans up. Tucking it in. *But I don't think I like it.*

Vera sits up at the edge of the bed. Looking away. I pull down my nightgown, latching a button or two up top. Sitting up behind her.

You smell like the woods, I say. *Like her.*

That's a terrible thing to say. What gives you the right to speak to me like that?

Her being here gives me the right. Before she came here, it was just you and me every night. Then it was every other night. Then it was once a week. And now, its been a month since you touched me.

Its because I have a life, Elizabeth.

Its because you been suckin' her tits!

Vera turns her body towards me. Sliding closer to me on the bed.

How dare you sit there, trapped in your own little do nothing fantasy world, and accuse me of something like that.

Words carry the blade of a sword. Piercing the heart. Cutting through to the marrow of bone.

Was this a do nothing, fantasy world when you raped me five minutes ago?

Now you listen here, she says sharply, pulling my hair harder than I've ever felt from her. Holding my head back. Staring at me in the pain of frustrated anger. Flashes of my mother's hand buried in my hair blaze the theater of my mind, to overwhelm me in emotional memory.

And when Vera sees the fear and longing echoed in my features again, the return of my characteristic expression, the resurrection of sadness in my eyes, the melancholy of tucked in lips, she is all at once burdened again by her calling, remembering who we are, and who we have always been to one another.

She releases my hair. Touching my face gently with both her hands. Staring. Gauging the manner of tears that might betray a soul of pain, a single one having flowed down my cheek. I see her wince as the agony passes through. Standing up, both hands in front of her mouth. Moving those self-same hands, that I may see her mouth open. But what words are there, when the stem of the rose flower is bent and broken? There is only the shock and awe of regret, when fragile barriers have been irrevocably breached, with trusts and promises irrevocably broken.

Through a watery haze, I see the wealthy woman's hands back at her mouth, while I blink for clarity, feeling the flood of quiet tears flow, seeing her hands tremble as she tries hopelessly to speak again. She turns as slowly as she can, swearing to herself that there will be no running and crying into the night, but having to at least hurry out of the gray nighttime cottage and to the end of the concrete walkway, into the yard beside the asphalt road.

What does a person do, when there is nowhere to go? Nowhere to turn? When it seems that every bridge in life has been flooded or burned? When one sees the floodwaters of Discord and Chaos rising, threatening to overtake one's only overpass to Hope and the future?

Vera gazes across the Great Lawn, to the statue of the music goddess. Feeling the sudden loss of strength and power in her spirit, leaving her helpless and devastated in the wind—though the trees are silent, and there is no nighttime breeze on her face. These are the Winds of Eschatology. Those that blow the breath of ice and doom, as a warning of what epic tragedies loom, and dire consequences for foolish choices come and gone. The path to her greatness in this life, to her tranquility of the mind, body and spirit, this path is suddenly overgrown with weeds and treachery, trees made barren by sickness, flowers wilted and burdened by death.

Vera looks at the gray cottage behind her, and the lighted monstrosity of a mansion before her, understanding that there is nowhere to go, and that twice this very night, she has crossed the barrier of the forbidden.

Giving in to her hands' own fervent will and desire, she undoes her pants and pulls them off in the open night air, ripping at the straps of her deviance with frustration and disgust, sliding it quickly down and to the ground. With only her white collar shirt barely covering herself, she stumbles past the gray brick house in the dark, into the forest grove of trees nearby, tossing the bundle somewhere deep inside.

Vera goes from the forest grove to the road, leaving the jeans and shoes of her night's diversion where they lay. Walking barefoot in the night, down the asphalt road of ashen gray regret. Pulling off the gold hoop earrings. Tossing them into the field of nighttime grass just off the side of the road. Fully aware now of her destination. Down the road of recollection. To a house she has not set foot in since it was abandoned four years ago, when the last part of the mansion was built.

Vera hurries the long walk through the night. Passing under the line of trees in the dark, at last crossing from the road to the old lawn. The lawn of the brick farmhouse, the ghostly remains of a past she had once sworn was dead to her. It seems that the harder she tries—the closer she gets to the brick house, the further away it seems to fade. But Vera commits herself to this mirage, this nighttime refuge barely seen in the country dark. Above her, it seems that every star in the Heavens is clearly visible, a single point of light multiplied into thousands, all of which are dedicated to observing her foolish cause, and mocking her flight from wisdom.

As if lifted into the flow of Fate, breezed along the cushion of moving History, she runs lightly in her white cloth, at last arriving to the old brick farmhouse, where the hopes of a former life has lived and died. She opens the perpetually unlocked back door, stepping into the musty, middle class kitchen where her husband was shot and killed. These spirits of Regret weigh hard and heavy, on the woman who walks unafraid of the ghosts that stare, from the kitchen brought to life by the switch of a light, down the hall to the old Gray Palace (bedroom), the place where clinical depression once sought to kill and bury her in.

In sackcloth and ashes remorse, Vera undoes the buttons on her white collar shirt, pulling it off and tossing it to the bed unused, the bed so long unslept in. Getting on her hands and knees in the middle of the gray carpeted floor. Crawling before the tiding of judgment in her mind. Saying *Oh God... please have mercy.* Grunting the words in pain and submission. Being transported backward through time, to where there is a naked young woman on a kitchen floor. Her long black hair unkempt, hanging nearly to the floor beside her hands. The young woman's massive breasts hang down as she crawls. And Vera suddenly feels the lash of what she sees, when the woman's Mother brings the hard leather belt down on the crawling woman's back. This mother follows her crawling daughter from room to room, bringing the belt down onto her bloody back and buttocks, admonishing her to slow down, or to stop, or to *crawl faster bitch.* Telling the twenty year old woman to crawl to the kitchen again and stay still. Lashing her over and over again on her back, enduring every angry scream from her daughter's mouth.

Now sitting on her daughter's back—telling her to *crawl like the stupid mule bitch* you are. And in trembling, the girl crawls like a beast of burden, carrying her mother who is fully clothed in the long, pioneer skirt and favorite purple blouse faded to lavender. This 37 year old beauty, with long, back hair and piercing gray eyes, and an expression burdened by frustration and sorrow. Admonishing the daughter that if she falls, she will get worse. Pressing all her weight on the weakening girl as she crawls, her arms trembling from the strain. The twenty year old carries the thirty seven year old on her back, crawling continuously, slowly from room to room, her back itching and aching and burning from the belt, and the mother's blouse scraping against her raw skin. The mother pulls the daughter's hair like the bridle of a horse, enjoying the weak, trembling ride from room to room, feeling the motion of her daughter's body where she sits straddled on her. Guiding the girl to every corner of the house, her body in the agonizing pleasure of her calling, even closing her eyes during part of the slow journey—telling the girl *did I tell you to slow down?* Immensely enjoying her feeble attempt to speed up. Feeling the girl's trembling grow under the strain. Knowing that her arms will soon have to give. Wondering what nature of pleasure can this be, where the breathing, straining, and grunting of her daughter tickles such a sublime feeling in her body. *If you fall before I tell you to stop, I swear you'll get worse.* But, as it is written, the spirit is willing, but the flesh is weak. Though the girl struggles to the end of endurance, shaking, crying out repeatedly for mercy and saying *I can't,* the strength in her arms soon gives way, and she drops her nude body flat to the floor. Crying under the weight of the long punishment, the agony of the floor's incessant scraping against her knees, and the impending cloud of devastation pressed down on her back. *I didn't tell you to stop,* the mother says. Feeling the girl tremble and strain to rise again to her hands and knees, but being unable.

The mother gets up from her nude daughter's back. Walking to the center of the kitchen. *Come here to me*, the mother says. Watching the twenty year old daughter slowly, stubbornly oblige, Which is the stubbornness of exhaustion, and the resistance of inner denial. On your knees, the woman says, to which the daughter complies, with a stubborn slowness that her mother patiently endures. *Hands behind your back*, the mother says. After which she brings the tip of the unfolded belt down on her daughter's breast one full time, enjoying so much the loud scream and cringe. *Put your arms down.* Repeating it only once more by necessity, with loud, boisterous authority in their mid-sized country kitchen. She whips the belt down hard onto the girl's breasts one, two, three times more, until the girl's scream comes out on its own this time, and her arms go back in front of her breasts, where they do not stop the belt at all, but are attacked enough to cause redness and welting. But the mother's patience wears as thin as her daughter's tolerance for pain. *If you don't put your hands behind your back and straighten up, I'm going to tie your hands behind your back and put a safety pin through both of your nipples.* Do you want that?

No, Maam.

Then do as I ask. Put your hands behind your back and leave 'em there. And to great avail, this most effective request is given. Whacking each one of her daughter's mammoth, hanging breasts one hit at a time, back and forth, until the girl begins to try to block the hits with her shoulders. *Safety pins*, her mother says, bringing her daughter back to her senses. Perfectly still, her mother says. Then, a single blow across the nipple brings the words screaming from her mouth…

It hurts!

Mother's response, each word in time to a whip of the girl's breasts… *of… course… it… hurts… that's… why… I'm… doing… it… you… stupid… bitch!* And the last word brings the last welt across the daughter's big, flopping breasts. Going to her bedroom, for the safety pins that lie in wait. Getting behind her daughter on the kitchen floor. Piercing her breasts in screams and blood. Leaving her there on her knees in the kitchen, face contorted in the classic ugly cry. Arms loosely bound behind her back.

This classic, ugly cry of the soul and spirit traverses time and space. From the little farmhouse surrounded by the Carolina woods. Across the prairie green to the abandoned rancher house of brick, where the wealthy woman rests on her knees in the nude, her hands clasped behind her back, as the ugliness of grief contorts her beautiful expression.

$\mathscr{T}$he ninth month of Eve's arrival looms heavy in the heat of August, two months after the fervent Night of Independence, when the stars of Vera's greatest suffering have come and gone. Activity is perhaps the mourners best remedy, keeping her occupied with problems opening another Elizabeth Peele House somewhere in Martin County, another woman's refuge from violence and pain. Plans to turn Brenda's house into a shelter have been delayed by threats of a lawsuit from Brenda's family, though it will likely have no merit if it ever happens, being that Vera was smart enough to remove Brenda's name from the house, when she rescued the mortgage after Brenda's divorce. But these silly threats are like blanks out of a machine gun, I think. They make a lot of noise, but can do no real harm in the long run. The house in Grand Harwich Estates belongs to Veranda May Evans, and as soon as the family stops chasing and harassing her about it, she's going to give the beautiful, half million dollar home to our cause. And this is the ultimate focus of her life, when I am not burdening her down—to bring as much comfort to as many battered women as she can. I think that were it not for me, lurking around this property like a spirit, she would have already made it the flagship location for the charity she has mentioned many times in the past—a national charity called St. Carmen in the Fields, named after the mansion on our property, to promote awareness of domestic violence and child abuse across the length and breadth of this nation.

But are these the best laid plans of mice and men, which often go awry? Such things are decided by the Lord himself, whether charity and compassion will fall in a deluge of mercy, or as the waters of a trickling stream. And what more important line in the Lord's prayer is there, but that which begs God's mercy, and protection from the powers of darkness? *And lead us not into temptation, but deliver us from evil.*

Our Father, who art in Heaven. Hallowed be thy name, thy kingdom come. Thy will be done on Earth, as it is in Heaven. Give us this day, our daily bread. And forgive us our debts, as we forgive our debtors. And lead us not into temptation.

But deliver us from evil.

The rumble of afternoon thunder looms heavy over our countryside. Strong breezes overwhelm the sweltering, oppressive heat. Dark clouds of impending doom have gathered overhead, with flashes of brief warning to every hopeless inhabitant below.

Devastation looks through eyes of beauty. Winter gray eyes of hatred and disillusionment. Burdened by the realization of Opportunity's sudden arrival, and the notion that what must be done, must be done quickly.

Eve stands outside the mansion. Remembering Vera's silver gray departure a moment ago. Undone by the Third Part of the Truth, which is cataclysm.

Its not the end of the world, Vera had said. *You're not being abandoned. You'll just be living in another place.*

You mean, I'll have to leave this beautiful property? What about us?

There is no us, Eve. I've been acting as if either of us matter in this. But there's only one person that's ever been on this property that matters. And she's suffered long enough. She loves this house. The piano. This prairie we call a property. The Rose Garden. But since the night you arrived, she hasn't left the guest house once. Nine months, she's been trapped in that house. But no longer. Tomorrow, we're going to get your things, and move you into my best friend's old house. It's a beautiful house, even better than the guest house on this property.

Words have the power to phase through the human body. To take the form of an angel of doom, and penetrate the heart and soul with a flaming sword.

I understand that you're going to be hurt and angry. I hope that you won't. I hope that you'll forgive me for this.

In the warning breezes. In the rising, apocalyptic wind, the beautiful woman stands in her full length dress of midnight. Arms folded. Face betraying the inner disgust of Vera's betrayal. Turning her focus to the gray cottage of rough hewn brick, and of the task awaiting her inside. Of the calling that must at last be fulfilled.

Eve hears the word. The single syllable of what must be. Gazing into the clouds with hatred. Looking down at the ground, holding the repressed smile in check. Turning on the whim of revelation, going into the mansion which is no longer her home. No longer a place for her to hide in. A refuge blown down by a rushing, mighty wind. Gathered up as debris scattered and strewn.

The woman goes up the stairs. Stopping at the top, to gaze at the object of insanity. The subject of her craving. Rolling her eyes in the purest contempt at the woman in red, walking down the hall to her upper room. Opening the door, to where the tools of conquest are so richly stored. From underneath the bed, she slips the long bundle wrapped in linen, placing it on the bed to open carefully. Ignoring the long knife blade and white rope. Picking up the classic square blade sharpened, made for the felling of trees.

Chopping them to pieces.

79

The first drops of rain fall on my shattered nerves as I walk, no, as I pace the carpet floor of my house. When is Vera coming home? I have to tell her that I can't spend another—

A sudden *crash* sends shattered glass flying past my face near the music desk, as the bay window is blasted apart to the music of a scream. It is the death scream. The otherworldly shriek of a woman at the jaws of certain death. This, which is the blade of an axe through the giant window pane, and the white hands of the truth that wields it. The face of my past is come to life in the late afternoon thunderstorm, undeterred by the arrival of a deluge of sorrow and fury. Through the space of the open window, I see the woman whom I have always known, by the backdrop of the asphalt road and great lawn, and the towering white statue lit up in the fast and violent storm. And this woman begins to climb inside, her axe blade tossed onto the desk where my notebook is covered in broken glass. The image holds me immobile for a second of trying, of pushing hard to wish it away. But this is not one of my dreams or visions, but the manifestation of my worst nightmare into reality. I am awestruck by the spirit of fear, which heightens my intelligence of flight. Holding me still at the front door, ready to open it and flee once she gets into the room. Watching me like a staring bird of prey, she climbs slowly onto the bay window ledge, waiting to see whether I will stay or flee. But being unwilling, or unable, to stay still. Climbing all the way onto the ledge. Her hands uncut by the glass. Climbing inside. Standing up in regal strength and power. Moving suddenly towards me, prompting another scream of death as I hurry through the door. Running fast away from the house in the rainstorm. Running towards the safety of the open lawn, which to my dismay has been compromised by my clumsy, stupid self, slipping and falling on my way toward nowhere to hide, shocked at the weight I feel slamming onto the back of me, screaming again as if I've been stabbed.

The weight lifts immediately, grabbing me by the hair, and holding my arm behind my back in the rainstorm.

The mansion is alive with Fear and Hatred. The sound of my voice echoes with the thunder outside, as I feel the cold touch of Death at my neck. In the middle of the living room, nearby where my piano rests silent, I am held tight from behind, my voice becoming choked from the pressure, and growing hoarse from the screams of fear. My spirit is on fire with the dread and terror of my youth, where I was plagued by the Fear of Pain, and the Fear of Death and ultimately, the Fear of Abandonment. It is the Fear of Death that I feel, whether I am held by a supernatural being or no, understanding that her only purpose in life is to see me die screaming, and to feel me begin to die long before it happens.

"I'm going to have to rape you with the knife this time," she says. Releasing her hands from my neck, covering my mouth tight, to listen to the moans of fear muffled inside. Fear that causes pain in the physical body. Fear unassuaged by the pressing of the great soft bosom against my back, through which she draws the energy of her calling, the pleasure gathered from causing pain. With one strong hand at my mouth, and the other gripping me so tightly around the waist to where both my arms are held immobile, she cannot resist a shudder in her body, which I feel as a fervent twitching of involuntary muscle spasm at her womb and groin. With her hand tightly over my mouth, she returns her other hand to my neck, undeterred by my tears, nor those that have run from both her eyes in two single streams. As if resigned to the end of the world pain and death she must cause, the woman begins to escort me toward the stairs in something less than anger. Something from where rage hath not known. From where wrath hath never trod. Where the cutting of another's flesh brings a lightning bolt to the cutter's groin, where the fear in the victim's eyes, the disillusionment and despair of Death is meat for the body, and the nourishment of milk for the soul and spirit. As she begins to move me, I have to fight like the rabbit in the wolf's mouth, which causes her to stop and hold me again as I squirm. Uncovering my mouth just long enough to hear the fear come out of my voice, and echo around the room. She muffles my voice again, escorting us towards the staircase, where I know lies the beginning of my ascent, the start of where I must suffer the final passion, before I must be taken absent from this body, that I may be present with the Lord.

"Barbara Jean!"

The voice of angelic power reverberates our space, making me strain to look, wide eyed and dim witted with fear.

"Over my dead body," Vera says. Walking towards us. Her hand conspicuously behind her back. "Elizabeth," she says, "when I grab the bitch's hand, tear yourself away from her."

"In your *dreams*," the woman says. Holding onto me tighter as Vera walks toward us. "You think you're so fucking important… you're just another rich, perverted busy body! Pretending you care so much about people, when all you really care about is your own sick, twisted lust. You're keeping this little bitch as nothing more than a plaything for yourself. She's not worth it. She's garbage. You should be helping me put her out of her misery. I'll let you lay on top of her, Vera, while I lay underneath her. We'll get rid of this stupid little nothing together!"

The words seem to activate whatever strength and skill the farmer's wife has pent up in her muscles. She lunges at us, grabbing the woman's arm at my waist, causing me to fight and pull in madness to escape, while she grabs my hair to keep me nearby. Then suddenly, I hear a sickening, high pitched yelp from the woman, born from Vera's arm having brought her hidden knife down and around, plunging it into the woman's middle, causing her to let me go immediately, her piercing gray eyes wide with shock and disbelief, while Vera holds her long, black hair tight with her other hand. Vera pushes the blade deeper into the tall, beautiful woman, staring her in the eyes, holding her up to receive the reward overdue. "Thou shalt not suffer… a witch… to live," Vera says, pushing the blade a third time into the woman's stomach. On her way down to the floor below, the woman grabs at Vera's dress, her hand slipping in weakness as she lays down with Vera on top of her astraddle, holding the blade tight inside her, the woman turning to look at me with that cold, mountain witch's gaze, breathing in just once, but exhaling only the long, ghostly sound of a last breath, to parallel the rising of a white, misty form from her entire body, even passing through Vera on its journey upward, where the form comes to life as a being of otherworldly motion, seeming to glide on a single flapping of phantom wings from high above us, and out into the storm.

Vera stands up from the lifeless beauty. Coming over to where I stand gazing at the high cathedral window, where the spirit of what we know has come and gone. Hugging her tight, I look away from the corpse on the floor, away from the rain soaked window, resting my head on the shoulder of the woman who loves me. Trying not to remember the pain of the woman who gave me life, and then took it from me so abundantly. I close my eyes, hearing the rumbling voice of Cataclysm in the clouds, grieving for the end of the age, and to tell of where it is that my beloved mother could have gone.

THE END

ABOUT THE AUTHOR

Jonathan Lovejoy is a graduate of the University of North Carolina at Greensboro, with a B.A. in Religious Studies, and a graduate of Liberty University, with an M.A. in Theological Studies. He currently lives in Winston Salem, North Carolina.

For more info on the author's life and career, visit jonathanlovejoy.com